THE OUTSIDER

BARRY MERCHANT

First published in 2021 by Merchant Publishing
Copyright 2021 © Barry Merchant

Barry Merchant has asserted his right under the Copyright,
Designsand Patents Act 1998 to be identified as the author
of this work.

All rights reserved. No part of this publication may be reproduced,
stored in a retrieval system or transmitted in any form or by any
means (electronic, digital, optical, mechanical, photocopying,
recording or otherwise), without the publisher's prior permission
in writing.

Any person who does any unauthorised act in relation to this
publication may be liable to criminal prosecution and civil
claims for damages.

The book is sold subject to the condition that it shall not, by the
way of trade or otherwise, be lent, resold, hired out, or circulated
without the publisher's prior consent in any form of binding cover
other than that in which it is published and without a similar
condition including this condition, being imposed on the
subsequent purchaser.

This is a work of fiction. Names, characters, businesses, places,
events, locales, and incidents are either the products of the author's
imagination or used in a fictitious manner. Any resemblance to
actual persons, living or dead, or actual events is purely
coincidental.

ISBN: 978-1-9196369-0-0

A CIP catalogue record for this book is available
from the British Library.

Book Cover : Photo Credit: Sammy-Williams Unsplash

IN MEMORY
June Elizabeth Bailey (nee Merchant)
21st July 1937-22nd February 2020

I

CHAPTER ONE

It was nearly always the same time every morning that the internal reception desk telephone started to ring. Incessant noises from those pampered middle-class professionals living above, demanding immediate attention. No doubt frivolous, but lackeys must always be available to please the potential alcoholic, drug addict (prescribed or otherwise), insomniac and mentally confused. The night porter fitted the bill superbly. Rub your shitty feet all over him. Shout, swear and abuse—he must take it all. Does it really matter to anyone else that a lowly flunkey actually has feelings? That he would crave an independent life where he could choose to live, work or even have a family? Yes, a family of his own. No, of course it didn't really matter in reality. No one living at Oaks Lodge, or anywhere else for that matter, would give a porter a second glance. Cedric had tried when he was young to make something of himself, but all to no avail. Lack of confidence, never could rise above the constant fantasies he thought would one day materialise. You are but a loser, he kept reminding himself.

'Is that you, Bambridge? What took you so long to answer the goddamn phone?' shouted Ms Fulton, a spinster aged 75. The usual diatribe he received in the early hours. Never 'good morning' or 'how are you?' She spoke as if he was a thing to taunt. But he was used to it. Besides, where could he go now? Who would employ him? Keep a stiff upper lip and all will be well. Bambridge didn't want to anger his area manager.

'Good morning, Ms Fulton. How are you?' he asked through clenched teeth.

'Never mind that, come up to my flat at once. There is something wrong with the tap on my bath, for heaven's sake, man,' she demanded in a harsh voice. Her attitude to the porters, and others, was Victorian rather than the 21st century she actually lived in.

'I'll be there in a few minutes, madam. I won't be long,' he reassured her, fearing the tirade awaiting him. How pleased he was that residents didn't have personal alarms in their apartments. Otherwise, they would run him off his feet. If they needed them, they had to make arrangements with private companies. Let them share the lapdog regime. Cedric and his colleagues had enough to contend with.

'Be quicker than that, Bambridge, or else,' she spat through the internal phone.

'Yes, Ms Fulton,' he said quietly. Wouldn't it be wonderful, he often thought, if the educated, wealthy apartment owners could address him as Mr Bambridge... or beyond his wildest dreams, Cedric even? Why have people got to undermine you, make you feel as though you are just a worthless piece of shit? That has been his experience for most of his life. The only places he found civil were those frequented by people from a similar background to his. The local cafés, pubs and day centres. Cedric didn't expect things to change. People are just born that way, he concluded. Those that lived above him all possessed what he didn't. When you had nothing, you expected even less, people kept telling him. 'You'll get your just deserts in heaven, don't worry, boys.' That was according to the vicar who used to preach in the borstal he was once sent to. Of course, Bambridge knew it was bollocks. There was no God. If there was, he would have helped him out of the predicament he was in. His life was full of anxiety, loneliness and isolation.

'You've taken ages, Bambridge, for God's sake. Where have you been?' Miss Fulton asked in her usual condescending manner.

'Sorry, madam, I had to fetch my tools from the cupboard behind the ground floor reception desk,' he said, looking straight ahead, fearful of her glaring dark brown eyes.

'Well, don't stand around, if you go into the bathroom, you will see the problem,' she exclaimed. 'And I hope your feet are clean on my new Wilton carpet. Cost me a bloody fortune from Harrods,' she said. It gave her much pleasure to keep the porter in his place.

After a career in the civil service, most of that time in the foreign office serving under many ministers of state, she was skilfully versed in keeping those minor shits, like Bambridge, firmly in their allotted place. Other than a few old biddies, it was not surprising that she had very few visitors. Probably thought that most people were not worthy of her company.

After a few minutes, he reappeared in front of the spinster to explain her tap needed a washer. He shuddered at the thought of her wrinkled bag of bones lying nude in that light blue bath. She must use gallons of foam to cover that frail skeleton. Surely, not even her self-importance could withstand a petrifying glance into the life-size mirror attached to the bathroom wall.

'As your bath requires some minor work, I shall hurry downstairs to collect a few other tools to sort it out, madam,' he explained as she glared right through him.

As he got into the lift on the fourth floor, he fantasized about how he would love to have smashed her head with the club hammer he possessed. But that wouldn't happen to her, or anyone else, as he didn't want to end up in prison once again. Not that stinking hell hole that degrades humans beyond any kind of decency. Scums of the earth—nothing better. That was his experience of those human dustbins.

At least in this place, he had a job, regular wage and a basement flat. Even though it was sparsely decorated, consisting of three small rooms and a bathroom, it had been his home for nearly 13 years. Before that, a succession of cheap bedsits, where some tenants crapped on the toilet floor. Places full of people with tormented souls. Bambridge had painted the flat all light green several years ago. He bought second-hand furniture from a local charity shop. Most of it cheap and cheerful, fit only for the scrapheap. Similar to the other porter's flat opposite. He had been invited there many times over the years for a few beers with his colleague, Nelson Trussington. When he came to retirement, a persistent threat—obscurity in a council bedsit—always threatened his chronic insecurity.

'Where have you been? I'm waiting for a bath, Bambridge,' she shouted at the porter when he returned, holding a few tools.

As she spoke at him, standing on her Harrods treasure, he thought about the insurmountable void between wealth and the degradation he and many like him had to contend with.

'It will only take a few minutes to sort out,' he explained, hoping she would drown once he left her spacious, expensive abode. Similar to most residents, he was rarely asked to go beyond living areas and bathrooms. But what he did observe was luxury beyond his wildest dreams. Most apartments had chandeliers, thick carpets, various porcelain, mounted pictures and colourful furniture. The lucky bastards, he continually thought. Who did they rob to live in such opulence? Oaks Lodge, consisting of 16 apartments, was full of people whose lives were full of privilege.

'That's it, madam, completed.'

'Thank you, Bambridge,' the anorexic woman said reluctantly.

While he had been occupied elsewhere, another owner had left a message on his employer-owned mobile phone requesting assistance. He made his way to number six. He was another resident who continually phoned in the early hours. All of them—except one married couple—were single and lived on their own. Most had never been married or had a long-term relationship. If you saw them, it would explain the reason why most had retired to live a lonely life, within a self-made prison consisting of four expensively decorative walls.

Cedric hated the lot of them. Pampered and over-indulged; when he saw them, occasionally in public, he would do his utmost to escape their wandering eyes. He wouldn't give any of them the time of day. He wondered if they realised the suffering of others beyond their own self-obsessed existence. But they too must suffer sometimes, he grudgingly acknowledged.

Indeed, Bambridge had suffered much during his life, some of it self-imposed. But birth, beyond his control, being luck of the draw. Birth, not worth, was his maxim.

'You left a message on my phone, sir,' enquired the porter, anticipating another ear-bashing from Mr Black, aged 78—a rather dapper, fat, retired accountant. Usually drunk around 2 am, he would phone with the most spurious of problems. All he required—sometimes demanded—was attention.

Now retired and living alone, alcohol was his only companion. Apart from the occasional, and reluctant, visit from his young nephew who was hoping to inherit the old buffer's money, he talked incessantly to anyone foolish enough to listen. That included poor old Bambridge, whose short, slim build was made to sit on his large leather settee and listen to his scotch-induced vitriol.

'Hello, Mr Bambridge, how the devil are you?' he enquired. Mr Black was one of the few residents who addressed him with civility. Not much to ask of someone in his position, Cedric thought. What was the point of all this... loving family life, education, well-paid employment and so forth, if one was unable to treat your fellow man in a decent manner? Perhaps that was the idea of being superior, so that the majority were always available at your beck and call, he surmised. Outsiders like Cedric Bambridge.

'I'm OK, sir, thank you,' he quietly responded. Think of your station in life, Cedric, don't be too cocky or confident. Otherwise, fatty Black will put you in your place and start quoting Shakespeare or Dickens to bring you down a peg or two.

'That's good. Are you busy this morning? All those old girls got you clearing up after them? Have a goddamn drink, you deserve one,' insisted an inebriated Mr Black. His black wig, not tidy at the best of times, had slid to the side of his large head, resembling an army beret. He staggered over to his bar and poured out two large whiskies. At this stage, Cedric was craving for his phone to ring so he could escape the predicament he was in.

'There we go, my boy. Cheers.' Black had swallowed the drink in one gulp. His puce nose stood out like a road map.

'Thank you, sir. Was there a problem to sort out, by the way?' enquired Cedric.

'No, I don't think so, my dear boy. Not that I can remember. My old brain is becoming a bit confused nowadays,' he said.

Cedric Bambridge took a few sips from the drink he was given. It tasted awful and burnt his mouth and throat. He didn't want any more of it. After many years of drinking that gut wash, it wasn't surprising that Black's memory recall was fuddled. Must make a move from this place, he told himself, before the old boy pours another.

'What sort of life is it here for you? Do you enjoy meeting

all these affluent residents? I'm sure they treat you well,' he asked Cedric.

'It is interesting at times, sir. Hard work, but varied problems to sort out which I enjoy,' all cobblers intended for the ears of Mr Black. If Bambridge had his way, he would have bumped them all off with cyanide poisoning. Watch them groan and shriek in agony. The thrill excited him immeasurably, but it was no more than a mere fantasy, just like the other fantasies he constantly brought to his consciousness. He knew he needed to be careful about the extreme thoughts of harming residents as most were decent enough. Only a handful needed severe punishment, but he hoped that would never happen!

'Well, that's jolly good, that is, old boy.'

'I have to go now, sir. I have other residents to attend to. Thank you for the drink,' he said under his breath.

'Poppycock, you must stay and have another, won't you?' Mr Black stammered.

'Sorry, sir. I must go now.' He got to his feet and headed for the door before another drink was shoved under his nose.

'That's a pity, I was about to tell you about my holiday in Tanzania last year.' By this time, Cedric had opened the front door and bid goodnight to his host. As he walked briskly down the carpeted corridor, Cedric could only fantasize about the moneyed world he had just barely glimpsed. Just imagine, no more worrying about the price of food, wearing tailor-made clothes from Savile Row, holidays with scantily clad girls in Monte Carlo and watching his horse win the premiere King George race at Ascot. Fantasy, nothing but, Cedric, my son. Your allotted place is here at Oaks Lodge,

Mortingbridge, West London, with your superiors. Don't forget it because they shall keep reminding you of that cast-iron fact—no money, no power.

As soon as he arrived at the ground floor reception—dreaming of 8 am when his 12-hour shift ends—he received another phone call.

'It that you, Bambridge? I need some assistance right now. Would you please be a sweetie and come right up to my apartment? I'm number four, but I expect you know that, don't you?' she croaked to dear old Cedric.

'Good morning, Miss Holroyd. Yes, I know your apartment well. It was only yesterday that I helped you find your walking stick.' Over the years, he had found the bloody thing on numerous occasions. He vowed that the next time she bleats about it, he'll break it in two and dump it in the skip. Mind you, on more than one occasion, he had thought of something more treacherous but managed to dampen his feelings.

'That's right, my good chap. You're a bloody good indispensable social worker, that's what you are,' she said as she rather confusingly promoted Cedric to a position he knew nothing about. She addressed him, and most other people, by their wrong names. She had been doing this for some years. As a former barrister, she once had a sharp mind, but now it was failing her somewhat. At 80 years old, her productive years were long gone.

'I'll be there in a few minutes, Miss Holroyd,' Cedric reassured her. Incidentally, he thought to himself, not for the first time, he had never known whether she was Ms or Miss. That also applied to most of the other female residents. He had, of course, looked at their mail when the postman was late and would ask Cedric to deliver them. But even addressed letters were sometimes misleading. Over the years, some of the words affixed to surnames were rather scandalous. But his lips were sealed as always. Dependable Cedric at your service. Nevertheless, if he had the opportunity to make some rather underhanded money, he would not hesitate. But whatever you called them—shithead, shithouse or shitty—it didn't really matter, Cedric concluded. In his aimless existence, wandering worthlessly around Oaks Lodge, amongst old people who had lost any sort of aim long ago.

At the same time, Mr Flowers, aged 77, had let himself in through the front security doors. Cedric noticed that the taxi driver had physically supported him to the front door. Another night on the booze, probably been frequenting one of the many private members clubs he patronised. He had been well known in West End circles for many years. A first-class character, friend, drinker, punter and many other qualities, Flowers would, no doubt, have ascribed to his name. How many of those dubious descriptions could actually be reliably contributed to him was debatable.

'Good evening, old boy. How the heck are you this sunny day?' he incoherently asked Cedric. The occupant of apartment 16 was in a right old state. Alcohol stains were all down his shirt and tie. His coat buttons were all undone, as was the front zip of his trousers. Cedric noticed a large bottle of scotch sticking out the side pocket of his expensive, blue Crombie overcoat. He was a rather unsightly specimen, indeed. No doubt, like many living within the same concrete and glass confines, he was passed caring about the opinions of others. Although it must be said, when he was sober, he was always neatly attired.

'Good morning, Mr Flowers,' Cedric replied, appealing to a mind not in full control of its faculties.

'Morning already, Bambridge?' he asked the smiling night porter in front of him. Countless times he had asked Cedric this question.

'It is, sir. The time is exactly 4 am.'

'Well, blow me down, old chap. Where have I been? I've probably been drinking with those scoundrels in a club somewhere. God knows where. The taxi driver drove for bloody miles. How far out are we here, Cyril... sorry, Cecil... no, Cedric? Got it bloody right for once, I hope.' Flowers spurted and spluttered his words all over Cedric's face.

'From the West End to Oaks Lodge is approximately 15 miles, sir. Please, remember we are on the very outskirts of London here.' Nearly every time he is on duty and Flowers is drunk, the usual diatribe comes wallowing from his gigantic mouth, which, when in full flow, is like a building site digger—loud and aggressive.

'That fucking young prick is always overcharging. He thinks I'm a fool. One day, I'll catch him out with the end of my big boot up his arse,' Tom Flowers chuckled. 'By the way, Cyril, would you fancy a nightcap? I've bought a really handsome bottle of malt whiskey from Stewarts of Bond Street, I think. Yes, do come, Cyril, and put your feet up for an hour. I'm sure you're tired after so many hours of work,' he said, urging Cedric on.

At that moment, another phone call came through to reception. Bambridge knew who it was and was anticipating another ear-bashing.

'Where have you got to, Bambridge? I phoned ages ago requesting some assistance.'

'I say, how is that old tart, Miss Fulton? Saw her in town the other day buying flowers in Sharps department store. By God, she gets uglier every time I unavoidably cast my eyes on her. Scrawny neck reminds me of a Christmas turkey that Father once bought. I'm sure she will soon start gobbling her speech. And those fucking steel-framed glasses sitting on the top of her protruding bony nose do her very few, if any, favours,' Flowers spat out across the desk.

'I do apologise, Miss Holroyd. Another resident came in the same time as you phoned and he needed my assistance. But fear not, Miss Holroyd, I will be with you in two minutes.'

Turning his attention back to Mr Flowers, who was by now looking dreadful and in desperate need of sleep, Cedric thanked him for the kind invitation but explained he had to leave immediately.

'Goodnight, Mr Flowers.'

'What was that, Cyril?' inquired the old pissed chap, whose NHS hearing aid sometimes sounded as though it was playing music. Not surprising, perhaps, that he became confused at times.

'Goodnight.'

'Yes, have a good day, Sambridge.'

Instead of waiting for the lift, he sprinted to the second floor to where apartment four was. Panting heavily, he knocked on Miss Holroyd's highly polished front door. Five minutes later, after unlocking three locks, she opened the

door. Like entering Fort Knox, an irritated Cedric thought as
he was slowly ushered into the owner's lounge or dining room.
Residents had various names for this particular space. She was
slow on her legs due to severe arthritis, and without the aid of
a walking stick, she would have frozen on the spot like Nelson's Column.

Other ailments were absentmindedness, chronic short-
sightedness and false teeth. All these impediments she suffered from reminded Cedric that, one day, money or not, he
might end up like the old hag in front of him... walking into
walls or talking to the wrong person or trying to open the
wrong apartment door, as she constantly did. He had seen it
all. On one occasion, she flushed her cheque book down the
toilet.

It was the insufferable false teeth that he had been summoned to hunt down and find once again. They could be
anywhere among her legal books, bags, cookery magazines or
bundles of wool, of which there was enough to have opened
her own factory. Cedric thought he must be nice, kind and
polite to the old lady. You never know, was his persistent
thought, the slim doddery spinster might just leave him a
few bob in her will. He was prepared and willing, he had no
choice, to listen to her current woes.

'At last you are here, Bambridge. I thought you got lost
or ran away. I know you are not going to believe me but I
have lost my false teeth again. I've looked everywhere, but I'm
limited where I can look due to the arthritis,' she feebly explained.

Cedric felt like telling her to chain the fucking teeth
around her neck with some sort of musical attachment or bell

to remind her. Mind you, her memory recall had deteriorated noticeably during the last year. At that moment, he realised that not too many years ago, she was a criminal barrister. Sod that, he thought, pleased the incompetent old fool hadn't defended him, otherwise, he might still be behind bars.

It was about time she saw the visiting doctor, all privately paid for, of course. Dr Stern made periodical check-ups for dithering residents to be assessed, for numerous medical problems. He usually spent about 15 minutes at most with a resident, but did very little for them than have a chat and cup of tea. It was money for old rope, Cedric was convinced. Dr Stern had made a fortune from the insurance companies that residents had used for years. Even Cedric realised that some residents, including Miss Holroyd, had considerably deteriorated during his employment, yet few received the medical support they required. Perhaps the quack was hoping early deaths would bring forth bequeathed riches. An apartment or two would do nicely. Monies, jewels and pictures deposited in bank vaults in Switzerland. The devious old medic had it all planned. Furthermore, thought Cedric, how many more old codgers, elsewhere, does the doctor visit for personal gain? All being prepared by the good doctor for the day when they enter their wooden overcoats, and are lowered into English soil! Or self-interested family members, anticipating riches galore as the person is laid to rest.

'Firstly, I will look in the bathroom for them, Miss Holroyd. They may have fallen behind the washbasin,' he loudly explained to the old lady. He was also hoping to find some money or jewellery or any other small valuable item that she was unaware of. A nice little earner waiting to be had, he anticipated.

'That's fine, Mr Tambridge,' she said.

On all fours, he made a slow, thorough search of the large, pink decorated room. He scanned every conceivable space, which was more to his advantage than the resident, but found nothing. Not even an odd ten-pound note lurking among the dust.

'Couldn't find them in the bathroom, Miss Holroyd,' he stood talking, while she sat in her Harris Tweed covered armchair. He was praying that the phone would not ring during the search for the old girl's brown covered rancid teeth. This was the umpteenth occasion that he had been called out to find them. Cedric, given the opportunity, would love to have smashed them to smithereens with a 14-pound sledgehammer. Not to say, super glued them, once and for all, inside her rotting mouth. She certainly wouldn't lose them again!

'I will have a look inside your kitchen. Is that alright, Miss Holroyd?'

'Yes, yes, of course, please do what you have to but please find them.'

Cedric entered the light blue tiled room, consisting of a large fridge/freezer, washing machine of industrial proportions, an ageing gas cooker, sufficient pots and pans to feed an army and all the other essential paraphernalia. That is essential for some people, but Miss Holroyd rarely cooked. Her kitchen, similar to the owner, was largely a museum piece. She ate delivered food, and the rest was bought in town or prepared by one or two sympathetic neighbours. Mind you, she was so slim that she couldn't have eaten very much. Two mice and a budgerigar probably ate similar amounts of food.

Having passed his driving test many years ago—about the only minor merit he possessed—he was able, on occasions, to drive Miss Holroyd and others to buy various goods. He preferred that one of his colleagues drove her, due to the incessant desire she had to visit charity shops. She would dawdle and dally around, talking to anyone who would listen, buying anything, regardless of its practical purpose, and take them home. Once there, she used to wash and place them in any available empty space. None of the items were ever used. She made donations to the women who came weekly to clean, vacuum and polish the public areas of Oaks Lodge. From time to time, for a small fee, they cleaned Miss Holroyd's apartment, and several others. One of the women informed Cedric that her bedroom was stacked to the ceiling with charity shop-bought clothes. Enough, she said, to clothe the whole of Mortingbridge.

He looked high and low, under all the various machines. On top of one wall-mounted shelf, he found a tin of Argentine beef canned before the Second World War. On another, a high-heeled shoe, a rotten pineapple and mouse poison. The fridge was half full of out-of-date tins. When he opened the freezer, he saw the infamous false teeth, chattering away like a cemetery soul singer. He found them at last after an hour of fruitless endeavour. If the freezer had been big enough, he felt like stuffing her in there and permanently sealing the door. He returned to the lounge, feeling like a belligerent lackey, to explain the case of the missing teeth.

'Miss Holroyd, I have found your false teeth, of all places, in the freezer. I wonder how they got there,' said Cedric incredulously. Whatever she now said, he was going to emphasise, in the strongest of terms, that she take his advice on how to keep them safe and within eye distance.

'Miss Holroyd, we must permanently sort out your teeth problem. We are wasting too much time,' said an exasperated Cedric. He was also aware that Nelson Trussington, his colleague who lived in the other basement flat, and various agency staff, had dealt with the same problem.

'Yes, of course, Mr Bambridge,' she apologetically accepted. 'What do you propose?' she asked. 'Will I have to go and see that goddamned, four-eyed chap in the dentist again? He sticks all manner of things in my mouth and they are most uncomfortable indeed,' she complained. Cedric knew there was something unmentionable that he would like to put in her mouth.

'Yes, you will have to visit him again. They don't have mobile dentistry units small enough to visit you up here. What I propose is that you get fitted for two or three pairs of dentures. One pair you could wear, and the others you could store in a small light box around your neck. If you lose one pair, you will have another pair in reserve. What do you think of that idea?' he asked the confused looking old woman who, by this stage, was slipping down the armchair. 'Or we could have a spare denture in the cupboard downstairs behind the reception area where all staff would be notified and have easy access to them,' he suggested to the crotchety old dear.

As he was finishing his sentence, the mobile phone started ringing again—the last thing he needed right now as he tried in vain to explain the options available to Miss Holroyd. You couldn't make this up, he thought, trying to discuss false teeth with an 80-year-old at 6 am. The whole residential road will probably be asleep, not to say the whole town. Probably, most of Britain, other than essential workers, will be snoozing and, here he is, arguing about fucking false teeth. What had he done to deserve this absurd life? Always an outsider—that was Cedric Bambridge.

'Hello, night porter speaking.'

'Good morning, Bambridge. This is Miss Starling. Please could you come up and assist me with a problem? I'm apartment 15,' she squealed through the phone.

'If it's not an emergency, I'll be about ten minutes, Miss Starling. I'm assisting another resident. Thank you.'

'Well, Miss Holroyd, what do you think?' he asked after ending the call. At this time in the morning, now past 6 am, it was not surprising that he and his colleagues all prefer to work the 12-hour day shifts. He felt exhausted and hadn't had a tea for several hours. During the day, it is less busy; time for breaks and conversations with people. But did it all really matter as work promotion didn't exist at the Lodge, he thought for the millionth time. A different day, same old shit.

'Yes, I shall give the matter some thought and then phone that cretin dentist,' she informed Cedric after wasting his invaluable time. He was so enraged that he felt like throwing her out of the apartment window. He could imagine reading the national headlines: 'An invidious old lady, aged 80, found dead in the garden of Oaks Lodge, Mortingbridge. Porter arrested.'

Whenever Cedric became stressed to the point of self-harm, something he frequently avoided, his mind took him back to his teenage experiences. It was the era of punk rock. Cedric was heavily into punk culture. He loved the mad anarchic people he met in clubs, where any sort of outrageous behaviour was the norm. Cedric grew spiked hair, coloured blue and pink, wore leather jackets and beaten up jeans. Thick crepe sole boots made him look the business. He looked for fights. He got beaten up several times by various people, usually when he was drunk. Smoked cannabis most days until it came out of his ears. But most of the girls gave him short shrift. Too ugly, he reckoned. Never did he once have sex with a girl to this day. Plenty of gay punk sex about, but that wasn't for Cedric.

He was satisfied head-butting walls, security railings in clubs and other people's heads. The greatest thrill of his life was listening to his punk heroes, The Sex Pistols, Sham 69 and The Clash. He once had a beer with Jimmy Percy, of Sham 69, in the infamous 101 club. But Cedric's all-time hero was Sid Vicious who fronted the Sex Pistols. Though they only recorded four singles and one album, it was the lyrics 'God save the queen, that fascist regime' that had been imprinted on his mind forever. Given the opportunity, he would have kissed Sid's arse. Ever since those heady days, whenever he felt how absurd life was with all its broken promises and empty truths, he had something solid to fall back on. It was his coping strategy.

Cedric had pacified old hag Holroyd and was eager to move on to the next job. Mind you, that 8 am bell finishing time was ringing in his head. He now had to give his undivided attention to Miss Starling, another resident who was a 75-year-old single spinster. Similar to a lot of her cohort, she was short, thin, wore no cosmetics on her pinch-lined face, and involved herself in several local history groups. A former museum curator, one must say she was socially minded. She did her best for others by donating to various local charities. She had the money, no doubt. Due to her high level of energy and enthusiasm, Cedric thought she was smoking dope or taking acid.

Now over 60 years old, Cedric's slim frame didn't have the energy to run or walk up to apartment 15 anymore, where Miss Starling lived. Years of chasing up and down the stairs, assisting here, problem-solving there had expunged the life force out of him. Eight flights of steep stairs were for the youngsters. He'd stick to using the lift and, in hard times, useful for scratching his bollocks and head-butting the metal interior.

'Apologies if I'm late, Miss Starling. Only, the last resident has ongoing problems to sort out. How can I help?' he asked the sorry-looking specimen dressed in a black nightdress and cap. Reminiscent of a workhouse character, he thought.

'Well, Bambridge, please come into my lounge. As you can see, I have no lights working, only that emergency lamp on the table is giving me some light. When I pushed the light switch at 7 am, they all failed. Nothing came on. Fortunately, I keep that lamp for emergencies on the sideboard. Rather irritating, isn't it, Bambridge?' she said. Well, that may be but she should have experienced Borstal during the winter. Broken cell windows allowed snow, rain, wind and anything else in to freeze the soul into submission. He and his two cellmates regularly woke around 4 am covered in ice. If you found a willing partner, then a shared bed could be the difference between life and death in those Victorian slum cesspits.

By this time, all he needed was a hot mug of tea and two bacon sandwiches. Instead, he had to sort out her fuses in a cupboard barely big enough for an anorexic ballerina to move around.

'The problem is that your fuses have blown. I'll crouch down in your small cupboard sideways and replace them.' The fuse box cupboard was full of cobwebs, spiders clambered over his blue overalls, and crammed in one corner was about 50 brochures of Monet. Related to her former work, he assumed. Cedric looked several times but didn't see any long-forgotten money hanging around or anything worth nicking. 'That's it, Miss Starling,' he said as he turned the light back on. 'All finished for you.'

'That's marvellous, that is. Would you like a cup of tea or coffee?'

He thought the old Duchess would never ask. By now, he was parched, but never in a million years, he concluded, would she offer him any grub. I bet she had never heard of egg, bacon, beans and chips. For her, it was a thin piece of toast, oatmeal biscuit and black coffee.

'That would be most acceptable from such a kind resident, thank you.' Cedric gave her the old flannel treatment, hoping for once that she would offer hot sausage rolls or at least a few mouldy biscuits.

After leaving the apartment, Cedric took the lift back down to the ground floor. All was quiet at the moment. He pulled out the night shift diary from under the reception desk, which he had to use to record all activities for the last

12 hours. Cedric always found this arduous and laborious. From his earliest days at school, he hated sitting behind a desk, being shouted at by various teachers, trying to write and read. Teachers threw chalk at him, clipped his ear and gave him endless detentions to make him learn. Those memories evoked anger and resentment in him at the way his elders abused him. Cedric thought self-abuse, low self-esteem and isolation, and other things, originated from these experiences.

The thoughts of the last 12 hours of intense, frustrating work quickly receded as his colleague, Nelson Trussington, opened the lock to the front door.

'Good morning, brudder, how are you?' asked Nelson, a big, tall, balding first-generation Jamaican.

'Hello, Nelson, I'm so pleased to see you after 12 long fucking irritating hours working for these old biddies. I'm up to my neck in shit that these old wretches have just thrown at me. I've finished writing in the night diary, but could you ask the cleaners to spray all the oriental plants near the front doors and down the passage? The central heating keeps them vibrant but dust from those fucking thick shag pile carpets cling to the plants. That's what the area manager reckons. Anyway, it will brighten up the place on this cold, damp January morning.

'What the fuck does he know, the old pussy,' Nelson laughed.

'Not a lot, but if you get a minute, do mention it... not once, but three times to those women who have brains like sieves.'

'Will do, Cedric, get much sleep during the night?' asked Nelson.

'You must be joking. With old shit-face Miss Holroyd and piss artist Mr Flowers carrying on, the chance would be a fine thing,' Cedric explained.

'Of course, the night shifts are usually busier than the day shifts, brudder,' Nelson smiled at his weary colleague.

'Well, have a good day, my friend. I'm off to my flat for a rest, as we hoi polloi call them.'

'Don't pull that old plonker too much. Take care, Cedric.'

'I will, Nelson. I've got four days off soon when I can get out for a while and ride a few trains or buses or whatever,' he told his colleague with a rare beaming smile. All the years Cedric had worked at Oaks Lodge, he had never really got to terms with a rota system of four days on duty and four days off. But after 48 hours of night duty, when the early hours were the most difficult of any shift, the next four days to one's self were wonderful. He hadn't the gumption or knowhow, though, to work out if over 52 weeks he was working more than he should or, put another way, he was being underpaid. He certainly wasn't going to ask his area manager about it just in case he was being paid too much by his company, Cleanaway Ltd. They employed everyone, including the cleaners that worked in and around the building and gardens. As far as Cedric was concerned—keep your lips sealed. Instilled by the different institutions where he had been a non-paying guest!

Although a life-long fantasist, 60 years of age wasn't too old, Cedric kept drumming into his mind, to change certain things. Out of order to expect a woman to set up home with him, he realised. No way could he ever buy his own home, even though, due to his frugality, he had managed to save a few thousand pounds during his service at Oaks Lodge. Fantasy probably maintained his sanity and decline into hell. He had come to realise that he probably thought, felt and acted differently to others. Self-harm had its merits.

The most intense times for Cedric were watching the television. There were occasions when the rich and famous were appearing, when he fantasized about killing them with a machine gun, or flame thrower or even dynamite. This used to excite him, allow some relief from inner torment and gave him much-needed self-control. He hated them all. His fantasies, at times, went close to the edge. A part of him looked for revenge. But he managed to pull back and return to reality before the inevitable.

But Cedric had a clean driving licence and was experienced at several different practical skills. He wasn't unemployable elsewhere, not by any standard. All his life, people had told him he wasn't up to much. Fit really for very little. But during the last few years, he kept maintaining that he was a competent worker. Though undermined by certain residents, on the whole, he had carried out what was required of him. No, fuck it, he thought, he must hold onto that dream of getting a job somewhere—anywhere. Perhaps a resident gardener or chauffeur or housekeeper would fit his requirements. Whenever possible, he visited the job centre, registered with several private employment agencies and bought a monthly gardening magazine. His weary brow trod the pavements trying to find that suitable job for the rest of his working life.

2

CHAPTER TWO

Nelson stood in reception with his legs astride and his hands on his hips, looking like some giant gladiator. He was well-known and liked by all those who use the building. With hands like shovels, he could pick up a chair with one hand for a party trick. He laughed and joked with everyone, except some of the crusty residents. But to be fair, on their day, they too would crack their old, bent, distorted faces into a humorous smile.

Especially Mr Ford, the resident of apartment two, who loved to arm wrestle with Nelson on the reception desk. They used to have some right old ding dongs together. Even at 70 years old, many years younger than his opponent, he was a tough old cookie. Hated losing at anything, whether that was playing marbles or placing £5000 bets on a horse. In his younger days, he gambled real big for a hobby. His profession by day used to be a structural engineer. But at night, he lived and played hard with a lot of mean souls who would sell their grandmothers for a shot of whiskey. Although Ford was getting on a bit in age, he still had what it took to get by. He was shrewd and self-aware. Divorced for 30 years, after a succession of lovers, his former wife still came to visit occasionally in the town nearby. Ford had regretted not having children. He admitted that he was too preoccupied developing a professional career that took him around the world constructing bridges, stadia and ships. Made a fortune and lost a lot of it on gambling, sex and drinking. He had owned his smart apartment for at least 20 years; although he made sure his former wife was financially comfortable. He appeared to be a decent guy. He certainly called all the staff by their first names. No bullshit like most of the other residents who thought staff were a lesser breed.

'Well, Nelson, we've certainly had some good sparring on that desk, haven't we?' he laughed at the porter.

'We did at that, sir. Weren't they worth a million dollars apiece to watch?'

'They certainly were. Must have another arm wrestle soon?' he said enthusiastically.

'That would be great. Get the money ready, sir,' Nelson replied.

'Must get going, I have a taxi waiting outside. I'm off to meet a former colleague for lunch in London. I'm sure he'll try and tap me for a few hundred after I've soaked up too much brandy. Cheerio.'

All was quiet as the reggae-loving porter sat on his chair drinking coffee. The light shining on his bald head gave the reception area an added glow to counter the outer gloom. He was thinking of his parents that sent his heart in a spin. Boy, they were both great company. Yes, full of life, music, dance and romance for one another. They met in Jamaica, a small village called Jacob, where they were both born into large, supportive vibrant families. Neither their families nor anyone else had a bean to their name, but they sure did enjoy life to the full. Nelson was told stories galore of his parents' early life when he sat to eat evening dinner after a wretched day at school in East London.

Both his parents made the difficult decision to leave their loved families. Neither of them ever got over it, but to find a better life in England was their goal. They travelled as a part of the Windrush generation. They were accompanied by several friends, so they weren't alone in London. Both worked on the buses for most of their lives and bought their small council house. They made it into a loving home, the place where Nelson was born 50 years ago. Superficial tears came to his eyes as his feelings were consumed by their inner presence. But it wasn't all love, limbo and family legend.

He was near totally oblivious to the weekly cleaners pushing the security bell several times. He unlocked the door from under his desk.

'Hey, you had a heavy night or something, Nelson? It looked like you were on another planet,' beamed Emily, aged 58, and the oldest of the four cleaners,

'Morning, ladies. Well, if it ain't the Oaks Lodge scrubbers,' he said, smiling. 'Only joking, girls, really. You're the best bunch of cleaners I've had the privilege of working with in the years I've worked here. That's straight, girls,' he said, smiling from ear to ear.

'We've heard all that tosh before, haven't we, ladies?' said Hilda, aged 56, and the longest-serving cleaner.

'At least Nelson has a laugh with us,' said Gill, aged 45, who was blind in her right eye. 'Poor old Cedric doesn't say much. Looks a bit frightened of us women,' she said.

'Perhaps we should take his trousers down and rub his balls in cream,' said Emily, the cleaning supervisor—single with three grown-up children.

'Right, girls, I've been informed by the boss, rigorous, Richards, that he wants all the plants sprayed and cleaned of all the bits and pieces that lodge on them. And the rest, vacuum, etc., is on this chart that you are given from time to time. There might also be a few of the older biddies who may require personal cleaning, but don't charge 'em over the top,' Nelson winked at them.

'OK, boss. We've got the idea. We go through this rigmarole every time we set our eyes on your ugly face, Nelson,' Emily laughed to herself. 'By the way, who was the geezer here for a day, agency bloke, some two weeks back? He didn't have a fucking clue. You need to train 'em a bit before sticking 'em on that reception,' she said.

'Yes, I shall inform our lovely boss, but please do carry out what "Your Grace" has demanded. Otherwise, he will have my cobblers on a plate if you know what I mean, you gorgeous souls.'

After collecting all the necessary equipment to wash the QE2, the four pink-jacketed females trundled to their usual places for the next four hours or so. They had all lived locally for many years, with partners and children, except Emily. Several years ago, Emily hit her husband over the head with a milk bottle, which necessitated him being stitched up in hospital and her being fined for common assault in the local

Magistrates' Court. She made the front page of all the local newspapers when she said to the beak, 'I'd love to shit over your head.' If she wasn't before, she certainly afterwards became a bit of a celebrity.

Minutes later, two residents entered the reception area. Wearing their expensive overcoats, carrying leather bags and rouged, unusually, to the rafters. They acknowledged Nelson's presence.

'Good morning, Miss Perks and Miss Nobton. My, you both look delectable. Your presence has brightened up this rather cloudy day,' said Nelson, who was aware that flattery was worth a million dollars, especially for the two old biddies that stood right in front of him. In fact, he thought, they were two discarded mannequins thrown on the heap by Dorothy Perkins.

'Good morning to you, Trussington. We hope you are well?' enquired Miss Perks, aged 74, who was slim and short with multi-coloured hair. You could have assumed that she had been car sprayed by the local garage.

Nelson had a wicked sense of humour. Something he attributes to his early upbringing when his family were always laughing and joking at each other. He didn't take anything that seriously, unlike lonely dejected Cedric whose life existed of chronic anxiety. Nelson's late parents always told him to laugh and the world will laugh with you. That is why he told people—anyone, even a toff at Oaks Lodge—numerous jokes. He had the outgoing personality to get away with it. Now, if someone like Cedric had called Miss Perks delicious, he would have probably lost his job. The day porter was a showman, a show-off and could be outrageous, but most people, even Miss Nobton, lapped it all up.

'I'm a lot better now I've seen you fine women. Meeting young men in the local hotel for drinks, are we?' he teased them.

'Good gracious, Trussington, we are going out to play bridge with friends,' said a glum-looking Miss Nobton, aged 76. She was single and becoming slimmer by the day. Both women were spinsters, and had met at a preparatory school in Basingstoke. They had remained life-long friends.

'Please take care, ladies,' he said, smiling at them as they made their way through the door and into the waiting taxi, Ace cars, which made a small fortune throughout the year, driving residents and staff to numerous destinations.

No sooner had the two women departed, when another taxi pulled up outside the building. Nelson was pleased, as were his colleagues, that one didn't have to race out, especially with an umbrella if it was raining, and open the cab door. Nelson opened the security door (not obligatory) for the tall, well-built male, aged about 75 years with a thick head of silver hair.

'Good morning, sir,' said the porter who was curious to know of his presence. Something rather solid about him caught the porter's shrewd eye. Doctor, maybe? If he was, he certainly wasn't the usual quack, he surmised. Looks more like a lawyer or even a businessman of some repute maybe. It was the protruding firm chin and small dimple on his right cheek that made him distinguished in some respect.

'Good morning. I hope you are well. I've come to visit

Miss Holroyd. She is expecting me,' explained the gentleman dressed in a thick woollen overcoat.

'Thank you, sir. I'm very well. May I have your name? I will phone through to let her know you have arrived.'

After being told his name, he picked up the phone. 'Good morning, Miss Holroyd, the porter speaking. There is a Mr Matthews here on a visit,' Nelson said in his perfect English.

'Oh, that is wonderful, Bambridge. Please send him up immediately,' she said rather sourly. Well, she is over 80 years old and becoming immobile. Perhaps she needs to have her eyes tested or ears syringed, thought Nelson.

'That's fine with Miss Holroyd. Please take the lift to the first floor, apartment four, sir.'

'Thank you.' Nelson hoped he didn't have the misfortune, like several before him, of treading or sitting on her false teeth and crushing them into minute pieces.

Two hours later, the cleaners having finished their work and departed, the area manager drove up in his silver Ford car. Mindfully, he got out of his new acquisition, tightened his tie, and walked over to the communal garden. Inspection time had arrived, nothing will miss the prying hawk-like eyes of Mr David Richards—20 years employed, shareholder and provocateur-in-chief, he was here to kick arse, find fault and demean to the fullest. He had given many employees their marching orders to the front gate—like Hugh Preston, the former cleaner who wasn't scared of his frightful conduct. He chased him around the garden and car park, nearly clobbering Richards, who escaped into the building within inches of his life. The police arrested the unfortunate bloke after he had clobbered one of them.

Having inspected the garden, he made his way into reception. Beware, Nelson, he is going to give you a hard time. For his part, the porter had heard and seen it all before. Underhanded, devious and scheming were qualities that Richards only lived for. Although married, he spent little time with his children, it didn't surprise those who realised he was central to most things. They reckoned he lived in his car. He set up a sophisticated technological battery of cameras and microphones. Driving surreptitiously to different sites owned by Cleanaway Ltd, he hid in his car, in various places, to spy on employees. He also had a written logbook full of the foulest details—prepared and waiting—to use as evidence against anyone he deemed had wronged him. A head case of the highest order!

'Hello, Nelson, how are things around here? Did those women clean and spray the oriental plants? How about the two communal toilets down here next to the lifts? I've noticed pieces of orange peel, dead plants, cigarette ends, a plastic bottle, rubber doll and several artificial nails either in the car park or garden. Know anything about them?' he asked with a surly smile.

'Hello, Mr Richards. I hope you are well. Several times this morning, I emphasised to the cleaners that you required the plants to be immaculately cleaned and polished. I've inspected them. They appear fine and—'

'No, I asked you about the car park and garden litter,' Richards scowled without compromise.

'Well, boss, the women don't clean outside the building and I—'

'What did I just say to you?'

'Boss, I haven't had time to sweep the car park, I've been busy. Residents and others coming and going. And as you know, Cedric usually does the weekly garden clean, and during the season planting, pruning and mowing,' he explained to the hate-filled eyes staring at him. Nelson felt like knocking the shithouse to the ground using his 16-stone bulk. Had he done so, he would have been a hero within the company. But, also, he would have been sacked, prosecuted and unofficially blacklisted for employment. Though illegal in Britain, the invisible grapevine had long sticky venomous tentacles that stretched around the business world. This was expedited skilfully by well-paid individuals to spread that glue all over people like Nelson Trussington's character. His employment of 12 years will be ruined, he kept thinking, if he thrashed that bastard in front of him.

'Well, go out and clean the fucking car park now. It's not a very good advert for potential clients and visitors, is it?' barked the pit bull.

His clenched fists shaking, Nelson tried to remain focused on his work. Broom and shovel in hand, in full view of Richards smirking, he walked slowly out to the car park. Unlike Cedric, who would by now be on all fours, fastidiously picking up the detritus, this porter took his time. From the car park, he made his way into the garden so as to satisfy the prying eyes firmly fixed on his every move. After 15 minutes, he returned to reception.

'That's all clean, boss,' said Nelson, smiling. He wasn't going to be undermined. Don't show anger or fear, he kept repeating to himself. Play the hideous game that Richards thrives on. Don't weaken in front of power and control. Feed his insane ego, yet at the same time, keep mindful. Richards will soon get the message. He has played these immature games with him, and many other colleagues, for years.

'Right, let's inspect the plants and all eight floors for cleanliness. Those cleaners usually leave something in a terrible state. All they think about is getting down the pub to numb their tiny brains,' Richards said sarcastically. It was fortunate that Richards was unaware of the cleaners receiving cash in hand for carrying out work for residents. That would have been stopped immediately. Mean to the bone, he certainly was.

They slowly walked down the brightly lit corridor. Richards ran his slimy hands over most of the tall oriental plants. He didn't say a word. They walked up to the first floor and he ran his finger along the bottom of the skirting board, around the window frame and checked the lift was clean. Nelson's employee mobile phone started buzzing. Wonderful, he thought to himself. Hopefully, I can escape the proverbial ear-bashing.

'Good afternoon, the porter speaking.'

'Hello, Trussington, it's Mr Gates from apartment 14. I would like some assistance right now please,' he asked politely.

'Yes, of course, Mr Gates. Will be with you in a couple of minutes,' he said, smiling to himself. The phone call gave Nelson the opportunity to get away from his boss.

'You heard that, Mr Richards. Must get into the lift and visit Mr Gates.'

Nelson knocked on the front door of the apartment. Having a mobility problem, Mr Gates, aged 80, always took time to open his front door, hobbling on his walking stick.

'Ah, there you are. Please come in and close the door behind you,' they walked very slowly down his brightly painted passage and into the lounge. The room was full of books, photographs and fine-looking furniture. Nelson didn't have any idea of the value or names of the people who painted the pictures. Not educated enough, he concluded. He wondered, as Mr Gates was divorced and had no children he knew of, who would inherit such wonderful items. Nelson fantasized that those luxury items would buy him a house beyond his wildest dreams. 'My problem is this, Trussington. I have dropped my very small tool, which I use for carrying out minor repairs to watches, and it has rolled under my fine mahogany table. Becoming increasingly immobile, I am unable to retrieve it. Please could you do that for me?' he explained.

'Of course, sir, that is no problem.'

In the forefront of Nelson's mind was trying to keep healthy space between himself and Richards. On his hands and knees, he immediately saw the object but looked the other way to waste time. He ventured further under the table, wondering whether his boss had finished inspecting and left the building. He kept up a quiet running conversation with Mr Gates under the table, though he was slightly deaf. Nelson eventually emerged with the metal tool.

'There we are, Mr Gates. One tool found,' he said to a pleased old man, who was now rather housebound and becoming increasingly dependent on others for his well-being. One of the cleaners recently gave his apartment a fortnightly clean and tidy. Very handy £30 for Hilda, though she, no doubt, spent it boozing in the local pub. Why not, indeed! Mr Gates was still capable of using the washing machine and a catering company delivered his expensive meals. He had plenty of money to enjoy his life.

'Anything else I can do while I'm here, Mr Gates?' Nelson was desperate to stay away from his boss, who could give him a hard time, two hours before his duty ended.

'What say?' asked Mr Gates.

'Anything else need doing?'

'Well, my dear boy, yes, there is come to think of it. The washing machine is full. I completely forgot about it when I started playing with my tools of the trade. I used to be a jeweller in Hatton Garden. Did you know that, my boy?'

'Yes, sir, I did know that. Must have been very interesting, not that I know anything about it.' If he had informed Nelson once, he had informed him a hundred times. Of course, being the old chap's life's work, with many memories to reflect upon, he was proud of his achievements. Sadly, he reflected on occasions that he didn't have any other person whom he could teach the invaluable creative skill of jeweller. 'Do you want me to hang the washing in the bathroom, Mr Gates?' asked Nelson, who felt relieved he was in the apartment, hidden away from his boss who may well be lurking outside, listening to the conversation within.

'Yes, that's fine, dear boy.'

Nelson hurriedly hung the long johns, string vests, shirts and other moth-eaten old clothes. He sat on the side of the bath, occasionally making a noise or two for the ears of Mr Gates, thinking about whether he should have a beer tonight or listen to his reggae music. Divorced ten years ago, his two grown-up children lived in South London. He rarely saw them. They've never visited him in Mortingbridge. 'Too far, Dad,' they keep saying to him. He hasn't seen his former wife since the day he walked out. That was many years ago; two days later, he was ensconced in his present flat. Marriage, you can keep it as far as Nelson was concerned. Not worth the hassle. If he died today, no one would shed a tear. Sometimes, when he thought morbidly, he admired how Cedric had coped all is life on his own with no one to kiss, cuddle or have sex with. He must have a barren inner landscape, Nelson concluded.

'Well, that's all completed, Mr Gates. Is that all you need done?'

'Well done, my dear boy. Take a packet of biscuits here on the table. See yourself out,' he smiled at Nelson.

'Thank you.' The chocolate biscuits had expired by four years, but never mind, thought Nelson, it's the thought that counts. He had a brief look to see if there was anything he could steal. These old people, he and Cedric realised, sometimes drop cash or valuables on the floor. Perks of the trade they called it.

There was a loud thump on the front door. The porter knew who that was before he opened it.

'I've finished the inspection. I'm now going. Thanks. See you soon,' said Richards.

'OK. Thanks, boss. Goodnight.'

'Who was that, Trussington?' shouted Mr Gates.

'That was my area manager. He comes around from time to time to inspect the maintenance. Well, thanks for the food. I must attend other things. Goodnight.' Nelson shook his hand. He quite liked the old boy. If he had realised Gates' age, skills and growing disability, when he had first moved in, he could have asked for tuition when off duty. Better paid work might have materialised. A higher status job could have bought a small cheap flat somewhere in South London, near his kids. What a fucking idiot he was. Now, stuck in this porter job and living in a crummy basement flat opposite moronic Cedric. If Nelson had a gun to hand, he thought, he would have blown his own brains out.

Cedric went off duty 11 hours ago, but he had only managed to get two hours of sleep. That wasn't unusual for him. On this last occasion, he had sat in his beaten-up old armchair, eyes fixed on the dirty wall for two hours, reflecting upon his life. The more intensified it became, the more hopeless his position was. He had always been an outsider. No one, or very few people outside of work spoke to him. He felt lost, worthless and alone, but he wasn't going to self-harm. Those haunting thoughts never left him. He had never told anyone since he first experienced them in the children's home where his mother had dumped him as an unwanted, unloved baby. Cedric was about five when intrusive thoughts came to his attention. Even today, he still wasn't sure what they meant. No sooner that he is aware of them, he suppressed their power over him for a while.

His early life was spent in a Catholic children's home somewhere in Dorset. He had various legal papers that the nuns gave him to keep or, rather, they were given to him via his adopted parents. But most of the adoption spiel he had never bothered to read, and he had no intention of doing so. He thought the nuns tried to show him affection, but he didn't take any risks by reciprocating. From the earliest days, he realised that if he kept quiet and just looked to the floor, it gave him a safe haven. When he had occasionally spoke or laughed or played tricks on other children, the nuns smacked him hard. Once or twice—could have been more—those dreaded nuns, shrouded in their superior religious garments, had locked him in a room for three days. The only times he saw the nuns was when he was fed and they removed his toilet pot. On one occasion, he had diarrhoea and shit all over the floor. They made him clean it up and afterwards refused to let him wash himself. Brutal bastards they were. If there was a heaven, Cedric hoped that all those brutes at St Michael's children's home went to hell.

The nightmares began when Cedric was around four years old. He pissed his bed regularly. When thunder and lightning started, he immediately dived under the bed. He still hides under his own bed, or at work in the cupboard. If noticed by a nun, he was promptly dragged back into bed. Cedric was told by nuns that God was angry with him and was making him pay for his sins. It was this part of his life that he had tried belatedly to understand. He tried to grapple with its knots and binds. The pain, at times, had sunk into the deepest part of his inner space and time. The contradiction of various peoples' behaviour confused him to such an extent that he had to be alone whenever possible. The nuns would show occasional tenderness, then hateful inconsistencies. The only possible solution, although Cedric hadn't thought it out at the time, was to escape into his own world. It was a make-believe universe where he was safe—anything possible unto himself only. From those days, he proceeded to make a life of sorts. He always had a fear of being judged negatively.

It was not surprising, therefore, that Cedric Bambridge, his adoptive name, found life full of pain and suffering. That all it consisted of was injustice. He vividly remembers a man and woman smiling at him. He thinks he was about five years old. Standing there in torn clothes, shaven head, rotten teeth and snot running down from his nose onto his top lip, the woman held his hand and said, 'Hello, sweetheart.'

The couple, Tom and Tina Bambridge, who lived in Wiltshire, had visited the home seeking to adopt a child. They were unable to have children. For some unknown reason, they liked Cedric straight away. Probably felt sorry for the undernourished, sad looking youngster whose eyes craved to be loved. They drove Cedric to various places of interest. He stood back from this new world he had rarely experienced. But his instinct informed him it was for him. He tasted wholesome food for the first time in his young, under stimulated life.

It was a world that didn't exist within the grey walls of the home. The institution was the only world he had been led to believe by his carers really existed. No, they were wrong. He had tasted something potentially exciting, challenging and vast. Not long after the visits to the zoo, seaside and funfairs, the Bambridge's legally adopted Cedric. Within weeks, they had collected him from the home, along with his few meagre chattels and driven him to a new life.

Another grinding shift approached. Realising it was approaching 8 pm, he hurriedly jumped into his working clothes and ran from the back of the building to the front door. With porters living out of the way, residents and guests didn't have to experience the embarrassment of unwanted noise or smell. Nelson was standing, leaning on the desk smiling as Cedric unlocked the front door.

'Hello, Cedric. Enjoy yourself today? Find a bird or win the premium bonds?' he asked, laughing at himself, aware it was time to descent to the pit—the place he called home—for sleep. That small space, as gruesome as it was, separated him from homelessness. At least it was quiet most of the time. The only irritating noise came from Cedric pounding around the garden with the lawn mower. The blank walls depressed him. Must buy a few cheap pictures to liven the place, he reflected. But did it really matter? No one, other than Cedric, ever visited him.

'Alright, Nelson, what sort of day did you have?' he asked his friendly colleague.

'That pussy Richards came here with all guns blazing. I would have loved to smash his jaw for him, you know,' said an animated Nelson.

'I've been downstairs all day. Slept for a couple of hours then did a bit of thinking. A little reading,' he said.

'I've filled in the daybook. A Mr Matthews visited Miss Holroyd several hours ago. They're not at it, are they?' laughed both men. 'More importantly, he might have done her in.' They laughed even louder. 'Also, those two old hags, Perks and Nobton, went out earlier. That's about it. I'm off to my humble home. I'll see yer tomorrow unless I kick the bucket before that.'

3

CHAPTER THREE

Cedric looked out into the cold, dark night. That lonely world, at times, frightened him. He had always known loneliness even when in company. But for some deep, complex reason, possibly from his days at the home, he found being on his own, nonetheless, reassuring. If you're on your own with no commitments or responsibilities, you can't get into trouble. Besides, his parents had told him not to speak to anyone unless they spoke first. They were a very quiet couple. Never once did they show affection in front of Cedric. All three used to sit watching television, all night, without a word being said between them. Cedric loved being quiet. That's all he had ever known. He used to sit quietly on his own in the children's home chapel for hours. If a nosy nun entered, he pretended to be praying. All hypocrisy, he maintained.

'Good evening, ladies. I hope you enjoyed your day?' he asked Miss Perks and Miss Nobton, who had just opened the front door. Sour faces as usual.

'Good evening, Bambridge. Yes, absolutely, thank you,'

said Miss Parks who looked conservatively dressed in a long beige jacket and hat.

'No doubt you have both noticed the sky is full of stars this evening. One consolation the cold winter nights bring,' said Cedric, who thought that to hear Cedric or Mr Bambridge uttered once, only once, would have boosted his self-esteem.

'Absolutely, Bambridge, the kind of evening that I enjoy,' commented Miss Nobton smugly.

'My colleague informed me that you went to play bridge today. I hope things went well,' said Bambridge, who was trying to make conversation but always found it difficult with people he thought were above him. You suggest one thing, they another. Most people thought in terms of contradiction.

'Oh, yes. We always enjoy our weekly bridge with friends. We had a delicious meal and conversations galore, thank you,' said Miss Perks.

Both women bid Cedric goodnight and walked into the lift that took them to their apartments. A slight smell of lavender had been left by one of the women. Although most of the residents are difficult, one must remember all were aging, as he tried to ponder the nature of their respective lives. They must have achieved well to live here at expensive Oaks Lodge. Although he felt put upon by some of them, especially in the early mornings, they were all individuals. Besides, it was his job to carry out their wishes. All had once been a part of a supportive family, he presumed. That gave them opportunity to fully develop their lives. Education, well-paid jobs and expensive luxury apartments, but it all seemed so difficult to fathom out. Cedric constantly thought about the conundrum. He hadn't the experience, from his deprived background, to understand how things really work. For some fortunate people, living in a particular place, their lives appeared a mystery to Cedric.

However, what Cedric didn't realise, was that Miss Nobton had had a most tragic family life. Seeing her now, one wouldn't give her demeanour a second thought. Intelligent, friendly and, apparently, well-liked.

Her father had killed a young colleague when he was around 45 years old. It was said that he slit his throat with a knife one evening after they had been out socialising together. The motive for such a violent act is still unknown to this day. After her father was sent to a hospital for the criminally insane, her mother steadfastly refused to discuss the subject. Mr Nobton died in the hospital some 20 years later.

As the years passed, Miss Nobton's mother became increasingly depressed and withdrew from the world. This left her daughter isolated and most unhappy. But after graduating from university, Miss Nobton never returned to the family home. She occasionally phoned or wrote to her mother, who rarely replied. Her mother died when she was 30 years old. Only three people attended the funeral. After her shattering past, she was determined to succeed in life. One can only admire her brave determination to overcome the multiple suffering her father's action had probably inflicted upon innocent people.

Not expecting anything to change, Cedric was grounded in place and time. He had always followed orders from other people. Those people who had power over him. Until the last few years, he had never thought that he, Cedric, could change his life somewhat. It had dawned on him that although residents were difficult and demanding, he could learn from them how to use words to his advantage. Cedric bought a dictionary, wrote down the meaning of certain words and how and when to use them appropriately. His confidence had grown as a consequence. Although quiet and alone at times, he was more aware of verbal communication around him. During his days off from work, he often visited the local library to read about certain subjects. A new stream of words and their meanings had entered his inner world for the first time. He had attended part-time history and English classes at the local college, but after several weeks, he dropped out due to feeling inadequate of his peer group. But it was not in vain. A growing awareness gave him the confidence to look for other employment. Cedric was optimistic that he was capable of moving on.

The gentleman that Nelson had informed his colleague of—Mr Matthews, who visited Miss Holroyd hours earlier—came out of the lift. It was 10 pm.

'Good evening, sir,' said Cedric.

'Good evening to you. I hope you are well?' he asked with a sincere smile.

'Yes, thank you, sir.'

'Are you working all night?' he enquired.

'That's right, sir. I work 12-hour shifts from 8 pm to 8 am.'

'Well, that is a long time. I hope you have an interesting book to read. I bid you goodnight.'

'Goodnight to you, sir,' said Cedric. What a charming fellow, the porter thought. Cedric fantasized about various people he saw. Now, he thought that was the kind of man he would like to be one day. It wouldn't happen, of course, but it kept his faint hopes going. The man was alive, energetic, well-dressed and intelligent. They were the qualities that had attracted Cedric's inner desires. God, did he envy those people who oozed confidence. Most of them did not appear too arrogant, but it was something they had that the night porter had not fathomed.

Whatever it was, he would never find it in the social places he occasionally frequented. They were tough, ignorant blokes from his background. If Cedric tried to suggest something not on their internal radar, he was asking for trouble. Fantasy and observation, he thought, was more productive.

All was quiet for the next hour until an ambulance drove up to the front doors with lights flashing and sirens wailing. Two men jumped out of the vehicle with packs on their backs, and rushed to the door. Cedric was waiting, anxious, to allow them inside.

'Hello, mate. We've had an emergency call from a Mr Spelling. He has heart problems apparently. Where does he reside?' asked the breathless middle-aged male.

'Mr Spelling is apartment 13. I'll take you up there,' said an apprehensive Cedric. Although he had experienced ambulance personnel helping elderly residents many times, every time it made him confused. What was he meant to do, if anything, for the suffering? He often felt incompetent in these intense situations.

The three men rushed to the lift and were on the patient's doorstep within two minutes. After ringing the bell several times, Cedric opened his door with an official skeleton key, and the ambulance men walked in and found Mr Spelling sprawled on his couch.

'Hello, sir. We are here to help you,' said the worker. Mr Spelling had pains in his chest, was sweating profusely and had an ashen face. They carried out emergency procedures and put him on a ventilator, which stabilised him. He didn't look at all well. One of the workers returned rather hurriedly with a stretcher. After collecting his medications and other personal items, they pushed him into lift, down to the ground floor and into the ambulance.

Within a few minutes, the vehicle was on its way to the local hospital. Cedric became instantly anxious. He hoped the old boy lived. Please, no more funerals to attend, he thought. During his employment, he had been to many residents' church services and seen them buried. They were usually attended by very few family or friends. One old resident, Miss Khan, he remembers had no one except two staff at her last resting place. That experience reminded him of his own demise, expecting not one person to be at his side for the final time. He was convinced there was no God or heaven, even though the vicar had told him otherwise. He would be buried similar to a pauper. Unmarked grave, no identity, and when people looked at it in passing, they would wonder who that poor wretch was lying within.

Cedric was made aware years ago of Mr Spelling's medical problems. That also applied to several other residents. The main reason they were informed was that emergency procedures might have to be carried out. That meant staff were authorised to use the company car to facilitate the problem, otherwise, they had to call the appropriate agency. Cedric was extremely relieved that Mr Spelling had the good sense to phone the emergency services. All the staff were given was basic first aid training. In essence, that meant offering a few tablets. No rocket science involved. Cedric knew that if he had received a similar phone call direct from a resident, he would definitely have panicked. He found it difficult to act spontaneously under pressure, unlike Nelson and a few of the regular agency staff, who were confident and acted with forethought. Under these circumstances, he wished he had never passed his driving test. Always afraid of change, was Cedric. How he had constantly beaten himself up due to his inept attitude. Nelson constantly reassured him. But he was working hard to try and change the way he overreacted to normal circumstances.

It was now approaching midnight, and Cedric was anticipating phone calls in an hour or two, asking for something or another. The usual things like unable to sleep, overconsumption of alcohol or just plain loneliness. Meanwhile, he made tea and sat down to read the evening paper. There were various jobs available that Cedric thought he was competent enough to fill. His eye caught an advert from the job centre, where a local employer was looking for van drivers and gardeners. On his four days off, he must go there and find out the details. Could be the opportunity he was looking for. Move away from this place and, ideally, work out in fresh air once again. Most of his numerous jobs had been unskilled physical work such as building labourer, gardening and road cleaning. The outdoor life he loved. On his days off, he nearly always went out, travelled on buses, trains or walked through the large local woods that passed through the back of Oaks Lodge.

Over the years, Marsh Woods had been a kind of retreat

for Cedric. Ever since the beginning of his employment, he had sought a local haven where he could find solitude. There he had, indeed, found what he had searched many years for. The woods were nearly always quiet and peaceful.

The last time he had found similar enjoyment was in his own small bedroom, living with his parents. They were both now deceased. When he finally left home, aged about 21 years old and encouraged by his dad, he first moved to Devon. His dad found him a job working as a farm labourer. The mud, cow shit and putrid smells eventually became too much. Cedric left after about three years for the heady heights of Birmingham and a succession of unskilled frustrating jobs. But he loved his parents. They were good people, and he was sure they loved him. As a boy, they took him on holidays, by train and coach, to numerous seaside resorts. Cedric thought himself privileged. Over the years, his contact with them was irregular. He was rather sad about that, he had thought many times that he should have visited or written to them. At both of their funerals, he broke down and sobbed for hours. He was inconsolable! The only two people who thought he was worthy of his name.

Cedric nearly always tried to find a small clearing, log or fallen tree to sit upon, hidden among the many unused small tracks. There, he was at peace with himself. He was safe, concealed away from the absurdities of life as he saw them. Aimless wanderings would stop for a while. No need for fantasy and observation. Alienation had temporarily fled his clutches.

He and Nelson had walked through Marsh Woods on many occasions together. They both enjoyed walking, and it gave them a shortcut through to the town for a beer. It was during these walks that they would find a discreet place to drink a few cans of beer. His colleague was the one person he really trusted. Nelson was everything that Cedric thought he could never be. As a tall, big, strong and confident man, people treated him with respect. But he was also a sensitive man, similar to Cedric, in love with nature. The two of them, and Cedric on his own, found several wildflower bulbs that they replanted back at the Lodge. They have now colonised many areas of the garden. Colours galore, from March to October, can be found by residents capable of physical effort.

Cedric was shaken from his reverie by the loud phone shrieking in his ear.

'Good morning. This is St Pauls Hospital casualty department. I'm the sister here. As you are aware, Mr Spelling, your resident, was brought here earlier with chest complaints and other complications. After the doctor assessed him, we have decided to keep him here on the ward for a few days, under observation.

'Thank you, sister. Do you know how long he is likely to be in hospital?' he asked the nurse.

'We don't know at this stage. It's not the first time he has been here with the problem. As you might know, he has been on medication for some time, but we will let you know. We will be notifying his GP. Thank you. Goodnight.'

'Thank you for phoning us.'

Well, thought Cedric, poor old Mr Spelling. He had lived at Oaks Lodge for at least 15 years, no doubt longer. Didn't speak that much to anyone. Rarely ventured out and had few visitors. If he could recall, the old chap was about 77 years old and had been an accountant. His sister, who was somewhat older, visited on occasions. Observing his mail, it appeared he had been an ardent cyclist and theatre-goer. Things of this medical nature had to be written in detail, which Cedric hated doing, and sent to head office. If he wrote any detail incorrectly, no matter how minor, Richards would immediately be down to give him a grand bollocking.

He looked at the wall clock, just past 2 am. Another six hours of grinding work, Cedric thought as he pursed his lips. Time for more tea and a bacon sandwich he had cooked earlier. Re-read the jobs adverts and, if any appealed to him this time, he will follow them up later today. All the staff were mightily pleased that there was no CCTV around the place. It gave them all a little leeway when late for work. Smoke around the back of the building in a former air raid shelter, or a short kip in the small tea room at the back of the reception, just as Cedric loved doing whenever possible. No electronic big brother to keep an eye on them, except the outside camera fixed to the building above the main entrance.

One of his favourite residents, David Ford, arrived back at the Lodge around 3:30. A large saloon car, white flashy job, had driven him to outside the main doors. He got out of the car, opened by the uniformed driver, and tipped him goodnight. Always a few bob about when Ford had been clubbing.

Cedric electronically opened the door for him. Ford approached the desk as sprightly as he left hours previously. Upright, smart in his camel hair jacket and holding a carrier bag.

'Good morning, Mr Ford. How are you?' he asked the smiling chap of 70 years in front of him.

'It's been a great day with friends, Cedric. Blokes I've

known for ages. Lots to drink, excellent food and intelligent company, but sadly no sex. You can't have it all, can you?'

'You can't, Mr Ford. I'm pleased you enjoyed yourself.'

'By the way, Cedric, I've bought a bottle of hock wine and a box of chocolates for you and that reprobate Nelson. I hope you enjoy it. Don't get too drunk.'

'Thanks a lot, Mr Ford. That's very kind of you.'

'You both deserve it. Thank you. By the way, tell Nelson to prepare himself for future arm wrestling. I'm gunning for him,' warned a smiling David Ford.

'I'll tell him, sir,' laughed Cedric.

'Goodnight.'

'Goodnight, sir.'

The inevitable internal phone call happened 30 minutes later. Cedric tried to stiffen his body in preparation, anticipating a verbal bashing.

'Is that you, Bambridge?' asked the usual sharp voice of Miss Fulton.

'Good morning, Miss Fulton. How are you?' he asked politely.

'Never mind all that nonsense. Look, a person will be visiting me within the next 20 minutes or so. Please send the person up to my apartment immediately on arrival. Do you understand?'

'Yes, I will send the person up immediately when they arrive, Miss Fulton.' That undermining voice pierced his soul to the core. Why do they have to project such deferential insults?

'Good. Thank you, Bambridge.'

The person in question arrived not long after. Cedric saw her drive up to the main doors and park. She got out of the car with some sort of badge on a chain swinging from her neck. He let her in.

'Good morning, madam. Miss Fulton has asked me to send you up to her apartment, number eight, on floor four. She was concerned when she rang me,' said Cedric, not sure what was going on. Who was this woman? He should have asked to see her badge—his training required as much. But never mind. She must be important for someone to visit at this time in the morning. He'll find out later, or otherwise, he will be in trouble. Must keep the records up-to-date, Richards kept insisting. Fuck him, Cedric thought to himself. One day, that glorious day that resides permanently in his head, when he leaves his job, he'll give the boss a two-finger sign.

'Good morning. Thank you,' she said.

'The lift is to your right in the corner over there. If there is anything I can do to help, please phone the reception,' said Cedric.

The woman made her way to the lift to visit Miss Fulton. When he thought about it, he realised that Miss Fulton had been visited by her private doctor in the past but they were always day time visits. He had never attended her at 4 am. It must be something quite serious, Cedric assumed. That wasn't surprising, of course, the whole place was full of older people who had various medical problems. Most of them ready to meet their Maker at any time. He wished he had their money. You never know, was Cedric's mantra, one of them might just leave him a few bob. Most of them have not been married, nor had children, though most had extended families waiting, no doubt, with hands held out in anticipation.

Cedric gave some thought to the next four days. He was

free to do as he pleased. Look for a job... have a beer in town. He hadn't been to the Red Lion for some time. At least they were his kind of people. Blokes there had known Cedric for many years. He first used the pub when he arrived from East London with two cases in hand, the day before starting his present job. Most were friendly, helpful blokes from the outset. Cedric had lost his job at a factory and couldn't pay his rent. Luckily, he found his present job in Poplar job centre. Looking underweight and rather sad, the guys at the Red Lion realised Cedric was down on his heels. Sid, Bob, Harry and others bought him a few beers. After that, he became one of the gang there, although Cedric, though appreciative, didn't really see it like that. The drinkers accepted Cedric as he was. He was quiet, rather placid and very much a loner. But he enjoyed showing his face from time to time and buying his friends—his only friends, other than Nelson—a few beers.

Or, very occasionally, Cedric would visit former colleagues. But he didn't relish the 15-mile journey into the metropolis. The crowds, noise and bright lights nowadays overwhelmed him. His instinct, given the opportunity, was to head in the opposite direction into the country where he felt safe. That was one of his fantasies, to work in the countryside on a small estate, gardening or driving or housekeeping for a retired sympathetic male. As long as he was kind and friendly, wages weren't that important. Just a small room of his own and freedom to roam among the woods and seek wildlife was all Cedric required.

But he knew, of course, that wouldn't materialise without looking for jobs. That he must do with a vengeance if he was to fulfil his dreams. Not much to ask for a man who had possessed very little in life's maelstrom.

An hour later, the same lady reappeared in front of the reception, smiling at Cedric.

'Hello, once again,' she said. 'I've spoken to Miss Fulton. She is OK at the moment. Due to confidentiality, I'm unable to explain the reason for visiting Miss Fulton.'

'I'm sorry, but due to security, I do need your name and your company's name.'

'Yes,' she said. 'My name is Lillian Miller and I work for mental care services. We are a local company. Here is the company registration,' said the tall, shapely blonde, around 30 years old.

'Thank so much, Linda. I should have requested those details when you first accessed the premises,' he explained, his bean pole legs still shaking from his incompetence.

'That's fine. Good morning,' she said as she walked out of the door, her identification still swinging around her young muscular neck. A sleek neck kissed by many privileged males.

What a bloody fool Cedric had made of himself. He usually asked visitors for names, and if needed, identification. What confused him was that Miss Fulton had phoned early morning for something completely different than usual. The visitor could have been anyone visiting such a vulnerable resident. Miss Fulton could easily have been manipulated into allowing her access to her apartment. The worker could have robbed, poisoned or even killed her. Wake up, Cedric, if Richards found out about your incompetence, he would drop a ton of horse shit on you.

It was not surprising that Cedric hadn't done well in life

when considering his irresponsible behaviour. His own words. He must be extra careful in future. Avoidance had been an integral part of Cedric's history. Whenever things got overly anxious for him, he found the easy way out. But during his tenure, it hadn't happened, so far, to any detriment. He had tried hard to combat irrational fears.

Yet, nevertheless, Cedric's denial that he didn't self-harm anymore was delusional. Although his punk rock days had served as a supportive social interaction for him, it also re-inforced his self-hatred by, among other behaviour, head-banging. When stressed, he would occasionally continue head-butting his plastic-covered wall cabinet. It released him from utter despair.

'Hello, night porter speaking,' replied Cedric.

'Good morning, Mr Bambridge. Sorry it's early to phone, but my tall lamp stand and shade have just crashed to the floor. It's all broken,' said Mr Tressle.

'Of course, Mr Tressle, I'll be with you in a jiffy at your ground floor residence,' said Cedric, who liked the old chap. He was friendly and always addressed people with respect. Now aged 79, he had once worked for the local council. Man-ager of finance, Cedric thought. After a fall in the high street and a subsequent hip replacement, he hobbled around, using a walking stick. Most people liked him for his spiritual atti-tude to life. He had been a devout Catholic since his boarding school days. Ever since, he had tried to love his neighbour.

'Hello, Mr Bambridge. How are you? My lounge is bit of a mess,' he said. The tall wooden stand had broken in two.

'Hello, Mr Tressle. Never mind. I know where the cleaning cupboard is, I'll get the pan and brush,' said Cedric. He put the required cleaning items in the passage and then had a look around for any small items he could steal. There was nothing of any value worth taking. As the old boy sat reading, he quietly tiptoed into his bedroom and had a look for any rings or watches worth a few pounds, but nothing caught his eagle eyes. Two £20 notes winked at him from the dressing table. He might be old, but Mr Tressle wasn't an imbecile.

Cedric returned to the lounge and cleaned up the mess. He put it in a large bag and took it with him. At these times of trying to pilfer from residents, he felt guilty and wondered why he did it. If he were found stealing, then only one option lay ahead. Even so, if he noticed something worthwhile taking, then he would take a chance.

'That's all cleaned, Mr Tressle.'

Thank so much, Mr Bambridge. Before you go, I thought you might be interested in this small booklet,' the resident said.

Cedric let himself out and threw the rubbish in the large bin next to the tool cupboard. He fished out the booklet. 'The Catholic Way of Life' was the title. It certainly wasn't for him. That sort of trash, in Cedric's opinion, had been stuffed down his gullet in the children's home and prison. Yes, dear old chap he was, but they are always conniving how to convert the heathens, the non-believers. The contradiction syndrome, as Cedric called it. The overbearing bastards!

Near the end of his 12-hour shift, there was another call from Miss Fulton. He thought it might be Mr Black, who, teetering on alcoholic insanity, might be craving attention.

'Could you pop up for a minute or two, Bambridge? Thank you,' she said.

'Yes, certainly, Miss Fulton.'

As the lift doors opened on his way up to floor four, the postman walked out having completed his delivery.

'Morning, Cedric. How's it going?' he asked, his shoulder carrying a bulging bag of mail.

'I'm well, Jake.'

Cedric knocked on the door, expecting another ear-bashing from Miss Fulton, who was losing weight by the day. Anorexia had certainly engulfed her life.

'Come in, Bambridge,' she demanded. 'Would you take this prescription down to the town chemist for me?' she asked rather agitatedly. 'I've not been well these days, but I don't want you to say anything, do you hear? I've had a bit of depression but I'm sure it shall pass like all things. Confidentiality, do you know what that means, Bambridge?' she asked arrogantly.

Yes, I do, Miss Fulton.' He took the prescription and walked out of the apartment. Once again, he had been brought down to the level of lackey, first class. Who do these people think they fucking are?

There was great relief on Cedric's face when he saw the large bulk of Nelson making his way through the front door. Such a reassuring figure in every way, he thought. He could be open with Nelson, unlike any other person. Mind you, that confidence in one person had taken a long time to develop. Cedric had the next four days to himself. What a relief to get away from residents who are living above you 24 hours a day. He sometimes felt the pressure of tons of concrete and glass about to crush him.

'Morning, brudder, how are you?' he asked his colleague. He thought he looked mournful.

'A lot better now you're here,' Cedric smiled.

'Yes, brudder, you have the next four days off. Enjoy yourself.'

'I intend to. Have a good shift.'

'Play some old rock music or drink some rum, and dream of making love to Tina Turner. Know what I mean?' he laughed out loudly.

'I think we should be ungraded to carers, you know. We attend their every whim, clean up their mess and run errands like road side piss pots,' said Cedric

'Good point, brudder, but don't mention it to shithead Richards, otherwise, he'll tell us to go to a care agency for work. Just play the game with these shitheads, brudder.'

With that care question lingering, and eventually forgotten, Cedric made his way down to the basement flat. The bowels of the earth, he called it. It was top accommodation, compared to the large institutions and some of the doss houses he had slept in, where he'd had to tie his shoes to the bed and sleep in all his clothes in case of theft. One old tramp, he remembers, pissed in his boots. No complaints about his little abode. It was quiet and warm. Besides, it was warmer than most London libraries, where he used to go for a sleep during the days of homelessness along with a menagerie of dossers.

4

CHAPTER FOUR

The days were warming up somewhat, but Cedric was feeling rather dejected as the last three days hadn't been that fruitful. No jobs for oldies like him at the job centre. The personnel gave him the impression that he was unemployable. He wasn't exactly the Tom Cruise of Mortingbridge. Three days' worth of stubble, unkempt hair and charity shop clothes didn't project the ideal qualities needed by an employer looking for motivated team players. How Cedric hated those words: team players. That was all he ever noticed when reading jobs vacant in local newspapers, employment agencies and newsagents. The job centre staff kept encouraging him to use the computers and go online for far more jobs. He didn't want to go online! Fuck the online palaver. He wanted to speak to a human being. Besides, if the truth were known, he was frightened of computers. That was a world he didn't want to inhabit. Cedric knew nothing and didn't want to know anything about technology. The world had gone crazy. Wherever and whenever he was out in public, people would have their eyes glued to a little box either pressing something or talking incessantly. What has gone wrong with people? It's not surprising there are so many lonely souls. They are all preoccupied with those small boxes called mobile phones. He had no choice but to use one occasionally, which was supplied by his employer for residents to phone. And that was handed over at every shift to the next worker. He wouldn't go near the damn things given the opportunity. But on crowded buses, trains, London trams, and the underground, they were everywhere. That's why Cedric enjoyed walking. He had done so all his life because he could be on his own without being intruded upon, or overhear other people's sordid stories. He was an outsider alright, and at this stage in his life, he very much enjoyed the status. He'll see his days out at Oaks Lodge. Hopefully given a council flat or hostel and live off a small state pension. Not a fulfilled life by any estimation, but who cares whatever becomes of him? There are billions of people with less than Cedric.

It was his fourth day off before returning back to work the next day and he was still in bed. That was most unusual for him to sleep until 10 am. The sun shone through his moth-ravaged curtains onto his ageing face. He felt so warm and secure for once. Did he really want to put himself out there among the intense atmosphere where millions are trying to earn their next pound to survive? What a fucking jungle, he thought. He hadn't seen or spoken to any colleague or resident, and he wouldn't until he had to. Tomorrow, he was back on the conveyor belt.

Cedric hauled his slim white frame out of bed. One consolation working here was that the central heating and water were free. Unknown luxury until he arrived was a bath full of hot water whenever he wished. Walk around in his vest and pants without worrying about the coin meter being empty. Enough grub in his Oxfam fridge for a few days. Many years, he had lived like this, heaven compared to those days of slogging his body from one Salvation Army to another. Cedric slung his battered old frying pan onto the gas stove. He first bought it at a charity shop years ago for 50p. Similar to most of his pots and pans, they were all old, worn-out and obsolete, resembling their owner. Although his wages weren't that good, he had managed to save for a rainy day. Cedric had enough money to buy new pans, clothes and furniture, but life had taught him to be prepared for the unknown. He could be made redundant or lose his job and be made homeless tomorrow. Without money, he would be left to the ravages of dirty hostels or bedsits. In his position, the council did not have a legal duty to accommodate him. Now, the financial tide had turned somewhat. He wasn't going to live with people anymore. Not just dossers and tramps but anyone, regardless of who or where they came from. He'd had a gut load of sharing dirty, rat-infested toilets and kitchens. He had enough money to rent a decent comfortable place of his own. If nothing else materialised, he'd made sure his money was safe in the bank for that eventuality.

With a fry-up in his belly, Cedric made his way down to the local town. The small high street consisted of a mix of expensive fashion shops, estate agents, cafés, pubs, two charity shops and the job centre. As he hadn't seen his pub mates for some considerable time, he decided to have a beer. He couldn't really call them friends, although it was they who first spoke to him when he arrived in Mortingbridge, penniless. Friendships were too comfortable for him, it suggested being reliant on another. Mates were more appropriate. Though Nelson, of course, he did consider a friend. That was somewhat different. He had worked with him for over 12 years. Nelson was trustworthy and they had spent valuable social time together. He didn't feel uncomfortable in his company.

He walked into the Red Lion, an 18th-century pub built of red brick. It had one large bar. First impressions weren't promising. At least gone were the three bars based on rank. But it was not very well decorated compared to London standards, Cedric thought. He remembered the torn flower-patterned wallpaper and flaking brownish ceiling when he first walked into the place. This pub was for working class people. Builders, factory workers, navvies and the unemployed found sanctuary there. The other high street watering hole was more middle class, suitable for those who resided at Oaks Lodge. The English Oak catered for those requiring lunches and evening meals. In the Red Lion, you were lucky to buy egg and chips, or a bacon sandwich. Cedric had only ever eaten in the latter.

'Hello, stranger,' shouted Billy Ward from the other end of the bar. 'I haven't seen you for ages, mate. How you keeping?' he asked Cedric as they shook hands.

'I'm alright, Billy, how about yourself?'

'I'm alright,' he replied. 'The last time I saw you, it was about a year ago. Where the fuck have you been?' asked Billy, a local builder and former hoodlum. He'd been to prison a few times for theft and affray. Now married with two children, he had kept out of trouble since.

'I'm still working up at the Lodge. I don't drink very much, Bill,' he replied.

'That gaff up the road where all the rich people live? Must be alright there, Cedric, for a few quid from some old wealthy bird looking to leave her money to,' laughed Billy.

'You'll get fuck all there, mate,' was Cedric's response.

'Don't give me that, Cedric. By the way, two of the lads have died recently, Sid Chapman and Harry Carver, both victims of cancer. Most of the lads are working. They only come in the evenings. Like you and me, they are getting on a bit and prefer to sit at home with the old woman, rather than drinking this gut wash,' Billy said.

'Half pint of bitter please,' Cedric asked the surly barman. 'Those two blokes were really decent to me when I first came in here, Billy. I had fuck all, but they bought me pints and a meal,' he remarked.

'I'll buy that, Cedric,' Billy said, remembering the day he was broke and Cedric bought him several beers.

'Cheers to you, Billy. All the best,' he said to a bloke he first met about 13 years ago in this bar.

But there were only a handful of morose drinkers in the bar. Other than Billy Ward, he didn't recognise anyone. People die and others move on. Not even Jake, who delivered post at the Lodge, was in there. Cedric found it a claustrophobic and depressing pub. He wasn't going to waste any more of his hard-earned money in these worn-out places. After buying Billy a drink, he left the pub and walked down the high street. Several people were smoking outside the job centre. They all looked lost of hope. Cedric walked inside to find a job, any job that could give his shallow life some interest, challenge, not to say more money. Three workers sat behind their desks reading newspapers. There were no punters requiring their attention. Not surprising as the jobs were very few and badly paid. Other than shop work, the only jobs available were at Turners factory some 15 minutes from the high street. They always had vacancies for machine minders, cleaners and labourers. It was mind-numbing work in a noisy, smelly environment. Locals preferred to collect the dole money, which was pittance, and work cash in hand for various small builders. Who could blame them? Fuck their jobs, Cedric thought, I've already got one.

Realising the place was a waste of time, Cedric jumped on the first bus. With a bus pass, he could ride up and down to any destination and get off when the ubiquitous mobile phones got too much for him. Cedric thought they should be banned in public. Your life is not your own nowadays. Intrusion was everywhere—a constant depressing thought of Cedric's. Barking dogs owned by scum kids sniffing glue, security cameras and lights at every turn. Loud music and the offensive smell of Indian curry that permeated every fibre of your clothes. At these stressful times, his mind returned to those peaceful days, walking down the high street with his quiet, placid mother. Being an observer even then, he noticed how people acknowledged each other with a nod or handshake. There was the occasional kind word in passing, but all very formal. People queued in silence. People always said thank you.

On the top deck of the 79 bus, which was littered with

human rubbish, he headed west out of Mortingbridge and, within two miles, was in the countryside. That was the one small consolation of living in the area. As he had travelled these ways many times before, he knew the green lanes of Buckinghamshire would open up before him. In no time at all, there were less houses, vehicles and fresh air galore. It was all worth the effort, dragging himself out of bed to experience beautiful scenery. Large detached houses surrounded by high conifer hedges for exclusive privacy, for the rich and famous. Not intended for hoi polloi like Cedric. He was way down the pecking order in the scheme of things. These were the type of large lush gardens where Cedric would have loved to work all day contentedly tending his flowers. Just the fantasy of it all took him close to self-harming on the bus. He wanted to head-butt the window. His impulse to carry it out was so intense that he ran downstairs and jumped off the bus. Having crossed a narrow road, he sat down on the grass in a spinney, full of oak and ash trees. Safe at last! Over the years, he had slept in many similar places. But the land he sat on, like most other land on this planet, was owned by someone. Wherever one trod, there was wealth belonging to the rich.

Cedric eventually made his way back to Oaks Lodge. He was back on duty in the morning at 8 am, replacing Nelson who will be chomping at the bit for a rest, no doubt, after being at the beck and call of those greater than himself. After alighting from the bus, Cedric walked the final mile through the woods so close to his heart. Dusk falling, he loved to stand, stare and listen to pigeons, blackbirds and the various calls of those mighty insects who hold the food chain together. He was mesmerized by the size of the universe above him. As a child, he had spent many nights just looking at the stars and thinking about how insignificant he was. Given the opportunity, he would have loved to have bought a small caravan and placed it in the middle of Marsh Wood. Alone with nobody to interfere with his existence, free from rules and regulations that dominate modern man.

Cedric awoke at 5 am. It was still dusk. Birds were singing in the nearby trees, anticipating the food that was thrown to them most mornings by some residents. He lay in bed thinking of the past and future. It was all confusion. What was the point of suffering for most of your life, and at the end of it all was death. Echoes from Widburn prison kept haunting him. The vicar informed the many that God put us here to suffer so we may learn the Christian way of life. God had chosen all of them specially, standing before him, to save humanity. What utter bollocks, Cedric thought. If he wants to save people, then give them a home, job and hope!

He got out of bed, made himself breakfast and ironed his working clothes, ready for the onslaught. Another day, same old shit, he thought, as he walked into reception.

'Morning, brudder. How are you?' asked Nelson who looked tired.

'Not so bad, Nelson,' he said. 'How about yourself, busy night, was it?' asked Cedric.

'Yes, man, it was busy at times. It's all in that fucking diary.' The old girl Fulton phoned twice. Mr Ford came back around 3 am a bit pissed, good luck to him. He was in no fit state for arm wrestling,' laughed Nelson. 'Lots more, brudder, you know what night duty is like'

'I certainly do, mate. Been at it for over 13 fucking years, I think,' Cedric said. 'It's my 61st birthday today. The 1st of February. Anyway, I think it is. Not quite sure,' he added, looking at the floor as though who cared anyway.

'Happy birthday, my son,' said Nelson in a carefully reassured voice. 'You're a good man, Cedric. We'll have a drink sometime, brudder,' he said quietly.

'That would be good. But not in the Red Lion, it's falling to pieces. We'll try that posh gaff up the high street for a change,' he quipped.

'That's a deal. Well, I'm off. Meeting some old buddies in London,' Nelson said as he put on his jacket and walked out the door.

Birthdays, celebrations and whatnot, Cedric pondered to himself, what is the point in being told you are a year older? Other than his colleague, he didn't have a clue when any of the residents had a birthday. By the number of cards delivered at Oaks Lodge, he could guess the birthdays of a few of them. But on the whole, he could not care less about the subject. Besides, they will all be dead in a few more years, he speculated. One thing he could forecast—he would not, and never had since his childhood days, received a birthday card. Fuck the cards, he thought. They are meaningless, commercial drivel... that was Cedric's limited experience of cards. Words like love, happiness, best wishes and hope all written by the pen of self-satisfaction. He knew, from his own experience, that people are inordinately fickle. If you say the wrong words or disagree with what others say, you are ostracized. That's the scheme of things for the self-righteous power seekers. And Cedric knew all too well that it is usually based on class or money. He had always been aware of being judged, which probably reflected his lowly status. Institutional life is full of judgemental monsters, he reflected. Everything directed by the book, and very little of the heart.

While sitting at reception, he had once again drifted into his inner feelings, while anticipating another saga at the Lodge. He was pleased that those loud cleaners weren't due until two days. They tried to undermine him by reeling out their hideous jokes, which were usually based on sex. The women knew he was single and hadn't much experience of relationships. How they knew, he didn't really know, but women have an instinct for such matters. He wouldn't give them the time of day outside of the Lodge, but here he had no choice. Cedric thought they were all worthless old slags. Nelson, of course, wouldn't hesitate in shagging all of them. Perhaps he had already.

The mobile phone rang.

'Good morning, Oaks Lodge. Day porter speaking,' he said in his perfect English. With outside calls, you never know who it might be. Got to be on your guard, he constantly reminded himself.

'Morning, Cedric. Hope all is well at Oaks Lodge,' said the masterly voice of Mr Richards.

'Yes, Mr Richards. All is well,' he said apprehensively.

'This afternoon, Cedric, I want you to take out Mr and Mrs Sternberg for a drive to Coronation Park, and take them for tea in the café there. You've driven them several times before since driving became too much for Mr Sternberg. You know the procedure. Keep them safe as they are both 80 years of age and have mobility problems. Both have made a considerable contribution to our society, and Mr Sternberg, previously an Army Captain, has the Victoria Cross. But you know the score, you have done it many times before, including for other residents. Enjoy yourselves and be fucking careful. OK?' said Richards in his usual stern manner. 'By the way, Cedric, I have arranged for an agency worker to replace you, about midday, until Nelson is back on duty at 8 pm,' said the boss, who didn't have a high estimation of Cedric. Mind you, he thought, he isn't paid very well and lives in a gloomy flat. He had similar feelings for Trussington. Who else would do this sort of work for pittance?

'Yes, Mr Richards. I understand,' said Cedric.

'You have my mobile number in case of any problems. Keep the company phone with you, and get the other one from the cupboard and give it to the agency worker,' Richards said, hoping Cedric was still competent enough to drive two of Oaks Lodge's wealthy residents out for the day.

'Right, Mr Richards.' What a fucking palaver, Cedric thought to himself. Mind you, it gets him out of the Lodge for a few hours.

The postman came whistling in through the front door with his usual full sack dangling on his right shoulder. He had been around for ten years and was known to some of the residents. Decent bloke. Thick as shit but wouldn't do you a bad turn, unlike those above him.

'Alright, Cedric, my son, got a rare letter here for you. From a lost lover who has found you at last,' Jake spoke in jest as he handed the white envelope to him.

'You must be fucking joking, Jake, what old bird is going to write to me?' Cedric said, narrowing his eyelids.

'You never know who—'

'I know alright,' he muttered. Cedric put the letter in his trouser pocket.

'Must get this lot delivered, See yer.'

Cedric was praying that someone, anyone, would phone or ask him for his assistance right now. Anything at all that would distract his mind from the letter. He felt rather apprehensive. Cedric made tea and toast in the small musty workers room. Still, no one turned up for his services. The place was so unusually quiet. Cedric noticed his hands were shaking. The only letters he ever received were from the benefits agency. He received the occasional charity flyer, but nothing else. He couldn't carry on like this thinking the world was going to collapse, due to a white envelope stuck in his grimy pocket.

He marched out to the reception desk and, resembling a man possessed, marched back into the room, where he pulled the letter from his pocket and opened it.

The letter was from a Joe Swift:

'Dear Cedric, I hope you are well. You probably don't remember me, but you and I, probably, attended All Saints Infants and Juniors School together in Wiltshire, many years ago. Three years ago, my wife and I moved to a small village near to you. When I was poking around for something recently in the Town Hall, I happened to look at the voters register. There, I saw your name, but thinking it was just a coincidence, I carried on. But as your name is unusual, there are no other Bambridge's in the local directory, I decided to delve more. Anyway, I have written this letter assuming it might be you, but if not, I profoundly apologise.'

Well, Cedric was speechless for minutes until the desired desk phone started ringing. He rushed to answer it.

'Good morning, Oaks Lodge, day porter speaking,' said Cedric, quietly pre-occupied.

'Good morning, I'm the ward sister at St Pauls Hospital. Mr Spelling, who was admitted a few days ago, is now ready to return to Oaks Lodge sometime this afternoon,' she said.

'Thank you, sister. I won't be here but I will inform my colleague,' Cedric said.

With that over and written in the daybook, the mystified day porter went back to thinking about the letter. It had been a shock, that was for sure. He was trying to place Joe Swift at All Saints School. It must be some 55 years ago that Cedric first attended. What had remained in his mind was the fear that the teachers had instilled in him. He was never intelligent or studious, although he attended nearly every day for lessons. Though always near the bottom of the class when it came to academic achievement, Cedric did well at school sports. That made him popular with a few of his male classmates. Beyond that, Cedric Bambridge was rarely recognised in the school hierarchy. His masculinity never impressed the girls. Today, that hasn't changed.

As Cedric's parents moved a few miles away, due to his dad being promoted, he attended a different senior school than the one attached to All Saints. No great academic or sporting achievements there either. Although, he did represent the school football team for four successive years, and he received a small trophy. His parents were mightily proud of their son the evening he was presented, along with the whole team, with his reward from the headmaster, in front of several hundred parents, teachers and pupils. That was about the sum total of Cedric's successes. He left school without any qualifications.

But the daydreaming took him back to that name—Joe Swift. He couldn't place him. There were a few boys and girls he vaguely remembered, but not the aforementioned. Cedric remembered the school photographs. There was one taken of the class every year. Some were ugly kids with rotten teeth and moth-eaten clothes, their parents earning poor incomes working the land. His mother bought all four photographs. They sat proudly on the mantelpiece for years looking like important figures of repute. He remembered a wooden figure of Christ on the Cross took centre stage higher up on the wall. Incidentally, he now remembered how religion played an integral part of his mum's life. She assiduously attended church every Sunday, even when they went on holiday. As his dad was an atheist, he waited for her in a pub.

Cedric saw Mr Matthews drive his silver Daimler into the car park. What a magnificent looking car! It must have cost him a small fortune. Lucky bastard, he thought. But is he happy? Cedric had surmised many times of all those in a similar position. What has happiness got to do with it? You can't eat it or buy it. It doesn't really exist, the only thing that is actually important is money! Without money, and all that affords, the worldly conditions would be completely different for the dapper Mr Matthews, Cedric concluded.

'Good morning, Mr Matthews. How are you, sir?'

'Hello, Cedric. I'm well, thank you. And your good self?' Mr Matthews enquired.

'Yes, I'm well, sir. Have you come to visit Miss Holroyd?'

'Yes. I hope she is relatively well,' he said eagerly.

'I think so, sir,' whose pronounced chin had always fascinated Cedric.

'Well, I'll go up and see her. Thank you.'

Cedric returned to the puzzling letter. Who was this Joe Swift character? He registered to vote many years ago and gave the Lodge as his address. Perhaps that's how he contacted him. Anyway, the bloke left his mobile number in case Cedric wanted to contact him. He'll give it some thought.

An hour later, the indefatigable Matthews re-appeared in reception. Smiling, neat, and poised as usual. He was mindfully assured of his presence in the world. Focused and self-directed, life for him was enjoyment.

'Hello, Cedric. Well, Miss Holroyd appears to be OK. She has been a bit down recently. Please keep an eye on her for me, would you?'

'Of course Mr Matthews,' said Cedric who thought it wasn't his job to do that.

'Thank you so much. Goodbye,' said a smiling Mr Matthews.

What does he do up there with Holroyd? Is he a doctor, friend, bank manager, former colleague or conman? One could only delve so far. They were just passing thoughts, anyway. She meant nothing to the resident porter.

Time was moving near to taking out the Sternbergs—the only married couple living at the Lodge. He had driven them to various places of interest before. They particularly enjoyed historic houses and gardens in full bloom. Today, Richards' instruction was somewhat different. Anyway, the company car was clean and full of petrol so he didn't have to negotiate the small local petrol station. On three occasions, he had nearly knocked over the pumps and scraped another due to the narrow exit. The owner had asked Cedric if he had a full driving license, insinuating that he be re-examined. Fortunately, Richards hadn't noticed the missing paint on the side of the car.

Ten minutes before midday, Miss Holroyd phoned reception.

'Good morning,' said the porter.

'Hello, Hambridge. Sorry, Mr Bambridge, how silly of me. Please could you come up for a moment?'

'Yes, of course, Miss Holroyd. I'll be up to the second floor in two minutes,' he quietly said.

In Cedric's usual energetic manner, although on the wane, he walked up the flight of stairs. He liked to keep active and enjoyed moving around wherever he was. He disliked too much physical confinement. It reminded him of the claustrophobic children's home.

'Good morning, please do come in,' said Miss Holroyd, who walked slowly back to her lounge with the aid of a stick. 'Please, sit down. You have no doubt seen Mr Matthews visiting me. Well, he is a counsellor. I have a long-standing problem called post-traumatic stress disorder. He has been very supportive. At some stage, I will probably visit him in his consulting room. Briefly, it means I was emotionally abused by my stepfather. When my father died quite young, mother remarried. I was 14 years of age when the abuse began and continued for many years thereafter. In retrospect, it probably impacted my years as a barrister. I took prescribed pills to help me with panic attacks and other things. In essence, Mr

Bambridge, and I'm sorry to waste your time, PTSD, as it is called, started by constantly being undermined. He withheld love and affection, frightened and intimidated me so much that I used to hide in my bedroom. He emotionally abused me for years. I was so pleased when I went to university, and out of his grimy clutches. After Oxford, I never returned home. I didn't inform my mother as I didn't want to hurt her feelings, but I was greatly relieved when my stepfather died. I'm 80 years old and still having to sort out the abuse that was inflicted upon me all those year ago, Mr Bambridge,' she said reproachfully.

'I'm very sorry to hear it, Miss Holroyd. I've read about PTSD, but don't understand, really,' he said humbly.

'The reason I'm explaining all this to you, and I'm sorry to burden you with it, but if I phone you at times, like early morning, it's because I'm not feeling well. I know, I have phoned you many times before but it was out of sheer frustration. At long last, with the great support from Mr Matthews, I have a diagnosis. That bloody stepfather. Thank you for listening, Mr Bambridge,' she muttered apologetically. She sobbed uncontrollably into her handkerchief.

'That's alright, Miss Holroyd. Just phone me, I'm only downstairs.'

Cedric left the apartment confused. Why would an educated woman like Miss Holroyd explain something most personal to an obedient lackey like him? It boosted his confidence somewhat to think that a former barrister—he had been defended by them—would confide in him. He must not undermine himself. He too was a mature man with the 'University of Life' under his experienced belt. You must like yourself, Cedric, he kept thinking to himself. You have a lot to offer, use it.

Due to the meeting with Holroyd, he was late, so rather anxious about meeting the Sternbergs. He phoned them immediately to explain.

'Good afternoon, Mr Sternberg. I'm a bit late. Apologies about that, another resident required some assistance,' he said.

'That's alright, Mr Bambridge. My wife and I shall meet you at reception in about 15 minutes. It takes time to hobble down there,' he said with a jovial laugh.

Cedric was looking forward to the next few hours. A bit of a doddle was assured if the past was any guide. Before they arrived at the reception, he went to the car park and started the green Ford. Only three years old, spacious and warm for elderly residents requiring it for personal activities. As the car was being reversed towards the building, the agency worker arrived just on time.

'Alright, Danny?' asked Cedric.

'Hello, Cedric. You alright?' Danny was a regular agency worker. A young family man, he lived in Hellum some ten miles from the Lodge.

'I'm taking out the Sternbergs for a few hours. Tea, toast and chitchat, you know what I mean. Use the other mobile phone. Look at the diary, Danny, Mr Spelling is being discharged, from hospital, so he'll arrive sometime this afternoon, OK? And don't forget the quack is visiting two of his old fogeys. Write everything down, mate, OK? You know the ropes by now,' emphasized Cedric.

'All in hand, Cyril, no bother,' he said.

'Cedric, you prick.'

'Are you both ready?' Cedric asked the couple who were waiting outside, leaning on their walking sticks. Who would have thought, Cedric thought to himself, that not too long ago, Mr Sternberg was a rampaging Army captain prepared to kill anyone in the line of duty. Where and how he was awarded the VC he didn't know. And he wasn't prepared to ask either.

They got into the car, their bones cracking and creaking, and were whisked away out of the short driveway and west through the busy town. Cedric drove sedately along the only main road, the A476, to Coronation Park. All three occupants knew the place well. The large Georgian house, with added Gothic facades, was closed to the public. However, the owner, Lord Barky, gave the public permission to wander around his colourful gardens six months of the year. Several years ago, the old buffer splashed out on building a delightful café. He had even gone as far as to supply wheelchairs, but the Sternbergs resolutely refused to use them. Although he had a permanent and debilitating limp, the former Army captain stood strong and proud. The thought of such a contraption, once suggested by Cedric, had sent him into a near rage.

With the good porter alongside for support, the Sternbergs walked painfully slow towards their favourite seat opposite the rhododendrons. Though not yet in flower, they were rewarded by young snowdrops just popping out of their winter coats. They had sat there for hours over the past few years as both gradually physically deteriorated. Neither had spoken very little to the other. They held hands, smiled and occasionally commented on the beauty of the natural world.

The captain had a remarkable understanding of topography. Having fought in some of the most inhospitable places on earth, he could name rare plants that grew in deep mud, rock and marsh. Both appeared to be eternally grateful for the treasures that life had bestowed upon them.

Cedric always sat alongside them—that's when he wasn't going to the toilet every few minutes to allow them to enjoy their silence. When he wanted a brief change of scenery, Cedric would rise and ask if they would like refreshments. He was comfortable with it all, it was their day out.

'That's jolly nice of you, Mr Bambridge,' Mr Sternberg usually commented.

'How about tea and a slice of cake for you both, sir?' was Cedric's parlour verse.

'That sounds grand,' added Mrs Sternberg.

'Or would you prefer to sit indoors?' asked the willing lackey.

'No, no. It's just fine sitting here, thank you.'

They would have sat there if it was snowing, raining or bombs were dropping, thought Cedric. So, off he would trundle with his order to the café. Inside, it was full of ageing people. Most were so old, he concluded, that they made him look like a teenager. Some had carers to support them to consume their refreshments. Mind you, most of the food and drinks either ended on their laps or on the littered floor. It was reminiscent of a monkey house at London Zoo. Cedric loved all this sort of nonsense. He didn't have to work back at the Lodge with all its frustrations. No, he didn't mind if the Sternbergs sat out there all evening until the groundsman closed the gates.

'Large pot of tea, cups and three slices of cake, please. Could you put them on a tray?' asked Cedric.

As he didn't want to rush back straightaway, he brought a sandwich out of his pocket to eat. It resembled a doorstep. It was full of cold fried eggs and chutney. It was usually followed by a mug of tea. He had done this many times before while waiting for the Sternbergs. No flies on Cedric. The refreshments expense was refunded by Richards as was always the case whenever he or anyone else took residents out.

He returned to the quiet, isolated couple. Nothing bothered them. There was certainly nothing amiss mentally. In their Russian hats and Harris Tweed jackets, all was well with the world as far as they were concerned.

'Here you are, Mr and Mrs Sternberg,' said Cedric.

He placed the tray on the small metal table and gave them their tea and cake. He sat with them. It was all rather genteel, thought Cedric. They looked a ridiculous site just eating and drinking, but not a word was spoken until Mrs Sternberg raised her voice.

'Now I remember the name of that piece of music, darling. It was a piano sonata by Stravinsky,' she eagerly reminded her husband. She was referring to music she heard on Radio 3 the day before last. They were both avid listeners of classical music. Not so long ago, they regularly attended concerts in London. Mrs Sternberg used to play violin and taught at the Royal College of Music.

Along with other musicians, Mrs Sternberg had performed around the world in her younger days. It was while on one of those travels that she met her husband, who, along with Army colleagues, had attended one of her recitals. Love at first sight.

The subject was never mentioned, but a profound sadness remained silent over the death of their only child, Paul, aged 30. He had died in a motor accident while travelling through France. His body was returned to England and buried along-side his paternal grandparents in Yorkshire's limestone country.

The mobile phone rang from Oaks Lodge. This was most unusual. The last time it happened must have been several years ago, Cedric recalled. He stood and moved away from the two residents as he didn't want to intrude into their silence.

'Hello, Cedric speaking,' he said quietly.

'Hi, Cedric, sorry to phone but the old quack, sorry, doctor has sent Miss Knight, that's apartment ten, to hospital for an injection. She has diabetes and apparently needs an injection to sort her out,' said a flustered Danny.

'OK, thanks for phoning. That's no problem. Write it in the book under the first commandment.'

'Sure, Cedric. See you later,' he said. He didn't know why Danny had to phone him while out with residents. Pretty straightforward injection, it's happened many times before. But as she was getting on a bit, as they all are, and being rather heavy, she was vulnerable after a lifetime of excess, he thought. Cedric realised that at aged 86, Miss Knight was one of Oaks Lodge's oldest residents.

Cedric returned to the Sternbergs. They finished their refreshments and were having a conversation about plants. So frail yet so knowledgeable, he thought of the old couple in front of him. You can have it all, but they were not immune, unfortunately, to the suffering of old age, just like anyone else.

Observing the couple, the notion of love came up again. All his life, Cedric had wondered what it really meant. What was one meant to do, how does one explain love? His parents were kind to him, but did they love the little man from St Michaels? Tough love, he had always called it, where you have to stand on your own two feet to survive. Nobody ever gave him anything unless he earned it. Sleeping rough, with friends, he was once beaten up badly. Later in hospital, the kind attention the nurse gave him was the nearest he'd been to love. It was the contradiction that made him confused. It was similar behaviour to the nuns. And many others he had briefly met. They give you their attention and then take it away. He knew he had always been confused about the behaviour of others. What were their intentions? What were his expectations? This was where fantasy, he had surmised for many years, had helped him cope.

By now, the temperature was dropping. It was becoming coldish. He must ask the Sternbergs if they would like to go back home. Besides, the main gates would be closed in 30 minutes. Time to hit the road, he thought, otherwise, they'll all freeze.

'It's nearly 4:30, Mr Sternberg. Shall we walk back to the car and drive home?'

'Good idea, Mr Bambridge,' he said with a smile on his pale, ageing skin.

They walked slowly back to the car. Once Cedric had manoeuvred them into the car—not an easy exercise—he drove back out onto the main road and headed for Oaks Lodge.

He didn't mind driving residents out every day. Any kind of work, elsewhere, signified that he could escape the drudgery and predictability of the Lodge. Accompanied by ageing residents, who were usually quiet and thoughtful, Cedric was excited by the prospect of having the opportunity of driving to new places. They didn't mind where they went, most didn't realise where they were. And besides, no one else knew of his whereabouts. Cedric stopped in lay-bys to buy tea, drove up country tracks, visited old farm buildings and took rare photographs of wildlife. At the end of the day, he wrote the same old shit for the eyes of Richards in the rock edit, called a diary. It was a worthless, subjective pile of garbage that no one, except David Richards, read.

The car pulled up slowly in front of the building. That institution loomed large in front of him. Cedric, once again, managed to pull and haul them out of the car in one piece. All three slowly walked to the lift. The old couple, smiling in unison, went up to their home. He had enjoyed the day out with them. Nice old couple. Outside the Lodge, they certainly would not have associated with someone like Cedric. Oh, no, when you're a lackey, that's different, of course.

Cedric shook hands with his colleague. He kind of liked Danny. Wasn't flash, lippy, know-it-all or a jack-the-lad. He had his feet on the ground.

'Alright, Danny,' asked Cedric.

'Yeah, I'm well, mate. The old girl Knight hasn't returned yet from the hospital,' he explained. 'But the quack thought it wouldn't take long,' he added.

'Well, we are both working until 8 pm, then Nelson comes on shift. So, we should be here when she arrives,' Cedric thought to himself, or otherwise, he would have to help move her ageing bulk on his own.

'I like Nelson. He's been about in life, hasn't he?' asked the agency worker.

'He sure has.' Cedric didn't say any more than that. As much as he liked Nelson, he wasn't prepared to make him out to be some fucking hero or shrewd operator. Like most people, he had none of those qualities. Nelson was a victim of the precariousness of life, just like anyone else. His life had been one of dependence on chance, danger and insecurity. The wee man from Dorset had experienced them all himself.

'He told me about his Jamaican background. Problems he had with crime in London when he was a young man. I think he even served a few years in the nick for robbery and other things,' Danny added.

'That's right, Danny. He was a tough bastard, make no mistake. He still is no fool, I can assure you. On one occasion, he was inches from chinning that Richards. I'm pleased he didn't though because that would have finished his working life. He's over 50, and getting another job, even a wanky one like this, would be extremely difficult. Richards would make sure he never received a good reference. If that happened, Nelson would have no option but to return to a life of crime. That ain't easy at 50. There are many young dudes out there willing to fuck you up for a few pounds. Even big Nelson would find it tough to play around with kids who have no conscience,' Cedric said contemptuously.

'Yeah, I understand, mate.'

'Besides, even though he doesn't see them much, he's got his children and grandchildren to think about. He told me only a week ago that he must make an effort to visit them all in London. When he gets his next four days off work, Nelson intends to stay with his children and take them all out for a meal and a trip to Thorpe Park, or something similar. Spend a few quid on the children. Buy 'em some toys, you know what I mean, mate?' he added. 'But Nelson quickly forgets things, between you and me. One day he's shagging in Ilford, the next he's at it in Battersea. Such is life, mate.'

'Yeah, yeah sure, Cedric.'

'By the way, have you completed the paperwork for Knight's outpatient appearance? Richards loves finding fault, bro.'

'It's right up to date. Mr Ford went out for the day. He's a decent bloke, gave me a £5 tip. Mr Flowers was picked up by a taxi, probably out to one of his clubs. Must be worth a few bob?' Danny asked.

'They've all got a right few bob, mate. To live in these gaffs, you have to. Take David Ford, for instance. He made a fortune as a structural engineer. He now cavorts in various London clubs, gambling. Knocks around with some shady characters, I reckon. But I've never seen him with a woman on his arm. I think he's too shrewd to be taken in by that anymore,' he said.

'By the way, Cedric, those old biddies, Perks and Nobton, returned after a couple of hours in the Towns hotel, so they informed me,' said Danny.

'Sound like a Victorian stand-up comic duo, don't they?' he said with amusement.

It was nearly 8 pm. Time for changeover of shifts. Nelson walked into the reception with a book and food in hand.

Smiling to himself, as he generally was, he shook hands with his colleagues.

'Good evening, brudders,' he invariably said.

'You alright, Nelson?' asked Cedric.

'Me? Great, chaps.'

'Well, we are both off, Nelson. We've had enough for the day. The diary is up to date. I know you're dying to read it,' laughed Cedric.

The two workers walked out into the cold midnight air. Danny drove off and Cedric walked around to the dog kennel. Nelson began drinking his coffee, laced with rum, in reception. He was pleased all was quiet, gave him some time to read the gossip in the evening paper. The front page had 'Inflation Dips' emblazoned across it. Would those headlines make any difference to the night porter, his colleagues or most other people who own next to nothing? Of course not! It's a game for the wealthy, he concluded. He'll be here tonight, tomorrow night and the foreseeable nights until he retires or drops down dead. They'll dig a hole—a big hole in his case—say a few prayers and throw him in. That's what becomes of us all, he said to himself. Another day, same old shit. Mind you, he would rather be sitting in one of those warm, cosy, wealthy apartments above him right now, drinking a large rum and listening to Bob Marley. He always tried to remember those powerful lyrics, 'Free yourself from mental slavery,' that the Jamaican sang so powerfully. Ultimately, we hold ourselves back but it's easier said than done if you've got fuck all to start with.

Instead, Nelson's fate gave him a job working here. Your £10,000 per year pay and self-contained dog kennel wasn't that bad for an ex-convict. Don't forget free heating and lighting. His employers were most generous, he thought contemptuously. He knew he had nowhere to go. Stay here and see out your time, or find a cheap room, hostel or B&B where social life, in essence, finishes.

Earlier, Nelson had been hobnobbing in the local high street hotel, which was frequented by some of the residents occasionally. They'd wander in for afternoon tea and fairy cakes. The dotty ones used to sit there all afternoon sipping a cup of tea. Lodge staff had been summoned several times to collect those residents, who had either fallen asleep or forgot where they lived. Cajoling and pulling them into the car, they'd eventually be driven back to their apartment, under protest and shouting; some of this fit for the West End Theatre.

Mindful of the old biddies watching his every move, Nelson thought he might find a woman whom he could have a drink or two with. Sane, any size, and preferably with money to spend, he scoured the hotel without success. Similar to those aged women who lived at Oaks Lodge, most were interested in their clothes, books and families. He could understand why some married men committed murder or suicide. After an hour of overhearing intense nonsense, sex eventually evaporated from his mind. Even Nelson had some self-respect when it came to conversation. After two hours of prevarication, he did manage to have a decent chat, encouraged by a few drinks, with an older man who used to be a gamekeeper for Lord Barky's father. Right old bastard, he told Nelson. His arse squeaked every time he paid your wages.

Nelson, like most of us, found it difficult to come to terms with his own repression. The hotel provoked unwanted feelings. Surrounded by people from a different background, it made him aware of his own failings. Buried deep were unwanted or unacceptable desires and impulses that haunted his unconscious awareness. He gave the impression of a smiling, jovial happy man who loved the world just for its own sake. Big, burly Nelson, the man they found friendly and helpful. Of, course, he did have those qualities, but chasms of unchartered psychological pain lurked not far from the surface he showed the world.

His earlier life had had its moments of fun, laughter and desire. Family parties were a regular occasion in his household. Dancing, drinking and love making made a heady mix at a time when his parents and their friends were coming to terms of leaving loved ones back in Jamaica. It was inevitable that his young parents would experience personal friction in their relationship. Most young married couples are travelling unchartered waters. Losing their internal map led Nelson's parents to experience turbulent times.

When the colourful parties subsided, violence reared its ugly head. His father battered, bruised and bullied all those who got in the way of his alcoholic drenched brain. Occasionally, his father left the house and then returned sometime later full of remorse. His mother, fearing the worst, lived with her friends when she feared for her safety and sanity. As a young boy, Nelson witnessed all this upheaval. It confused him psychologically. He witnessed love and kindness. He also experienced the other side of human emotions that ripped into his frail inner life. Outwardly, he withdrew from his parents, his friends and eventually from school. He grew wild, like some semi-feral animal lost in a concrete wilderness. In his teens, he stayed away from home, took drugs and alcohol. He got in with a crowd that would eventually torment his soul to shreds. Crime, violence and prison became a way of life. After many drug-induced relationships, he eventually married. But it didn't last long. His confused earlier experiences taking charge of anyone, or anything, that tried to crack open his repressed feelings. Divorce, recriminations and isolation soon followed. Many had suffered at his hands.

Subsequently, he had tried therapy to help him come to terms with his past. Similar to Cedric, regular work and a secure home, with all its limitations, gave him the opportunity to find some kind of equilibrium. Now at 50 years of age, he would constantly delve into his inner life and try to understand those demons that held him back. His ambition was to develop a psychologically mature relationship with his own family.

Miss Knight arrived back at the Lodge around 9:30 pm. She had been treated by a private physician whose practice was ten miles from the Lodge. The agency worker had thought she attended the local hospital. Nelson corrected that mistake before Richards descended upon him. Being a self-made millionaire, she could afford to look after herself with the best available treatment—another resident that Nelson, Cedric and the cleaners envied. Who wouldn't? There was nothing you could do but accept it.

Knight, aged 86, had sold her successful advertising business, after being found not guilty of fraud. Her co-defendants were all found guilty and sentenced to long prison sentences. More unethical practises were dangled in front of her eyes.

She was surely tempted to indulge again. But she was reluctant to get involved after the Old Bailey trial. It was the demise of friends and colleagues that finally convinced her to sell up. She had kept a low profile ever since. An apartment full of the riches resulting from her dubious practises; she now read, painted landscapes and supported local charities. But the judicial affair had a detrimental effect on many people whose lives would never be so comfortable again. Not so fortunate as Ms Knight's.

'Good evening, Miss Knight,' said Nelson.

'Good evening, how are you?' she enquired.

'I'm well. I'll be pleased when spring arrives.'

'Oh, yes. Lovely to see daffodils once again,' she said, smiling at the night porter. 'Goodnight.'

Goodnight, Miss Knight.' Nelson's eyes followed her to the lift. How he craved to be with her, even being short, fat and ugly made no difference to his desire to be in a warm, professionally decorated cosy apartment. Mind you, to her credit, at 86 and, though not actually fit for ballet lessons, she certainly looked well.

5

CHAPTER FIVE

Two weeks later, Cedric found himself sitting in a small restaurant. He had arranged to meet Joe Swift, the person who wrote to him some time ago, but he had not been to Chadwell before. It was a small village about four miles from the Lodge. Very posh if first impressions were any guide. The table had been reserved by Joe Swift. Cedric was early. He was also very anxious, but after giving it much thought, eventually decided to attend. Looking around, he noticed a few couples dining, enjoying themselves, it appeared. Cedric had never used these well-to-do places before. He was comfortable in working men's cafés, eating bubble and squeak, where men laughed, joked and told stories. Floors full of dirt, dog ends and betting slips. The place where he was sitting now, with all its coloured walls, large chandelier and beige carpet made him feel inferior. He was only a lackey, he was out of place in this gaff, he thought. A few more minutes, and if he hasn't arrived, Cedric would do a runner. He was hoping he didn't turn up. Maybe the letter writer was a crank or one of his colleagues taking the piss.

'Would sir require a drink?' asked the tall young waitress.

'No thanks, love,' said Cedric, who thought she looked smart in her light brown uniform. Wonder where she comes from. Probably from a supportive family, secure home and has a warm bedroom all too herself. Lucky bastard, he thought. Mind you, he had his own bedroom—the dog kennel—but probably nothing like hers.

Minutes later, wearing an expensive tweed suit, a distinguished looking man entered the restaurant. He stood just inside the door way, waiting to be seated by the waitress. She pointed towards Cedric's two-seater table. The tall, thick set man approached Cedric, who was shitting himself.

'Hello, I'm Joe Swift. Are you Cedric Bambridge?' he asked politely.

Cedric stood up and shook hands.

'Hello there, yeah, I'm Cedric,' he said rather nervously.

'May I sit down and join you?' he asked.

'Of course, my ol' mate.'

'I must apologise first of all for sending you a letter out of the blue, Cedric. You must have thought it was a hoax or someone winding you up. But I can assure you I am genuine. To cut a long story short, Cedric, my family and I moved from Shropshire, where we had been living, to a small village nearby called Doveton, three years ago. I was in the Town Hall looking at the voter registration as I needed to take my wife off the list. She died last year from cancer...'

'Sorry to hear that, Joe,' said Cedric, who appeared deeply moved.

'Thank you.'

'She died from breast cancer. Anyhow, as I nosed through the list, I came across your name just by accident. You are the only Bambridge on the list. Afterwards, I went home. Now living on my own, my children and grandchildren live elsewhere, I thought hard about that name of yours. It suddenly dawned on me that the only Bambridge I had ever met was you at All Saints School in Wiltshire, all those years ago. Am I correct, Cedric?'

'Yeah, I think you are, mate,' Cedric said gingerly.

'Please forgive, Cedric, when I say, not only was your name unusual, kids can be very cruel, I was cruel, but people found out that you originally came from a children's home and had been adopted. I'm sure you are aware we're talking about the late 50s, early 60s, when confidentiality was unheard of. Teachers weren't trained to enquire after pupils' home lives, just their education,' Joe looked at Cedric humbly. 'I'm sorry for what I did.'

'I can't place you just yet, Joe, but you are right, kids teased and taunted me about coming from a children's home, even though I was, by then, adopted and living with my new parents. The bastards, at times, wouldn't leave me alone. That's one of the reasons why I did badly in class. I was frightened most of the time of being harassed. I sort of retreated to my inner life. These are words and ideas that have become familiar during the last ten years or so at adult education classes. I was a laughing stock, wasn't I?' Cedric said brusquely. The whole school experience had left Cedric very bitter. No one, especially at school, had given him any care or support. Various children hid his sports equipment, threw his cap down the lavatory and tore up his soccer annuals. Kids, instinctively, hunt down the weak and vulnerable.

'I can understand how you feel, Cedric. At first, I was one of your tormentors, but when I told my parents about you, they tried to explain that none of it was your fault. You didn't ask to be placed in a children's home. All the other painful things that happened to you were the result of other's nastiness. After my parents had explained things to me, I slowly began to understand how fortunate I was. I could go home to a loving family but for you, particularly in the home, it must have been painful not to have someone kiss and cuddle you. I'm very sorry, Cedric,' Joe said as he put his hand firmly on Cedric's shoulder. Tears welled up in Joe's eyes. What an awful fucking place life is for some people, he thought.

'Well, it's not your fault. I don't remember any faces from those days really. I suppose I wanted to be nobody. If I didn't remember people, I hoped they wouldn't remember me. I then felt safe. You know what I mean, Joe?' he said, bitter resentment burning through his body.

'I have a few photographs in my pocket taken of our class at All Saints. That's me sitting in the front row and that's you there, Cedric, on the end with bushy hair.' He handed Cedric the photos. The earliest one was taken about 55 years ago. Cedric was standing, looking confused, lost and lonely. The stigma stood out like a sore thumb. He was short, underweight and terribly frightened of the world around him. Although the damage inflicted by the children's home had left its ugly presence, his parents, being kind and decent, had helped him to grow. They themselves had deprived backgrounds but had done their best. Without doubt, they loved their son.

'Blimey, Joe, I can't believe it's all happening to me. I can recall a few of these faces now, I think. That teacher... what's his name?'

'Which photograph, Cedric?'

'This one where the teacher is standing next to me on the end.'

'That's old potty Potter, we called him. You may recall he taught us history. Occasionally, he took us for games and, if I am correct, you were a bloody good footballer, Cedric.'

'Yeah, that's right, Joe. It was the one thing I was good at. Even some of the girls watched me play for the school. My proudest moment, and for my parents, was when I received the football trophy from the headmaster, and in front of all those people. That high didn't last though as I was soon back down with the shit.'

'Look, Cedric, what are you going to have to eat? We've been beefing for ages and that young waitress is constantly looking our way,' he said, smiling.

'Anything, Joe. Egg and chips will do.'

'Have something more substantial than that. Have what you like.'

'What about this here, Joe... cottage pie, chips and vegetables. That sounds fine by me,' Cedric nodded approvingly.

Joe beckoned the young female waitress to the table. They ordered their meals and two large glasses of red wine. Very little was said while they were eating. Cedric was not, of course, an enthusiastic conversationalist. He would rather be quiet and let others do the talking. That word again—confidence. Something he had always lacked. He thought Joe was a friendly type of person, but he still couldn't remember him from school. He had repressed so much of his past. Cedric was hopeful that in time he might remember some of it.

'Have another drink, Cedric?' asked Joe.

'Yeah, that'll be great, mate.'

Both men drank in silence until Joe thought he would like to understand a little of Cedric's life and, if time permits, talk about himself. Joe wanted to use his limited time here productively. Once Cedric left the restaurant, he assumed he wouldn't hear from him again. Instinct informed him that Cedric had had an impoverished life. One didn't have to be a rocket scientist to realise that, he surmised. But he had to be tactful, sensitive and honest with Cedric.

What's the work like at Oaks Lodge, Cedric?'

'It's OK,' said Cedric, who felt intense unease being in a restaurant with people he didn't know. He felt exposed, self-conscious and anxious. He had been in those establishments no more than a dozen times during his life. He didn't fit in there. He now wished he had been more thoughtful and suggested they meet in a pub or café.

'How long have you worked there?'

'About 13 years now. Something like that.'

'Fancy another, Cedric?' asked Joe, who was genuinely trying to help Cedric relax.

'Yeah, thanks, Joe,' said Cedric with a wry smile.

The young female waitress returned with two large glasses of red wine.

'Cheers, Cedric.'

'All the best, mate.'

'What do you do at the Lodge, Cedric?'

'Well, I'm a porter. I work different shifts like. Each shift is 12 hours. I work four nights with a break of four days. Then four day shifts followed by four days off,' he explained.

'And you've got your own flat there?' he asked

'That's right. What about yourself, Joe.

'Leaving school, I did various jobs like driving, labourer, hospital porter and so on. In my 30s, I got a break driving for a local haulage company. Once I got my HGV license, the governor then allowed me to drive his large lorries. After ten years, I had saved enough money to branch out on my own. First, I bought a decent second-hand lorry, then two and, two years later, I bought three new ones. I was lucky that a new bypass was being constructed nearby and I was one of the haulage contractors to get a contract. I went on from there to develop a successful road haulage business. I was fortunate, some aren't through no fault of their own,' Joe explained.

'Well done, mate,' said Cedric, who by now was feeling the positive effects of the alcohol. He felt less anxious, more confident just sitting listening to Joe Swift talk about his business. Joe had been successful in his life, unlike Cedric, who was a complete failure. That was the main reason, thought Cedric, why he had become a fantasist. He internalised everything. He could be like Joe, or anyone else, but only in his head. Cedric could have whatever he liked, but not in reality. Fantasy, no doubt, helped him with the external challenges of everyday life.

'Has your business been moved to your new address?' he asked.

'No, I sold it a few years ago before we moved to Doveton.

My late wife thought the fresh air would be beneficial for her here. My grown-up children and grandchildren often visit me. I am very fortunate, Cedric,' Joe shrugged his shoulders, but refrained himself from hugging his old school buddy opposite. Although Joe's feelings were sincere, he didn't want to frighten him off from meeting again. He assumed that close emotional and physical contact was something Cedric wasn't used to. He didn't want to impose too much.

'What do you do with yourself all day now then, Joe, with all that money and whatnot?'

'Well, Cedric, I enjoy gardening and meeting a few friends for a beer. About four years ago, I bought four racehorses. They take up a lot of my time. I visit the stables quite a bit to see them and talk with the trainer, Sid Price. I've always enjoyed racing and have visited quite a number of racetracks through the years. Good fun, but not when you lose money gambling, it isn't,' he said with a smile on his large round, smooth face. He wondered whether Cedric would enjoy visiting the stables or going to a racetrack. Dare he ask?

'What about yourself, Cedric, any interests or hobbies?'

'Nope, not really. Well, I enjoy bus and train journeys. And walking in the country, especially in woods and listening to bird songs.'

'That sounds interesting. My grandson, Toby, loves tenting on the downs and takes photos of wildlife,' Joe said, thinking once again about whether or not Cedric would be interested in visiting the stables. He might just be attracted to animals. They could help him to express himself emotionally. Several disabled children he knew about had been helped by having regular contact with animals. Be careful, Joe.

'I was wondering, Cedric. Would you, at some time, be interested in coming over to the stables with me?' but he was concerned whether the stable staff would be a bit to boisterous for Cedric's placid personality. They were a wild bunch, at times, but they were good fun. Joe wanted to expand Cedric's experiences, but he was mindful that he wasn't his social worker or counsellor. He could intrude too much into a life that didn't want or need intense personal contact.

'Well, yes, that would be good, Joe,' said Cedric half-heartedly.

The two men finished their drinks. Joe dropped Cedric off at Oaks Lodge. They agreed that they would phone about meeting again soon.

They went their separate ways that evening after an intense few hours. Naturally, both men wondered about the other person. It had been a long time, over 50 years, since they last met. Cedric was convinced he was genuine when he was showed the school photographs. Now that Joe had lent them to him, he could look deeper into those faces from long ago. He had remembered, as he sat comfortably in his armchair, that his parents had bought the photos he was now holding. They used to laugh at his mop of hair that he refused to have cut. That was it, his mum and dad used to call him Mopper due to his hair being so thick that it could have cleaned the chimney.

But he still couldn't recall Joe as a child. He vaguely remembered some of them. It was all a blur to him. Much water had passed under his forgotten bridge. One day, he hoped that all or at least some of the names would return. It was only the first meeting, yet he thought Joe was a good bloke.

Hadn't he been successful? Cedric kept thinking about the racehorses he owned, and the invitation to visit. He, Cedric, has been invited to visit a stable full of horses! Though, he wouldn't confide in anyone, just in case he didn't go or Joe changed his mind. He must be rich though, having sold his business. Big house, racehorses, family and a new Red Jaguar, he had it all. What a success he was, Cedric kept thinking to himself as mental images of sleeping under Waterloo Bridge kept intruding.

Joe Swift for his part had been pleased with developments. Having given the letter due consideration, he realised the first steps into the unknown would be fraught with problems. But on the whole, things had gone well. There was potential for further meetings. That man in front of him, for four hours, was surely the young scruffy urchin he had played, fought, punched and kicked all those years ago. Joe could visualise him now, standing on his own in the playground, eyes on the ground looking sad. If you said anything to him, Cedric would invariably shout or run away. Once you made friends with him, he was a kind, friendly, sensitive boy who had been neglected emotionally as a baby. The moment Joe had entered the restaurant, he immediately saw that deprived child. That man of 60 years, slim with short grey hair, was unmistakably the child who craved for love and nurturing all those years ago. Joe Swift wasn't going to be an agony aunt, spiritual guide, counsellor, or throw lots of emotional energy at the man. No, given the opportunity, he would like to have a friendship with Cedric. If the contact didn't come to fruition, then so be it, he thought.

Days later, another evening shift was beginning at the

Lodge. Cedric was pleased to be handing over the keys, diary, phone and all to Nelson. He would have a few hours' sleep and then go out somewhere tomorrow, away from the Lodge. However, after his meeting with Joe Swift, Cedric felt that as brief as it was, hope was all he had. He had to try and make the best of conditions!

'Good evening, brudder,' Nelson said.

'Alright, Nelson?' asked a tired Cedric.

'Any excitement?'

'All written in that fucking diary,' said Cedric, who by now couldn't have cared less about anyone or anything to do with the place. He was shattered.

'I'll see you, brudder,' said Nelson, who had travelled to London today for a rare visit to see his daughter and her two children. He wasn't a good father or grandfather. This, by his own admission, had been his first visit in over two years. Although he had been sent photos, he hadn't kissed or hugged his granddaughters since they were babies. It's not far to travel... only 15 miles, he kept telling himself. Though his two children had visited their late grandparents many times, the bond with their father now appeared broken. Throughout the years, Nelson had lived a wayward life. His children were rarely in his sight. The emotional abuse he had experienced was something he now wanted to repair in his parental relationship.

'Good evening, Mr Flowers. How are you, sir?' asked Nelson.

'Good evening to you, Nelson.'

'Out gallivanting, sir?' quipped Nelson.

'Yes, I'm afraid so. Chess club, good friends and tasty wine. Have a good night,' said a happy resident.

Nelson went back to thinking about his family. At some stage, he wanted to plan a large party for them all. He wondered whether he had the motivation or desire for it. His repression went deep.

'Hello, night porter speaking,' said Nelson.

'Is that you, Trussington?' asked, Miss Fulton.

'It is, Miss Fulton. How are you, madam?'

'Never mind all that, Trussington, could you come up and help me with something? Don't be long, will you?' she said sarcastically.

'Be right there, Miss Fulton,' Nelson reassured her as he jumped to his feet, into the lift and arrived at the fourth floor in record time for Her Majesty.

He waited the usual few minutes before she undid the chains and opened the door. Those piecing brown eyes greeted him behind steel rim glasses.

'You're here, Trussington. Do come into the lounge. I've not been well recently. Anyway, those darn books have fallen from the top of that bloody shelf up there. Could you put them back?' she asked abruptly.

'Of course, Miss Fulton.' Nelson wished that all the books had fallen on her head. He made a brief glance towards all the pricey pictures and furniture. How he would have loved to get his fingers on all those goodies, he thought to himself. His desire still focused on other people's belongings, inevitable in the light of the status quo.

'There we are, Miss Fulton, all the books back on the shelf.'

'Thank you, Trussington,' she said sparingly.

Nelson left the apartment and walked down the stairs to reception thinking of his family. His 51st birthday was in May, yet he hadn't much to show for those wasted years. His view of his parents, at times, he knew, was sentimental. Most of the good, happy times had overridden the real problems that dominated the household. His father, although a hard worker and provider, was a hard drinker and womaniser. Nelson hadn't realised this until later on in life when his mother told him the truth about a father who had many lovers. Naively, Nelson assumed his father to be untouchable when it came to honesty. Having left home when he was young, he assumed his parents were happy whenever he rarely visited them. But all was not well. Things rarely are with most families, whose waking lives are pre-occupied with survival. They are usually fraught with problems. But he realised, to a certain extent, mirrored the behaviour of his father.

It was 11 pm and quiet as a graveyard when the reception phone rang.

'Hello, night porter speaking,' said Nelson, who hoped it wasn't anything too serious. He just wasn't up to it right now. Night and day shifts fuck your body rhythms to pieces, he thought to himself. He needed a holiday but that wasn't due for months. Most of all, Nelson was desperate for a new job. To be able to live in London once again among the people he knew was his immediate goal. But they were only dreams which, at his age, wouldn't materialise. Unless he changed his attitude towards various people, those four walls of the dog kennel would consume him. His aggression needed an outlet, it was imperative that he found new interests.

Hello, Mr Trussington. It's Miss Holroyd. Would you phone for a taxi? I'll be ready in 15 minutes,' she quietly asked.

'Yes, of course, Miss Holroyd. I'll phone right away.' Nelson thought it odd ordering a taxi at this time of night. She's over 80 and uses a walking stick. But she's the resident and knows what she wants.

'Thank you. I will be down in reception soon,' she said.

True to her word, she arrived not long after she had put the phone down, wearing a thick overcoat, hat and fur gloves. She looked so vulnerable, especially at this time of night. It was cold and frosty. The night air, surely, wasn't healthy for an 80-year-old disabled woman. But it wasn't Nelson's responsibility to ask her where she was going on such a wretched night. Lackeys like Nelson were there to serve, not ask questions. At least she had her false teeth in, Nelson chuckled to himself. Hopefully, the other pair, or pairs, were in her handbag.

With the taxi waiting just outside the main doors, Nelson helped her into the blue Vauxhall vehicle. She waved goodbye as the taxi drove out of the Lodge. Nelson was most concerned, but what could he do other than enter her departure in the diary? Perhaps she was meeting a friend or visiting a local all-night shop for something urgent. All he could do was await her return.

The usual resident phone calls began around 1 am. Two were brief, unimportant and he didn't have to visit their apartments. However, the third, at 2:30 am raised Nelson's internal alarm bells. It was from Miss Rees, who lived at apartment seven and was a friend of Miss Holroyd.

'She's not been well lately, Trussington,' said the 81-year-old spinster. 'Three times she has phoned me recently about problems relating to her past, I'm afraid,' mumbled Miss Rees.

It was now 4 am, and by this time, Nelson was most concerned for Miss Holroyd's safety. There must be a rational explanation, he thought. Even though she was elderly and disabled, she was an intelligent woman who could speak up for herself. She had been a barrister and her mind, at times, was as sharp as a pin. Mind you, he'd just remembered she had problems with her memory. Fuck it, he thought, why didn't he think of that hours ago? Problem was that the porters weren't carers or nurses and they didn't have, nor were they meant to have, detailed medical or personal information about the residents. The porters, with scant personal information and limited memory recall, were not responsible for personal well-being.

'Yes, I think I understand, Miss Rees,' said Nelson, who thought he must act immediately.

'Hello, night porter.'

'Trussington, I think I heard Miss Holroyd leave her apartment late last night but she hasn't returned yet,' said Miss Fulton.

'Thank you, Miss Fulton, we are onto it right now,' said Nelson.

Without delay, Nelson phoned the police to explain Miss Holroyd had been missing for at least five and a half hours. He was asked numerous questions about her departure from the Oaks Lodge, the contact details of the taxi company and so on. Due to her age and disability, the police sent out patrol cars immediately to look for her.

Within half an hour, the police had arrived at the Lodge.

Tension was palpable in the reception area. What had happened to her? Where had she gone? Nelson couldn't help but worry. He opened the door for the two young police officers who arrived to question him.

'Good morning, officers,' said the night porter, worried he had not done his job correctly. Richards loomed large in his imagination.

'Hello. When did Miss Holroyd leave last night?' asked one of the officers.

'About 11 pm. I phoned the local taxi firm we usually use, Ace Taxis.' Nelson gave the officer their card from under the reception counter. 'She is over 80 years of age, uses a walking stick and a bit absentminded. She constantly loses things in her apartment,' Nelson explained to them. 'There's not a lot more I can tell you about her,' he added.

'Is this the first time she has taken a cab so late? Does she have local family or friends where she might have visited?' asked the officer.

'Not as far as I know,' he said. Nelson gave him Richards' contact details, as well as a number for the head office. 'She lives in apartment four, which is on the first floor, but we do have a skeleton key to it here. Head office does as well,' said Nelson eagerly. He was trying to butter up the young skinny copper in front of him. He knew what they were like, he'd seen so many of them, all trying to climb the police promotion ladder. They were so predictable, all of them.

The police departed after their brief enquiries. They gave little indication of what they intended to do. Nelson forgot to inform them of the phone calls he had received earlier from the two residents. If Richards found out, another bollocking

was guaranteed. He delighted in dishing out misery to anyone deemed incompetent. Not another incident that had to
be recorded in the infamous diary, Nelson heaved. That pathetic diary, he would love to have burnt it to ashes. Everything had to be recorded, Nelson thought, like some military
establishment preparing for war.

Nelson sighed with relief as his shift was coming to an
end. He had made up his mind, regardless of sleep, that when
Cedric arrived, he was going to visit his daughter and her
children. No more prevaricating, he was determined to phone
and explain his visit. His daughter, Marcia, aged 25, will be
flabbergasted to see his big bulk on her doorstep. At last, the
stranger came in from the cold. Besides the thought of old
Miss Holroyd out there, possibly alone and frightened, and
the police presence had jolted him into action.

'Morning, Nelson, alright?' asked Cedric.

'No. Old Miss Holroyd is missing, man. She took a taxi
late last night to somewhere and hasn't returned since. I informed the old Bill who are looking for her. They came here
to question me about the incident. What a fucking palaver,
man. The police have the taxi company's details. It's all written down in the bible there,' he said as he pointed to the diary.

'Anything else I should know about it?' asked Cedric, who
recalled the conversation he'd had with Miss Holroyd when
she explained her painful experiences when she was young.

'That's it for now, man. See you later. I'm off to visit my
daughter in Peckham. She's recently moved due to the expensive flat. Her benefits aren't enough to cover costs. The poor
are getting poorer, man. See you,' Nelson shouted.

Well, the police are certainly going to question Cedric.

Whether they find Miss Holroyd or not could determine if Cedric willingly informed them of his personal conversation with her. Wait and see, he thought. The idea of old bill mooching around Oaks Lodge made him anxious. They might just decide to look at the Lodge staff and their criminal records, if any, to see who they were dealing with. Again, it probably depends if they find Miss Holroyd. Mind you, both Cedric and Nelson had spent convictions. They didn't have to inform their employer and weren't asked anyway. He didn't know about the cleaners.

Nelson walked through the woods to Mortingbridge rail station. He loved the quiet and peace, especially after the last 12 hours. Similar to Cedric, he hated the police asking questions. He had served his time years ago in those rundown Victorian hellholes that provided fertile ground for future villainy. Recidivism was rife in many cities. Nelson had resisted the temptations. It was now all behind him, no more cell bars for him!

Most of the busy commuters had already barged their way onto the trains for London. The station was now near deserted except for a small group of noisy teenagers. Cropped hair, torn jeans and flashy trainers—the youngsters reminded Nelson of his once gregarious confident, cocky nature. He hoped they didn't end up like him.

It was only 45 minutes to London. He knew the journey well enough from the past, when visiting friends. Occasionally, he visited family, but that was going to change. He thought of the power of place, how London kept attracting him. Full of temptation, once in the metropolis, he had to be mindful not to enter any drinking den. If that happened, he could be back at square one.

He jumped off the train at Peckham. That familiar market din penetrated his ears. All was available for the many that pushed and shoved their way looking for bargains from gangsters who sold them under-priced. Not for Nelson. Acknowledging a few old faces as he walked through the market, his thoughts returned to the Market Trader pub he used for many years. It was in that den of thieves that he and many others had planned and robbed innocent people of their personal belongings. Some of those criminals now deceased, a few still in the nick and the rest too old for action which applied to Nelson. He was ashamed of his criminal past. Although he never physically hurt anyone, he nonetheless stole what others had legitimately worked hard for. That infamous pub had now been cleaned up by the authorities of its past deviant history. The guns, drugs, gambling and sex all gone, now replaced by a friendly family atmosphere. Or was it?

Nelson's daughter lived 200 yards to the north of the market. He could see the small block of council flats from the corner of Market Place, where he had once stood as a brazen youngster when he thought he owned the world. Pork pie hat, black leather jacket and pink shoes, Nelson thought he was the jack-the-lad. His good friend for many years, Benny Tramp, had been fatally shot just 300 yards down the road to his left. Memories, and there were many more, now belonged to the dustbin. He was now a more mature man, who would try and make the best of what he had. Financially potless, but he had a goldmine just in front of him—his beloved family.

He bought a bundle of flowers, a box of chocolates and a large bag of sweets, and marched up to that front door.

'Hi, Dad, how are you, love? So good to see you,' his daughter said as she hugged her father for the first time in ages. Nelson's two granddaughters also kissed and cuddled him. Was it all a front based on guilt? He hoped it wasn't because, this time—it's always this time—he craved to be a regular granddad. Well, that's what Nelson aspired to, anyway. Time would be the arbiter.

'My word, you girls have grown since I last saw you both,' said Nelson, forgetting they were babies when he last visited. 'There are some lovely yellow daffodils for the room, chocolates and sweets for all of you,' he said, trying to make up for lost time. He felt guilt, pain and useless inside of himself. Was he sincere about visiting with his empty gifts, or was it all a show and shallow performance?

'Fancy a beer, Dad?' asked Marcia.

'That'll be great, sweetheart,' he said. 'Are you pleased with your new flat, love?' he asked, smiling.

'Yeah, the girls and I have been here six months. Quiet block of flats unlike the place where we moved from, which was full of drugs, gangs and violence. The girls love their new school down the road. They dance, play music, make coach trips out to various places and have a very good canteen,' Marcia explained in an excited and enthusiastic manner. She loved her daughters, that was obvious to anyone. She wasn't going to allow anyone or anything to hurt, upset or hinder their progress through life. That also meant, although she hadn't mentioned this yet, her father.

'How is Paul doing, Marcy?' asked Nelson, who hadn't seen

his son, or grandson, for at least four years. He had moved away from London, fed up with high rents and everyday living, to Bournemouth.

'Enjoys life in Dorset, but with no car, he finds public travel to work expensive. Less intense than London, he tells me. But he phones me, or I phone him, regularly once a week. Both he and Sandra are working in a local supermarket. With two wages coming in, they have a decent life. His son, Errol, loves the openness of the place. Always swimming in the sea with classmates and plays football for his local team,' said a smiling Marcia. She dared to feel that, gradually, her family was coming together, but bitter experiences warned her of previous, premature meetings with her dad could be painful. So, be realistic, girl, not too many expectations at once. One step at a time was the way forward. Her dad had a track record of unreliability. Nelson hadn't discussed too much of his personal history with his two children. The deeper side to it was for another time. They knew of his criminality, but not about the earlier times before they were born. Nelson would have to discuss those with a more skilled listener before letting them loose upon the ears of his children. If he ventured down that road of repression therapy, Nelson would need to understand the potential repercussions. For the time being, he was in chartered waters that felt safe and, hopefully, benefitted others.

He was just contented to sit there with his family. The children ran downstairs and played in the communal playground. Marcia could keep an eye on them from the third floor. Nelson and his daughter drank beer, talked family and hoped he wouldn't take so long next time to visit them all. He was also given his son's phone number, which pleased him. He was optimistic.

However, they barely discussed Marcia's mother. She had remarried and moved away to Yorkshire. They had met four times in the last three years but it was a long journey for either person. She had seen her grandchildren, including Paul's son, twice. Understandably, she was overwhelmed by family dynamics. But now settled, living in a small village and working in a shop, she keeps herself in the background. Being around Nelson had left its mark on her.

Summing it all up, Nelson thought he wasn't too badly off after all, living and working at Oaks Lodge. He had a regular wage, small flat big enough for one person, quiet middle-class area and few frustrations. Plenty worse off than him. He kissed his family goodbye. The past few hours had been the happiest for many a year, but he was sad to be leaving it all behind.

'Bye, bye, Granddad,' the girls shouted and waved from the balcony as the big man walked out of the building, crossed the road and headed towards the station. The market was nearly empty. The punters had spent and retreated to the pub for another session of alcohol. There was a part of him craving to be in that market pub, downing a few pints and chipping a few jokes from yesteryear. But it had all gone. He had been replaced by a younger, more vibrant generation. You are yesterday's man, Nelson. He knew that and had accepted it long ago. Age, money, energy and whatnot had all taken their turn to supersede those falling down the handicap.

The station was packed with workers, school children, shoppers, crooks, tramps and the miscellaneous. The warriors of the roads, he called them. It appeared that very little had changed over the years, except the faces. He was at an age where people start to reminisce. How things used to be, why did it all have to change? Thoughts from the past began to overwhelm him. He stood thinking of them, of the rogues that he would never see again.

He sat quietly, reading a newspaper on a packed, noisy train heading out of Paddington station. Would he return? He didn't know. Most of the workers he saw were heading home after earning their few bob in the human jungle called London. How they make this packed, noisy, smelly journey five days a week baffled him. Fear is the word, he assumed. There were the elderly, the disabled, the children and so many more to accommodate, feed and clothe, and all dependent on those earning enough money to keep them alive. He shuddered at the thought. The quality of life for most must be poor, he assumed. His life so far, he thought, had been so completely different to most people. He was doubtful that he could live such a prescriptive existence.

Meanwhile, the local Mortingbridge police had ramped up their search for the missing Miss Holroyd. Over 18 hours ago, she had left the Lodge and serious concerns for her safety were now paramount. The taxi company, who had driven Miss Holroyd to the edge of Wayhill Woods, were interviewed by police. It's very odd, indeed, that a vulnerable old lady using a walking stick would be dropped off that late at night, nearly midnight, with no questions asked by the driver. It's beggar's belief that an 80-year-old person, short-sighted, arthritic with a poor memory recall should have been left on the side of a road in the cold dark of night.

According to the taxi driver, Miss Holroyd informed him that she was visiting a friend down the road. The nearest houses were at least 100 yards away. At that time of night, she wouldn't have been able to see that far, let alone visit a friend in the dark with very little street light assisting her. Now, it must be remembered, she was a very plausible woman. Brought to the legal bar as a young woman, she had been a ferocious advocate during her time there. Many a judge had scolded her due to a sharp tongue and witty presence. When she did legal battle, in the intellectual bear pits, women like her were a rare sight. So, it was understandable that she could fob off the young male driver with a most plausible concocted story. But why did she have to do that, and at a time when even most of the wild animals would have been asleep? Why didn't she leave a message with Nelson, who was on duty that evening, when at 11 pm, she left the premises?

When Nelson arrived back at the Lodge at around 6 pm, the police were interviewing Cedric in the back office. Richards stood at reception resembling a senior military officer in civilian clothes. Standing stiff and tall, with his hands behind his back, angry flames appeared to leap from his nose. After being informed of Miss Holroyd's disappearance, he had immediately driven to the Lodge. He was now in charge of the place. Couldn't leave anything to these morons, the porters, he constantly told himself. Regardless of the police presence, he would sort things out, he kept reassuring himself.

Richards beckoned Nelson to reception before he had the chance to walk around to his basement flat and prepare himself for 12 hours of work ahead.

'Where the fuck have you been?' shouted Richards.

'Why are you shouting, Mr Richards? I've been out all day visiting my daughter in London,' he said, who was a little angry and somewhat confused by Richards' attitude.

'Have you heard about Miss Holroyd?' his tone now not so aggressive.

'Yes, of course, I have. I was on duty when she left at 11 pm by taxi. She didn't say where she was going and it's not my responsibility to ask. When she hadn't returned by 4 am, I called the police. They came here to ask me questions. It's all written in the diary.'

The conversation went on for half an hour until Nelson insisted he get some rest before going back on duty at 8 pm. He felt that his boss was out of order by the way he had spoken, as if an inferior person to himself. Nelson, once again, had come close to chinning that fat bastard. If that happened, then he knew he would lose his job, home and possibly be charged with an offence. Fuck the world, he raged, as he kicked the kitchen door, in utter frustration, off its hinges. He felt really trapped, like a growling animal, for the first time in his life. If he left the job, where could he go? Council wouldn't give him accommodation, made intentionally homeless, they would inform him. His options were dirty cheap bedsits, crowded hostels, expensive hotels or the park bench, if he left the Lodge. The big man's image of his fair London Town was evaporating in front of his eyes. He looked at the dirty brown wallpaper, brown stained ceiling and charity shop furniture. He had virtually nothing that he could call his own. The big smiling image was a front for a person deep in shit, and it was sinking fast. But Nelson was no quitter.

Cedric's police interview lasted about an hour. He explained that Miss Holroyd had asked him up to her apartment. She told Cedric personal things about her past. He felt he didn't understand some of it, and was pleased when he left her apartment. He had felt uneasy and anxious listening to an intelligent woman explain that her stepfather had emotionally abused her. It had detrimentally affected her throughout her life, Cedric told the police. Miss Holroyd had taken pills in court, had flash backs and had misused alcohol earlier in her life. Mr Matthews, who was her counsellor, had been visiting her for some time. She informed Cedric that without his guidance, her life would be unbearable. Mr Matthews was another potential source of interest that could further explain her disappearance.

Later that windy evening, at around 10:30pm, two males accidentally found a female body lying across the path they were walking in Wayhill Woods. Being dark, they nearly trod on the body, not a hundred yards from the road. Their torchlight revealed an elderly woman holding a handbag. They immediately phoned the police and ambulance, but realised after feeling her pulse that she was dead. The two different agencies arrived within minutes of each other. Lights flashing and vehicles wailing, their presence took over the immediate vicinity. One of the young men stood on the pavement to hail the emergency services. He led them to where the body lay. Forensics was summoned in case of foul play. By this time, alarmed people from down the road had started to converge on the lighted scene before them. Areas were cordoned off. Personnel carried a tent to cover the body until a pathologist arrived. After inspecting the body, it was carried out to the ambulance and whisked away to the local hospital mortuary for a post-mortem. The atmosphere was sombre and subdued. Instinctively, people thought the worst after what they had just witnessed.

'Hello, night porter, good evening,' said Nelson

'Oh, oh, Trussington, have they found Miss Holroyd yet?' asked a concerned Miss Fulton.

'I haven't heard anything yet, Miss Fulton, but as soon as I do, I'll let you know,' said Nelson, who anticipated a lot more questions from residents to come.

'Thank you. I'm most concerned,' she said.

Minutes later, another concerned resident phoned to ask about their missing fellow resident. Slowly but surely, her disappearance was growing through the Lodge grapevine.

'Hello, night porter.'

'Hello, Trussington, have we found out anything about our dear Miss Holroyd yet?' asked Miss Rees, aged 81, spinster and near recluse. Her only contact with the outside world appeared to be Miss Holroyd and one or two other women.

The rest of the night, and most of the early morning, residents phoned reception enquiring about their missing resident. Nelson's ear was left ringing by the time Richards had re-appeared on the scene, not long after leaving for his home.

'Good morning, could you please go at once and get Bambridge? The two of you must meet me in ten minutes. It's too bad if he's in bed, it's very urgent. I need to speak with you soonest. Besides, he'll be on duty in an hour. Hurry up, thanks,' said Richards in a rather grave manner.

6

CHAPTER SIX

The two porters rushed in through the main doors and presented themselves to the boss. Both had anxious faces as if they were about to be told the unpalatable news that they had anticipated. From inside the closed door, Richards explained to them, in a rather intense atmosphere, what he had just been informed by the police.

'I'm sorry to say that Miss Holroyd has been found dead in Wayhill Woods late last night, by two young male walkers. Post-mortem found that she had died of hypothermia, exposure to the cold. According to the pathologist, she had been there for a considerable length of time. He couldn't be exact. It appears nothing was stolen from her person or bag. There is no need, therefore, to go in front of a coroner. One can only imagine how she suffered out there in the freezing cold left exposed to the elements. The poor dear must have been desperate to end it all. Head office will deal with her estate, church service and other matters,' he said in a quiet and humble manner not seen before.

'It's a terrible experience for all of us. With regards to the residents, I would like the three of us to place one of these sensitively written flyers through each resident's letter box. Keep a few of them for yourselves in case you need to refer to them later. The flyers don't inform about church service dates, etc. If residents phone and want to speak to you personally, in detail, about any matter, please refer them to head office or my phone number. Also, give a flyer to cleaners and agency staff. Thank you, lads.' With his head bowed, Richards walked silently out of the room trying to feel the suffering Miss Holroyd experienced.

'Well, Cedric, what did yer make of that, brudder?' asked Nelson, who had spoken to the deceased many times over the years.

'I'm fucking speechless.'

'In hindsight, perhaps I should have made earlier enquiries about her activities from the taxi firm,' said Nelson, quietly.

'She was only telling me, me of all people, the other day that her stepfather gave her a hard time when she was young.'

'Life surely is a funny ol' place, brudder. I'm pleased I saw my family today, it reminds me of how precarious our existence is. In the blink of an eye, my two sweet granddaughters will soon be grown-up,' said Nelson.

Miss Holroyd's death had focused their minds. The two men exchanged conversation about how they had found their way to Oaks Lodge for work. Chance had brought these two decent individuals together. Life itself was based on chance—take the right turning and you were heading in the right direction. The other direction led to obscurity.

'I'm off to my flat, Nelson. Have a good one tonight, hopefully without incident,' said Cedric, as he walked slowly out of the front doors resigned to living in the dog kennel for the rest of his working life. Headbanging helped at these times when worthlessness consumed him. All around him was wealth, yet he could only catch the mere morsels that others threw his way. He now realised that killing himself—something he had thought about intermittently—wasn't an easy way out. Meeting with Joe Swift recently reminded him that brighter things could materialise if he persisted. Keep at it, Cedric, he could still make something of a difficult life.

The flyers highlighting the sad death of Miss Holroyd had been given to every resident. There was an uncanny silence about the place. Words couldn't describe that depth of feeling and remorse for a resident of many years. Loss reminds us that nothing is forever. Some residents now wish, painfully so, that they should have made that effort to spend more time with a person suffering from many ailments.

'Hello, night porter,' said Nelson.

'Isn't it tragic? Poor Miss Holroyd,' said Miss Knight.

'Yes, it is, Miss Knight.'

'You don't know anything about the funeral, do you?' she quietly asked.

'I don't. The head office or Mr Richards, area manager, have all the details, Miss Knight.'

'Thank you, Trussington.'

Nelson was sipping his rum-laced coffee in peace when the exuberant Mr Ford walked out of the lift, humming a tune. Upbeat, well-dressed with a smile on his roguish face, suggestive of another foray into the clubs of Soho.

'Good evening, Nelson, how are you?' he asked.

'Hello, Mr Ford. I'm well. And how are you? You look dressed to kill 'em dead tonight,' said Nelson, smiling from ear to ear.

'Sad about the old dear, Miss Holroyd,' he said.

'Yes, very sad. Found frozen to death, apparently.'

'I shall attend her funeral. I didn't really know her. I only spoke to her on occasions,' said Mr Ford.

'Out gallivanting, sir?' asked Nelson, who wished he was shoulder to shoulder with the confident man in front of him, drinking in one of his well-endowed clubs.

'Yes, I'm meeting friends in London. There's my taxi out there now, Nelson. I've not forgotten our arm wrestling by the way,' said David Ford as he walked briskly to the parked Hackney Cab.

'Good evening, night porter.'

'Good evening, Mr Trussington. Just to say how sad I was to read about the death of dear Miss Holroyd. Such a lovely person, though we spoke occasionally, I knew very little about her. Bless her soul,' said Mr Tressle, whimpering into the phone.

'Yes, sir, very sad.'

'Goodnight.'

'Goodnight, sir.'

The good porter returned to his rum and coffee. He only drank Appleton's rum. Strong and deep, it was made in Jamaica. At least it used to be, thought Nelson. He nearly always kept a bag of scented sweets in his pocket in case Richards arrived unexpectedly. Or, for whatever reason, he had to visit a resident. He didn't want his breath overpowering them. He knew it was a sacking offence, and that would place him in a perilous situation.

'Good evening, night porter speaking.'

'Hello, Trussington. Miss Perks and I are most sad upon hearing the tragic death of Miss Holroyd,' said Miss Nobton.

'Very sad, indeed, Miss Nobton,' said Nelson, who wouldn't mind getting his hands on the old dear's money.

'Goodnight.'

Goodnight, madam.'

Wasn't it absurd when you kept hearing painful expressions or deep sincerities from residents who lived years beside each other, yet rarely spoke? Nelson wondered how many of the ageing residents actually met in each other's apartments. Probably not that often, he concluded.

Several more residents phoned reception to express their feelings for the deceased. It was natural that they felt for a neighbour whose last hours must have been painful alone in a cold dark wood. One could only guess the torment of exposure as one's life is slowly ebbing away. Her wretched abuse eventually took the final vestige of her identity.

After 4 am, the whole building was quiet. Nelson received no more phone calls until the cleaners arrived just before day shift began. When his shift was finished, he intended to catch up on a few hours of sleep. As Cedric was off duty, an agency worker would take over from him, which was useful when staff were not available. Mind you, Richards begrudged paying out the extra money that the agency charged. Due to the shift patterns and increasing costs, the boss had alluded to Nelson and others that he was thinking of employing another full-time porter. But it would have to be a non-residential post. There had been occasions when night coverage was unavailable due to sickness. Cleanaway Ltd had written security into residents' expensive contracts.

'Morning, ladies, how are you all? I hope you haven't had too much sex and booze the past week?' asked a smiling Nelson, who, given the chance, would like to indulge, in particular, with Gill.

'The chance would be a fine thing, Nelson. Better now we've seen you, sweetheart,' said Emily.

'You lot are early today. I thought you started at ten?'

'Boss man says we can start between eight and ten, but we must all start at the same time,' said Hilda.

'Where's lover boy Cedric today?' asked Gill, who enjoyed constantly ribbing him.

'His day off,' said Nelson. 'The agency worker, Terry, is on shift until I'm back on at 8 pm tonight, darling.'

'All work and no play, ain't it, Nelson?' said Emily.

'There he is now, parking his yellow car. He is young and handsome, you would fancy him, Hilda,' laughed Nelson.

'Very nice indeed, I hope he's well packed,' she said, laughing.

'Welcome, Terry. meet the scrubbers of Oaks Lodge.' That was Nelson's nickname for cleaning ladies.

'Hello, Terry, how are you, darling? Welcome to the Oaks,' said Hilda.

'Hi, ladies, good to meet you.'

'Right, a serious matter I have to inform you all about. Please follow me into the lover's room,' said Nelson.

Once inside and away from prying ears, Nelson gave the typed letter to everyone. He explained the brief circumstances surrounding Miss Holroyd's death. In essence, it was information that Richards had told him. The cleaners were visibly upset, especially Emily as she had cleaned her apartment many times and found her to be a kind and friendly woman. Miss Holroyd often used to make tea for Emily, and occasionally the other cleaners, where she had the opportunity to chat about anything. Nelson suggested that they all chip in a few pounds each to buy a large bunch of flowers to send to the church. They all agreed.

'Right, girls, I'll leave you to clean the place. Please spray the reception plants, gives them a bit of a shine just like the top of my bald head,' roared Nelson.

Nelson explained work requirements to Terry. To read and write anything relevant into the diary, walk around each floor to check all is well and answer the phone politely. He warned him that the Oaks, for some residents, had been lost in a time warp. He told him not to take it seriously, although he had worked a few shifts before.

Tired and fed up, Nelson walked slowly to his flat below ground. Just as he was about to put the key in the door to his flat, he heard banging noises coming from Cedric's flat. Bang, bang, bang, half a dozen times at least. Nelson wondered what was happening. He stood still, quiet and listened to a few more bangs which appeared to be on the inside of Cedric's front door. Nelson was literally only three or four feet from the door. What should he do? Nelson just stayed where he was for another few minutes listening. After several more minutes, he heard Cedric shouting and swearing. What was happening to his good friend, he didn't know. But Nelson was concerned and decided to knock on the door. Cedric eventually opened it.

'Morning, Cedric, you alright, brudder? I heard lots of banging and was a bit concerned, my friend,' he asked.

'Yeah, problems, mate,' said Cedric, rather despondently.

'Wanna talk about it, mate?'

Yeah, come in.'

Both men sat opposite each other on dilapidated armchairs. Cedric remained quiet for a minute or so, his eyes were fixed on the floor.

'Yeah, sorry about the noise, mate, but I've got this problem. I've had it since I was a child in the home. When I get stressed, I start banging my head against anything that is hard like a door or wall. It relieves the pain in my head. I've never seen anyone about it like a shrink or local GP. I don't want those bastards interfering. They only bring more trouble.

'Well,' said Nelson. 'You need some sort of support, mate. You could do yourself some permanent damage.'

'No not for me, Nelson. I learnt from an early age to keep my mouth closed. I hid my feelings away from those who had power over me. That's what institutions do for yer. Someone told me it's called repression. I suppose that's why I fantasize and imagine things. I know that they are not real but it gives me a bit of hope, I suppose. Lack of confidence, that's what the teacher explained to me when I attended adult evening classes. I look up the meaning of all these words I'm told, or overhear what others say.'

'That's good, mate. Look, Cedric, anytime you wanna talk about it, just ask, OK? Try not to hurt yourself, mate. I'm your friend, what you do will remain confidential. It's between you and I,' said Nelson reassuringly.

'Thanks, mate,' sighed Cedric. His inner torment, whatever its origin, continued to make his life difficult at times. But he was making ground in trying to understand why he suffered so. Fancy talking, as he called it, and pills weren't for him, but it demonstrated the resilience of a person who had experienced only a glimmer of life's expectations.

Cedric found the talk with his colleague reassuring. But being an outsider, as he saw it, he was reluctant to talk about himself. Indeed, he had tried occasionally with others but found it all too much. He felt exposed and vulnerable expressing his feelings to others. They had a hold over you, Cedric thought.

Today, he was meeting Joe Swift for the second time. Cedric had plucked up the courage to phone him, though still convinced, at some level, that friendship wasn't for him. They had made arrangements to meet at about 10 am in Mortingbridge high street. It was nearly deserted, only the road sweeper whistling and fish monger singing gave the place any sort of life, not surprising as the place was near full of ageing people. Children were very much the minority. Joe had promised Cedric a visit to where his four horses were stabled at Lewton, ten miles from where they met. Uncharted territory lay ahead.

It was during a social occasion, visiting Sandown racecourse with business friends, that he got hooked. It was only Joe's third visit to a race meeting. He had watched a little racing on the television, like the Derby and Grand National, but hadn't given it that much notice. But something lurked in the back of his mind that attracted his personality. He was excited by taking chances, the thrill of pitting your wits against the odds. That's what he had done for over 25 years in road haulage, undercutting and outdoing others to win contracts. The racing fraternity had that competitive urge to succeed. Joe wanted to be a part of those people who were prepared to push the boundaries further. They had won and lost big gambles. Every time horses, jockeys, trainers, racetracks and big money gambles came together, it excited Joe to even greater endeavour.

After that third race meeting had finished, Joe approached a trainer, Sid Price, for a chat about ownership. As usual, Joe had done his homework. Shrewd guy was Joe Swift. He had discussed horse ownership with his friends. They recommended him to read about trainers, their successes, training fees, location and, most important of all, how to buy him a decent horse. Price appeared to fit the bill. He arranged for Joe to visit him at Lewton stables a few days later to discuss business. After explaining the many pitfalls that owners had experienced during his tenure—some had lost a fortune—the two men discussed financial arrangements. There were fees for that, fees for this and many other unmentioned fees along the way. Joe was prepared for this. Several horserace owners had educated him about how to proceed. Besides, now that he had sold his business, he had become a millionaire. Most of that money he had invested for his family, and others who had supported him when times were difficult. Mind you, he was only 60 years old, and longed for a new beginning now he was on his own.

Besides, Joe didn't need another sexual relationship or

marriage. His late wife had been his partner since the day they first met, aged 16. She was his one and only woman. Mind you, he had dabbled a bit! His late wife would have been pleased that he had bought new homes for their children, who were educated, and all had well-paid, challenging jobs. No doubt, motivated like their father. Joe and his wife had grafted to provide them with a secure and pleasurable future, if such a thing exists! One or two major setbacks... well, Dad was there to sort it out.

'Morning, Cedric, how are you?' asked a smiling Joe Swift, who, no doubt, had already planned the day ahead. His self-awareness quickly cutting through anything deemed waste of time, energy and money.

Hello, Joe. I'm alright, thanks,' said Cedric, who was still apprehensive about the day that lay ahead. New faces, places and words to contend with, his anxiety levels rose. New words, on second thoughts, he reckoned could be useful to him. Words had the ability to boost his confidence, demonstrate that he understood things and communicate more effectively. If he could get that right, then people should take him seriously. Confidence was the problem. He found that emotional gap, when trying to talk to people he didn't know, insurmountable. Cedric was desperate to have friends, at least acquaintances, but childhood conditioning had placed a psychological concrete wall in front of him.

On this occasion, Joe drove a sleek silver Mercedes with red leather interior and all modern technological gadgets. Cedric had not seen anything like it before. So many confusing dials, it reminded him of the cockpit of a modern aircraft that you can see on the television. Must have cost him a fortune, Cedric surmised. Mind you, as Joe drove out of the village and onto the main road, he felt, for the first time, good about himself. People were looking at him in the expensive car, he thought, thinking that he, Cedric, must be someone important or rich or powerful. How inanimate things can delude. Fantasy—this was one of Cedric's many defence mechanisms used for coping with unwanted or unnecessary thoughts and feelings. What they were, he was unaware of. This automatic response was something that Cedric had done unconsciously all his life. It was probably triggered by feelings of losing control in front of Joe's friends.

'Have you been busy, Cedric?' asked Joe, who was genuinely interested.

'Well, same old stuff at work, Joe. An elderly female resident was found dead in the local woods the other day,' he said.

'What happened to her?' Joe was taken aback by Cedric's attitude to someone dying as the same old stuff. But he understood what he meant.

'She died of exposure, I think. She was a decent old bird.'

'How tragic,' said Joe, who had just remembered that his late father's friend had died of exposure to harsh conditions while on a winter holiday. The stables are just another hundred yards up this bumpy old road. Most of this land around us belongs to a wealthy landowner but he isn't here very much. He lives in Dubai. Most people have never seen him. Some even doubt his existence. An agency looks after half of it. The other half is worked by a tenant farmer, Richard Bryce. He's a really good bloke. Started here with nothing, the whole 50 acres was full of small trees, shrubs and weeds. It was a wasteland. He ploughed the whole lot several times un-

til he could start planting vegetables and feed his livestock,'
explained Joe.

A few young, fresh faces acknowledged Joe's presence as
he drove into the stable yard. He occasionally gave the lads
£100 each if he had a winner. Their tongues appeared to be
hanging out their mouths in anticipation. In one corner of the
yard was an almighty pile of steaming horse manure. Fresh
from the horse boxes some 50 yards away. Other expensive
cars were parked nearby. Both men got out of the car.

'Morning, Ted. How did your horse run at Newbury the
other day?' asked Joe.

'She ran like she had three legs. Finished nearly last,' he
said, his frowning face told the whole story.

'Meet my friend, Cedric.'

'Hello, Cedric, nice to meet you.'

'Hello, mate,' said Cedric, who felt uneasy but looking forward to what was ahead.

The two men walked slowly down through the yard. Horse
boxes either side of them. There were large, powerful horses,
who stared at Cedric, sticking out of each box. Instinct informed them there was a new presence in the yard. They
could sense Cedric's fear of them. Joe said hello to three Jodh-
pur clad stable staff cleaning out their muck. The animals
snorted and shot their heads forward as they passed by. A
world that was totally alien to Cedric. He was surprised by
how short everyone was. He eyed with interest how comfortable the horse boxes could have been during his days of sleeping rough. Four-star luxury, he thought.

'These are my four horses,' said Joe.

'Have they won any races?'

'Yes, they have. The most successful is Blue Pearl. She is five years of age and has won... yes, she has won seven steeplechase races. All the horses jump over fences. They don't run flat races like the Derby.'

'That's a lot, Joe.'

'Between them, they have won about 18 races. Not bad going. They are expensive to keep, mind you. There are many different fees I have to pay to various people. And, of course, they weren't cheap to buy, but I've won a few good gambles on them. So, they don't owe me any money. Besides, it is now my full-time occupation travelling all over the country watching my horses, accompanied by friends, race on different tracks. The owners, stable staff and trainer meet regularly for an evening of excess. We have great fun and laughter. Occasionally, the trainer ends up dunked in the water trough outside the pub. The racing mob is full of energy and devilment. Always willing to try something new, that's what appeals to me,' Joe explained.

'Sounds interesting, Joe.'

'Come down to where you see these younger animals being broken in. They are trained to go through various methods or techniques until they are deemed fit enough by the trainer to race in public.

'You alright, Dave?' Joe shouted to one of those training a horse.

'Hello, Joe. Good result for the yard last Saturday,' he said, referring to Dark Star's win at Bath.

The two men leant on the fence to watch the horses being schooled. Cedric had not seen this kind of thing before, in fact, it fascinated him. It reminded him of the power some people have over others. Tied to a metaphorical financial rope, similar to that in front of him, controls how people can conduct their lives over others. They are limited by the length of rope, or money, they have to make choices about where they live, work, educate and so on. In fact, as Cedric looked on, he was horrified by the power of the man constraining the natural instincts of a young animal. Naturally, it put as much distance as possible between him and the master. It snorted loudly, bucked, jumped and terror filled its bulging eyes. Cedric hoped the animal would jump over the high wooden fence to freedom. Failing that, he fantasized the horse fighting back, kicking and biting the prison guard who held him tight. Cedric wanted to shout out loud, to stop the suffering he witnessed, but he realised where he was.

'It's called lunging, Cedric. It helps the horse learn to be more flexible and balanced. Look, I've got business to sort out later, Cedric, so I'll drive you back to your village, or town, isn't it? Have you enjoyed the experience?'

'Thanks very much, Joe. Thanks for showing me all this. I've not seen this sort of thing before.' Cedric realised he hated the spectacle of the cruel methods used to train animals he had just experienced. It was all in the name of racing, although he wasn't convinced. It wasn't for him, but he had to be careful about what he said to Joe.

Joe dropped Cedric off at Mortingbridge high street. Cedric got out of the car feeling more confident about himself than he had hours previously. If only some people, he knew, realised where he had just been, they would be flabbergasted. No, not Cedric, they would have said, in a racing establishment.

'Thanks, Joe, I appreciate going to your yard and seeing your horses.'

'My pleasure, Cedric, would you like to go racing one day when one of my horses is jumping?'

'I would love that,' he said enthusiastically, but deep down, he wasn't convinced about it at all.

'Take care. I'll be in contact with you soon.'

Cedric stood on the pavement waving at his friend as he sped off like the Lord of Doveton. He stood there for minutes wondering about the contrast of their lives. How well Joe had done—successful business, money, big house and supportive family. What had Cedric done with his abysmal life? Not very much if today was any genuine guide.

He decided to buy a coffee in the café across the road. Cherry's was quite a posh place where middle-class women go for tea and a chat about their inept cleaners or useless son-in-laws. He was in two minds... would he have a beer down the road? No, that place is dirty, cold and sold overpriced beer. Cedric thought a late afternoon tea should be enjoyable among the chattering menagerie. He would also have a cake, full of cream and jam as a treat for navigating his way around anxious moments with Joe.

The horses were enormous, just think of those little men riding that muscle machine at 40 miles an hour on a rain and windswept racetrack. What nerve and confidence they must have, surmised Cedric. Just one look at Joe's brown horse, with bulging muscles and iron veins, had frightened him. But Joe had reassured him that the powerful, mean looking beast couldn't get out of his box. Although Cedric had thought it didn't actually belong there, the wild beast should have been galloping free, amongst its own, in natural surroundings. But, man the master, having domesticated the breed centuries ago, wouldn't have cut any ice with him. All living beings should be free to live naturally, he considered.

Cedric crossed the road and walked sheepishly into the small café.

'Good afternoon, sir, what would you like to order?' asked a young, fat, blond-haired woman.

'I would like a coffee and cream cake, please,' said Cedric, who thought the waitress was quite attractive in her red uniform and powdered face. He wondered whether she was married and had children. He hadn't seen her around the town before.

'Thank you, sir,' she said quietly.

First glances of the café were rather positive. About eight four-seater tables covered in white cotton tops and place mats. White ceiling, pale blue walls covered in drawings of various dogs stood out. There were two female staff serving and, no doubt, others preparing his order elsewhere. It was all very quiet and genteel. All the customers were women, sipping tea and mouthing softly spoken words. Cedric cringed at the theatre in front of him.

'There we are, sir. Thank you,' said the fat waitress.

'Thanks,' said Cedric. He felt obliged to say something.

As Cedric ate his cake and drank his coffee, very nice indeed, he thought, his mind wondered to those in the café. Their lives must be considerably different to the one that he lived. The sharp, multi-coloured, fine clothes they wore suggested that in an instant. Sitting there, healthy and secure, with very few problems to worry about except what to do on

their forthcoming holidays in the sun. If he had been educated, he too would probably have been in a similar position.
Big house, good job, sexy wife and spoilt kids, all demanding the last drop of spunk out of his tormented existence. No,
are they really better off, these people? Huge mortgage, long
hours at the office, the husband's piles causing endless pain
and driven to near insanity by alcohol as his wife struts the
spiel with her friends. Poor old husband, family need him to
supply one thing only—money.

It was this type of environment that occasionally caused
Cedric to think of his biological mother. At these times, he
hated her for abandoning him. Vulnerable, unloved and unwanted; she just got rid of him like a piece of shit floating
through the night. How could he love anyone, or be loved, after such a tragic start to his life? He often wondered whether
he had any siblings, but he certainly wasn't going to make any
enquires into the subject. Several people, during his life, had
encouraged him to contact various institutions. Cedric didn't
want to go anywhere near those places. Intrusive, that's all
they were. He couldn't give a damn if his mother, or any other
family member, contacted him. He would ignore any type of
communication. Just like they all ignored baby Cedric. Besides, his mother was now probably dead. He hoped she was.

But when his frustration and anger had subsided somewhat, he used to feel sorry for her. Perhaps she had no choice
but to find him a better home. Had she been a prostitute,
drug addict, alcoholic or abused by others? Perhaps she had
lived a homeless life, full of torment and suffering, he surmised. No identity, a waif-like figure stalking through the
shadows. At this stage, tears invariably came to his eyes for

a mother who asked for very little and received even less. He had seen so many people in similar terrible predicaments. Where was she born, did she have a family or was she thrown upon the vagaries of a loveless life, similar to her son?

Anyhow, Cedric knew that way of life wasn't for him. All front and no substance, he kept reminding himself. He looked at his watch and was reminded that his shift was only two hours away. He walked down the high street, crossed the road and came across Jake, the bloke who delivered post at the Oaks.

'Alright, Cedric?' asked Jake who had been drinking nearby.

'Yeah, I'm fine, Jake.'

'Where you off to?'

'Working soon, must go, Jake. Must go,' he said.

He shook his hand and walked on up the hill and into the woods, heading for the Oaks. Cedric didn't want to get involved in drinking with Jake, who was notorious for fighting anyone after a few whiskies. He was as wild as a bull when alcohol flooded his demented brain. Cedric walked slowly through Marsh Wood, taking note of the various wildflowers he had seen many times over the years. The wind blew through the trees making sounds like a harp playing a soft melody. About a mile long, the wood acted as a convenient screen from the gushes of rain, wind and snow that bombarded houses in Oaks Park Road. Council workers occasionally patrolled the woods, trying to catch offenders who degraded the beautiful green space with their rubbish. It was Cedric's sublime green space, where he could go and just be himself. In an ever-encroaching world, he cherished the trees, shrubs, flowers and animals that had made the wood an eco-logical gem.

Another shift had arrived at the Lodge. It was nearly 8 pm when he walked in through the doors. Terry was at reception.

'Good evening, Cedric. How are you, mate?' asked a smiling Terry who was pleased he would soon be leaving to go home, and baffled how anyone could work and live in the place full-time. His day wasn't difficult, the usual comings and goings. He was grateful for the agency work now that he had been made redundant after seven years working for a local printer. With a mortgage, wife, and two young children, any money was mightily accepted. He was going out of his way to help residents hoping that they would inform the boss he was a good and dependable worker. If he had to, he would clean shit out of cuckoo clocks!

'I'm alright. How are you?'

'Looking forward to seeing the kids, mate,' he said, smiling.

'Good.' Cedric wished he hadn't said that. He had no one to go home to, except a fucking dog kennel. The thought of opening your front door and being greeted by your wife and kids, he found too much to bear. A hot meal waiting on the table, tea and cigarettes afterwards added to his inner torment. However, the recent café theatrics reminded him of illusion.

'OK, mate, have a good night. See you soon.'

7

CHAPTER SEVEN

Sitting behind the reception desk like a lost soul looking for shelter, there was Cedric, as usual, on parade at 8 pm. He was now stuck to this place, like shit to a blanket. The nights were drawing out and spring was around the corner. Cedric rarely went on holiday for two whole weeks. He took his holidays, but usually went out for various day outings to the coast or visited a castle or large public garden. But he was always mindful of keeping his distance, if possible, away from crowds, they tended to suffocate him. Wherever that intense feeling came from he didn't know. There were many theories in his head about this sort of thing, but its exact understanding baffled him.

However, Cedric's meeting with Joe Swift had ignited something different inside him. Yes, he was 60 years old, uneducated, unskilled with few opportunities left for him. But if nothing else, he could change his mind set about the kind of person he could become. He was only late middle-aged, still time left for practical change. If he couldn't get a better job, so be it. The main thing now was to think about himself as a valuable member of society. He didn't want to be a woman-iser, frequent pubs, clubs or gambling joints. None of those things had ever excited him. He had come to realise that soli-tude had its merits. You don't have to live like a hermit away from the hustle and bustle of life. Scientists, artists and others had sought solitude, not to escape, but to develop their work. Many had left a great legacy that has benefitted the world. Cedric had no need to worry about being on his own. He probably wouldn't be a scientist or artist or engineer, but he could be himself. What was most important of all for Cedric was to be at ease in his own company. It was his life, time and space. His parents, who he had never known, had given him life. Now he must realise how invaluable that life was to become someone. Anyone, like a surgeon, accountant, driver or porter—they are all important in the dance of life. One couldn't live without the other. Joe Swift had made it from humble beginnings, Cedric too could improve his lot, so he thought.

'Good evening, Mr Ford, how are you?' Cedric asked with a smile breaking out on his face.

'Good evening, Cedric. Poor old Miss Holroyd, do you know when the funeral is?' he asked rather solemnly.

'I don't, sir, but when I'm informed, I will let you know.'

Thank you, Cedric. By the way, would you or maybe Nel-son be interested in driving me and my two friends down to Devon?'

'Well, yes, sir. I—'

'Please, call me David,' he insisted.

'Yes, I would be interested. I haven't driven that kind of

distance before but I'm sure it will be alright,' said Cedric half-heartedly.

'Our regular driver has retired. My friends and I have been going to Devon for years. I own a cottage in a small cove, not far from Exmoor. We go fishing in the local waters, do a bit of walking and visit a few pubs. It's enjoyable down there,' Ford said with great persuasion.

'When would you be thinking of going down, Mr Ford?'

'Four weeks.'

Right, that's a deal. I'll make arrangements with Mr Richards about my holiday,' he said, now rather excited after giving it a few minutes of thought. Just think, Cedric driving down to the West Country with Mr Ford and his affluent friends. He must get some driving practise in before they depart. Visiting pubs, walking on the cliffs and, well, he wasn't sure about the fishing. Just wait and see what unfolds.

'I'll be in contact, Cedric. Goodnight,' David Ford said as he jumped into the usual taxi waiting for him outside, ready to drive him up to one of London's posh drinking and gambling clubs. Well known for his gregarious drinking habits, among those with deep pockets, Ford was invited to many private parties, no doubt, frequented by young women seeking a good time on the knee of an old fuddy-duddy. But he had never invited women back to his apartment during the years he had lived there. He didn't like to shit, so to speak, on his own doorstep. Besides, living 15 miles from central London, he wanted to keep that distance between the two parts of his life, domestic and social, separate.

An hour later, Mr Long, aged 77, arrived at reception full of smiles. He infrequently ventured out, especially in the dark evenings, to visit his lady friend who lived nearby. That was his usual spiel. As it was now past 10 pm, Mr Long would probably stay the night with her. They had visited one another for several years. It was a platonic friendship, it was assumed. It began soon after Mr Long's wife died. She was a kind old soul, Cedric remembered. She often gave staff small gifts and Hilda regularly cleaned their apartment. Mrs Long had fought a losing battle with a pulmonary medical problem. Her one enjoyment was pruning the garden roses. She was occasionally heard singing soft lullabies inside her apartment, and sitting knitting in the garden.

'Good evening, Mr Long,' said Cedric.

'Hello, Mr Bambridge, how are you?'

'I'm well, thank you. Out for the evening, don't do anything I wouldn't do, will you?'

'Yes, I'm visiting Miss Sheedy. We enjoy playing whist and chess together. You've seen her, of course, on several occasions, haven't you?' Cedric wondered if she played with anything else.

'That's right,' said Cedric, hoping that he enjoyed his time there.

After Mr Long had walked out of the building and down the road to visit his friend, Cedric gave some thought to his recent fortunes. What a coincidence that Joe had contacted him after so many years,' and David Ford had given him the opportunity to have a holiday in Devon. Now was the time, if there was a right time, to fight back and fend off those frustrating demons that had held him back for so long.

'Hello, night porter,' said Cedric.

Hello, Mr Bambridge, how are you, my dear boy?' enquired Mr Black.

'Good evening, Mr Black. I'm well, thank you.'

'Are you busy right now? I have a minor problem to be solved, my dear boy, if you could,' asked Mr Black, who by this time, 11:30 pm, was becoming drunk and seeking attention. Similar to other residents, long lonely days leads to grabbing the bottle for comfort and support in the evenings. Oh, how the years fly by.

'Alright, I'll be up in five minutes, Mr Black.'

Cedric was anticipating the usual large whiskey and a lot of scholarly preaching from the good Mr Black, who, it must be acknowledged had done well, like most residents, in life. For a young working-class boy from Rotherham, he studied assiduously, under the tight tutelage of a strict father, from grammar school to the heights of Cambridge University. Years, thereafter, followed more study of accountancy until he gained employment with a top city firm. He had flown like a bird to achieve heights preserved for the powerful few. He was sending out, albeit subconsciously, the right messages, for others to follow those long, hard, deviating tracks to success.

Black had followed the same tried and tested track as those before him. It must be remembered a thousand times, if necessary, the rich, the powerful, the mighty are communicating to the poor to come and take it, just like they had. It won't be hand fed to Cedric and the millions like him on a plate. Possession is nine-tenths of the law. The aristocrat will laugh in your face, standing on stolen fertile soil, if you don't follow his lead and take what is available. But Cedric wasn't fooled that easily by those whose only purpose was to exploit.

That included the owner of apartment six. It was all a contradiction to confuse. To promise much but deliver little.

Cedric arrived at Mr Black's apartment a little earlier than his usual time. He rang the doorbell and a voice shouted for him to come in through the unlocked door.

'Good evening, my dear boy. How are you? You look overworked as usual. I think that deserves a large scotch,' slurred Mr Black, whose wig, as usual, had slid to the left side of his small bony head.

'Only a small one for me, Mr Black,' said an irritated Cedric. He hated the stuff.

'There we go, dear boy. Cheers,' he said, as he touched glasses with his visitor.

'Cheers.'

'Tell me, dear boy, do you have any hobbies or interests in your spare time?' he asked.

'Well, I enjoy rambling, riding on buses and trains. I've been doing these things for years and...'

'Yes, I remember you telling me that long ago. Ever thought of going to the theatre, cinema or museums?'

'Not really. I once went to the Science Museum in London, and someone nicked my rucksack from the toilets.'

'Oh, dear me, I'm very sorry to hear that,' said Mr Black rather apologetically.

'Never mind,' said Cedric. He had actually stolen it from someone else weeks before.

'Do you read much? I personally like Dickens. 'A Tale of Two Cities' is my favourite.'

'I read The Amateur Gardener.' He wanted to say The Beano, The Topper and Picture Parade but thought otherwise.

Talk rambled on for another half an hour or so. Mr Black got steadily drunk. He wobbled on his old legs and his wig slipped off his head. Cedric, steadfastly, refused any more alcohol. If he were aware, which he wasn't, it would have been the ideal opportunity to ask Black about the merits of education. Sitting there like a mass of blubber, one could forgive his pathetic appearance. His brain, usually sharp, aware and insightful, was soaked with alcohol.

'I must go, Mr Black. Thank you for the drink. There's nothing else to do, is there?' he muttered. Cedric hoped he wasn't going to suggest sex in his pink-coloured bedroom. He nearly retched at the idea.

Several hours passed before any telephone calls were made or residents returned home. Uppermost in his mind was the holiday with David Ford and visiting the races with Joe Swift. He had been to neither place by choice. He had read about the Cornish Riviera from various brochures. The scantily clad females sunning themselves on white golden beaches appealed to Cedric's fantasies. Small coves surrounded by high cliffs, where fisherman in boats caught their supper. The peace and quiet meant time to walk, think and collect shells. Cedric had conjured a haven not experienced before. His parents never took him that far west on holiday to Devon or Cornwall. But did such a place exist, other than in his head?

Racetracks, Cedric had seen plenty during his travels but had never actually paid to watch those large thoroughbreds thunder over hallowed turf, where many a gambler has met his doom. By chance, one day, he was walking along a public grass verge, when he saw the spectacle of jockeys thrusting their small energetic bodies forward, upon an animal many times their weight and strength. But the thought of being amongst a large cosmopolitan crowd, with huge amounts of money being gambled on horses, shouting and screaming their animal past the winning post didn't quite appeal to him. Many years ago, Cedric recalled that he and other dossers had stood on the public hill to watch the Derby. It was a depressing sight. Thousands of drunken people milled around him reading race cards. A line of bookmakers took lots of money from punters hoping to buy their freedom from the everyday grind of working. Very few collected their winnings, he had noticed. Just a fantasy as punters retreated to dream some more in the beer tents. Those big white laboratories that inspired people, with grand delusional plans, to place their hard-earned monies on some old nag, the only winners were the book makers and bar owners. The ragged majority, penniless and forlorn, stumbled back to the railway platform strewn with rotting food, discarded newspapers and broken glass. After recalling the Derby experience, visiting the races with Joe didn't seem like a good idea. He would give it some thought.

'Good morning, night porter,' said Cedric.

'Good morning, Bambridge. It's Miss Fulton here. Could you pop up and sort out my cupboard for me?' she requested. Due to her increasing problem with depression and insomnia, she resorted to more alcohol to help her cope. It must have been distressing for her. Age wasn't on her side, like all residents whose lives gradually, yet assuredly, were deteriorating by the minute. He'd thought that Black should be a good bedfellow for her.

'Yes, of course, Miss Fulton. I will be there in a few minutes along with my bag of tools,' he said with some concern. The intractable Miss Fulton needed careful assurance, thought Cedric.

'Good. Don't be long.'

He stood outside apartment eight, holding his bag of tricks, hoping to solve the problem quickly and return to reception for coffee. The last thing he needed was a lecture from the angel of Oaks Lodge.

'Come into the lounge, Bambridge. I don't feel well, you know. Here is the broken door,' she said as she led him into the kitchen to reveal a door hanging precariously on its hinges. The table resembled a small chemist shop cluttered with medicine bottles, lotions and potions. She must be in a bad way, Cedric concluded, but he wasn't her doctor and didn't want to interfere. He wasn't that interested anyway.

'That's no problem to fix, Miss Fulton. Just needs a few new screws and some glue to secure it,' he said. Cedric thought the woman had lost more weight since he last visited her. Her anorexic body and scrawny neck, which resembled a dying turkey, looked about to disintegrate at any moment. Her private doctor should have sorted out the problem some time ago. I suppose his only concern was collecting the fees he charged, not her well-being. Cedric thought that she should be in hospital right now, but he was a simple porter even though his conscience demanded otherwise. 'That's fixed, Miss Fulton. Is there anything else?'

'No, no, that's all, thanks,' she said quietly. Cedric had a brief glance to see if there was anything to steal. Brooch, necklace of pearls, silver rings, anything worth a few pounds was acceptable.

Within 15 minutes of each other, Mr Flowers and Mr Ford arrived in taxis back at the Lodge. Both had been to their respective drinking clubs in London. They stood there, in front of the reception desk, dressed in their expensive hand-sewn tweed coats resembling two overaged gangsters. Both men were a similar height and weight. Flowers' grey moustache was neatly trimmed, as always. Two old sex warriors worse off for alcohol, but straight and proud, and prepared for life's unpredictable consequences. It was due to their iron insistence for hard work that both had fought the best and been successful at their professions.

'How's it going, Cyril?' asked a smiling Tom Flowers

'I'm Cedric, Mr Flowers, but I'm well, thanks.'

'Sorry, old chap. How's business?' asked Flowers, smiling like a Cheshire cat.

'Busy sometimes.'

'Don't listen to that old fart, Cedric,' said David Ford, who was nudging the other in the ribs. 'By the way, Cedric, I've given you my mobile number to discuss the trip down to Devon, haven't I? I sold my car years ago due to alcohol consumption, otherwise, I would have killed someone sooner or later. I shall hire a decent four-door saloon. I will let you know so you can take it out for a drive before we depart,' said a reassuring David Ford.

'OK, Mr Ford.'

They ambled over to the lift. Flowers now aged 77, and Ford approaching 71, they pushed their health to the limits. Both had maintained early morning arrivals from club land, at least three times weekly, ever since they moved to Oaks Lodge. Their hearts must have taken a terrible pounding from the continuous flow of London's expensive booze. Their personalities were such that a driven man keeps going until he smashes into the proverbial crash barriers. Huge egos know no rational bounds. Cedric must take the golden opportunity that David Ford had given him, he had an emotional mountain to climb, he realised that. But regardless of that chronic anxiety, he had to break through to a level that could offer a better life. Only 60 years of age, Cedric still could break off those self-ordained shackles of victimhood, take the mantle like an Olympian, and run your guts out until you are unable to give anymore.

'Yeah, I went to London yesterday, brudder, for a few bevies with an old school friend. I enjoyed it. Percy is a head case and drinks like a fish. He buys a bottle of rum and hides it in his pocket. When he gets the chance, he tops our drinks up. Those pub prices are fucking wacko, brudder,' said Nelson.

'Good on you, mate.'

'What's on, mate? Busy night, was it?'

'Same old stuff. Black was pissed, again. All in that fucking old diary, I would like to wipe my arse on it,' said a smiling Cedric.

'Hey, that Richards pussy is visiting us today for a cleaning inspection, isn't he?' asked Nelson, who smiled scornfully. He shrugged his shoulders, expecting the usual ear-bashing from a man who never sleeps and thinks only of his work. Obsession had overcome his good intentions years previously on holiday with his family, when Richards insisted driving on home to inspect a residential home. His wife kept her intense fury safe in her intelligent head, pleased that most of the time she enjoyed being at home alone with her children. In fact, she would have been ecstatic if he could have stayed out all day, everyday away from a happy home.

'All the best, I'm pleased it's not me on the receiving end of his third-degree questions,' said Cedric with a slight smirk.

All life is absurd. Do not unwittingly let the influences of others detrimentally affect your behaviour, Cedric. The self-fulfilling prophecy mask has beaten countless people down to such a level that many are barely human. Through no fault of their own, Cedric, Nelson and the Lodge cleaners had been treated in such a way that they had nothing. They meant nothing to no one. Yes, it was utter futility.

Leaving his colleague to take over the shift for 12 hours, Cedric walked back to the dog kennel. When glimpses of light shone through intense anxiety, he could now understand how his behaviour had been shaped by his past. If only he'd had a good friend or mentor that could have taught him the way out of that continuous circle. His earliest days of having a rudimentary awareness stems from the children's home. The nun's expectations of Cedric, conscious or otherwise, he was becoming to realise, had been to act subserviently. If that had happened to him, he concluded, then it must have happened to countless people who were not in a position to challenge. He was going to have a few hours' sleep, then in the afternoon go to the library to read about human behaviour.

Nelson Trussington was also in a similar predicament to those around him. As a child, he had seen and experienced racism in London. He thought it had affected him badly, contributing to his wayward life of crime. But, he thought, many of his friends, black and white had experienced what he had, and they didn't resort to crime. They've led good, industrious lives. So, what was the reason for why he had gone astray? Nelson didn't have the answer. It was beyond his capability to think it out. Therapy, he continually thought, might just help.

'Good morning, Mr Long.'

'Good morning, Nelson, how are you?' asked the friendly former town planner who was returning after a night with his female friend.

'Not so bad, sir. You know how it is,' smiled Nelson who thought the old boy had been shagging his chess friend. Mind you, his frail body suggested otherwise.

'Have a nice day,' he said. As he slowly walked off to his apartment. Mr Long was an avid reader of history. For days, he would stay indoors without showing his face to the world. Self-contained, he crept slowly around his abode, like a house mouse, looking for the most comfortable place to sleep.

'Good morning,' said Mr Richards as he crashed his way into the reception area. He was making a statement that the boss was here to inspect Oaks Lodge. Any little dust or discarded piece of paper not picked up was to him like a red rag to a raging bull. Beware, you shower of shit, that's how he thought of colleagues, I'm here to make your life difficult.

Born in America, his parents moved to London when Richards was a young schoolboy. A succession of private nannies failed miserably to stimulate his interests. Not surprising, for Richards was a most precocious child. As such, he was often isolated and left to his own devices as he wandered the streets of a big strange city. His parents being both preoccupied with their own successful professions, Richards often, deliberately, failed to make an appearance at his private day school in Westminster. He was eventually expelled. At the age of 16, and with plenty of money, he often drank, smoked and gambled in Soho bars. Being tall, well built with a silken tongue, it was easy for him to buy anything he required to satisfy an ever-growing oversized ego fit for a king.

His financial troubles began when he got involved in gambling casinos. He lost big money, most of it belonging to his parents. They had little time for him, so by giving him handfuls of ready money, it compensated for their guilt. Due to continuing money problems, he fell in with small crooks. They broke into a few jewellers shops. The gang stitched Richards up over the proceeds. He protested out loud and ended up in hospital with a broken jaw and nose.

Soon after, he found his first full-time job working for an insurance company. His arrogant and confident personality propelled him forward to success. However, after a while, he was sacked for stealing money. A succession of similar jobs followed. None of them lasted more than six months.

He successfully applied for an area manager vacancy with Cleanaway Ltd. That was 20 years ago, and he hasn't looked back since. Richards had confidence, guile and panache in abundance. He donned the appropriate hat for each pretended presence. His was the art of deception according to the part you resembled on stage. It must be said that he was very good at what he did. He had no conscience, all that mattered was self-concern. Working for 20 years at Cleanaway had given him a near-untouchable status. The owner, James Clark, thought so much of him that he was rewarded with shares and a company car. Clark leant on his every word. If you wanted to succeed at any cost, then he was your narcissistic man.

'Morning, Mr Richards,' said Nelson, who wasn't looking forward to today's inspection.

'Let's start down here, shall we?' Richards said, pointing towards the plants and ground floor. 'I thought I asked you to make sure the cleaners removed the dust and dirt off these fucking rubber plants?' he said contemptuously.

'I did. Several times I saw them cleaning the plants,' said an exasperated Nelson.

'Make sure they clean them the next time they are about. Are those women up to it?' he asked disdainfully. 'The first-floor stairs could be cleaner,' said the boss.

The fault finding continued throughout the inspection. Any little microscopic piece of dirt was detected by his sharp eyes. Richards pointed here, there, anywhere, he could to find fault. In essence, undermining Nelson, even though he had nothing to do, or very little, with cleaning the place. Richards hadn't liked Nelson from the first day he employed him. The black man wouldn't go down well with middle-class residents, he had thought. Mind you, the wages were poor, and besides, it was difficult to get residential workers with a rudimentary ounce of intelligence. Trussington appeared to have below average intelligence, he thought, but he made up for that in size and strength.

An hour later, with a short period in between to help a resident, they had completed the bruising inspection. With so many residents and visitors, not to mention staff, around the place, it will be dirty once again in a day or two. But the boss must be obeyed. Why is it that power and control are bed mates? Why can't a person have power, yet be friendly, even spiritual?

They took the lift back to reception and walked into the tea room. Anticipation was high on the agenda.

'Well, I can't say that I'm entirely pleased with the cleaning. I realise you don't clean, but it is your job to inspect it,' Richards said curtly.

'Look, I do my best. I always have done so from the very first day I started here,' said Nelson, who was rather irritated by Richards' incessant tirade against him. 'What don't you like about me?' he asked.

'I've got nothing against you. All I want you to do—'

Nelson's brain went blank. A crashing right fist thudded into Richards' face, knocking him to the floor. Nelson stood over him like a gladiator standing over the bloodied defeated bull. His fists were still clenched in anger, and he was prepared for more action. For a few seconds, there was deafening silence in the room. Richards, blood pouring from his mouth, gradually hauled himself up from the floor. He pulled a handkerchief from his trousers and wiped the blood, which smeared his face. Richards regained his composure. He was fortunate his opponent had refrained from giving him a severe beating.

'You're in fucking big trouble now, Trussington,' said an angry Dave Richards. He immediately reached for his phone and contacted the police. They would be at Oaks Lodge as soon as possible.

'You had better fuck off to your room, or get off the premises. You have lost everything, you loser. Make sure you collect all your hand luggage together, and the furniture can be collected another time. Now, just fuck off,' he said angrily. 'And leave that mobile phone and front door key on the table.'

David Richards had got him at last. Never mind the blood or dented ego. He didn't want that scum, as he called most hoi polloi, anywhere near Oaks Lodge or any other Clean-away premises. If Trussington's furniture wasn't collected, Richards, would personally burn it. It would be a symbolic gesture of revenge. He would make him wait for his outstanding wages and under no circumstances would he give him a decent reference. That shithouse had crossed the line of no return.

Nelson made the lonely, slow walk out of the front door. He had acted impulsively and paid a high price for it. He felt defeated, empty and devoid of feelings at that moment. He wished that the ground would have opened up and swallowed him. With his hands in his pockets and his head nearly between his legs, he walked solemnly back to his flat. This place had been his home for over 12 years, but it was soon to be vacated. He looked at the painted walls and ceiling, old furniture, pots, pans and whatnot—all now useless. Items he bought all those years ago when he was desperate for shelter and work. He was homeless once again. He had let himself down badly. Where could he go to get a roof over his head once the police had charged him? What a fucking idiot, he thought of himself. Without delay, he packed two large bags with various things he might need in the tortuous days ahead... 50 years old and back in the proverbial shit once again.

Two police officers walked into the flat, one holding a pair of handcuffs.

'Are you Nelson Trussington?' the officer asked.

'I am.'

'I am arresting you for assault...' they carried on with the same old legal spiel that Nelson had heard too many times before.

'As I won't be returning back here, please could one of you carry my two bags out for me to the car?' asked Nelson. 'If I get bail, I will need to find somewhere to kip and those bags are my worldly possessions,' he said.

He was led to the familiar site of a blue panda car and driven off to Mortingbridge Police Station. Once again, the same old rigmarole played itself out. He was charged by the station sergeant, a surly old-time server, sitting high and mighty on his stool. Nelson was bailed on his own surety for £500 and told to appear the following morning at the local Magistrates' Court. That same old rancid station smell hit his senses from 30 years ago. Industrial soap and urine, the stench he smelt when he was first charged with a crime as a young man. He was ushered into a side room to sign the bail form. All that greeted him was bare grey walls, stained brown ceiling, and an old table and chairs. The privilege given to countless charged people over the years. Nothing had changed.

'Sign here, sir,' said the young male officer who wore glasses and a brace on his teeth. He was fortunate to be called sir, not too long ago, it was surname only, if you were lucky. Nelson had been called all manner of expletives. Some were unmentionable. The London police stations were manned by a rough and tough bunch of hoodlums.

Nelson walked down the well-worn Victorian steps of the station, onto the pavement not knowing where to go. It was too late to phone his daughter in London, she would give him a bed for a few days, but he didn't want to impose. She had her own problems. Besides, he didn't want to inform her that he had been sacked for chinning his boss. After explaining to her that times had changed, he also felt he had really let her down big time. After all the promises of giving his grand-children good times ahead, here he was, a few hours from ap-pearing in court once again. An old lag back in the stocks, he viewed himself at that moment.

He had no choice, now that it was 11:30 pm, but to try a small local family hotel at the end of the high street. It was ex-pensive but he must have a decent night's kip and full break-fast before attending court. After ringing the front door bell a few times, minutes later, a man opened up. He eyed Nelson rather suspiciously.

'How can I help?' asked the proprietor.

'I'm really very sorry to wake you at this time of night, sir, but I'm looking for accommodation for one night. I've been visiting my aunt at Oaks Lodge and forgot about the time,' Nelson explained. With two bags in hand, he resembled a travelling salesman.

'Ah, I know Oaks Lodge well. Lovely apartments, yes, by all means you can stay,' he said. They both walked into the passage area where Nelson wrote down in the visitors' book fictitious details. Mr Strange, the owner, gave his guest the bedroom key. It was sanctuary for a few hours.

8

CHAPTER EIGHT

The hotel internal phone rang sharp at 7:30 am. Nelson jumped out of bed and into the shower. He dressed himself in his only suit. He wanted to show the beak he was a smart man, who had been employed for 12 years, and had acted impulsively due to continuous harassment and provocation. But he was going to plead guilty. Initially, he thought grounds of diminished responsibility but that was a bit too strong to argue. No, he'd stick with endless provocation. Besides, he didn't want to get involved with meaningless reports. Stay away from professionals, they usually exacerbate things, was his attitude. He walked down the thick carpeted staircase and into the breakfast room, wearing a light brown suit and looking like a film star.

'Good morning, Mr Brown. I hope you slept well?' asked the slim, middle-aged owner. 'We are happy to have you here at Waverley Hotel. What would you like for your breakfast?' Nelson thought of a double rum and young pussy, but thought it safer to stay with Brown's sizzling sausages.

'Good morning. I would love a full English breakfast with white coffee,' said Nelson, being uppermost in his mind was the cost of his night's stay there. Having visited the Lodge, they probably thought he was a wealthy relation.

Half an hour later, with his worldly possessions by his side, Nelson appeared downstairs to pay the bill. It was the wrong time to do a runner without paying.

'Ah, there you are, Mr Brown. Was everything alright?' asked Mr Strange.

'Very fine, thank you.'

'Here is your bill, sir.' Nelson nearly collapsed at the £100 now required. Fortunately, he had withdrawn money yesterday morning. After settling the bill, he made his way back along the high street, crossed the road and carried on for another 15 minutes until the Victorian red brick courthouse loomed in front of him. It appeared to be the largest building in the town. The next hour or so would seal his fate. Although Nelson had form, he had gone straight for years. Richards couldn't deny that he had been a good, honest worker with few sick days. He intended to plead guilty. Nelson had no option, hoping for a fine, or at most a suspended sentence, and would get out of Mortingbridge as soon as his arse could fly to the station. He hoped to contact Cedric sometime soon, but first, if the magistrate didn't send him to prison, he must find digs in London.

'Hello, Mr Trussington. You are first in today. Leave your bags with me, and when told, go and sit in the dock. My colleague will be there. Don't speak until spoken to. OK? Be polite at all times. You'll be alright. You won't go to Dartmoor,' said the court sergeant, laughing on the other side of his face.

Two magistrates walked into the court. Everyone was instructed to stand. Nelson had seen it all before. The beaks in front of him were probably landowners, or former military, or wealthy merchants, he knew the kind of face that fit his experience of power. They occasionally looked over their spectacles at Nelson. Did they have a recidivist in their midst?

'How do you plead?' the court clerk asked Nelson, who realised that to his right, Richards had just entered the courtroom.

'Guilty, sir,' said the defendant.

David Richards told the court what happened that night. He added bit more manipulation to his evidence. Richards was a master at such matters. A few porky pies were unforgiveable, Nelson thought, but given the opportunity, he would have loved to knuckle his nose once again. It was all over in 40 minutes. Nelson was given two years' probation with £200 court costs.

Outside the courtroom, he signed various papers and was given three months to pay the fine. Fuck their fine, that's what he thought. With his bags firmly in his large hands, he flew across the road and down towards the station to take the first train to London. As far as he was concerned, that was the end of his time as a lapdog. They could trash the dilapidated furniture he bought when he first moved in. He had a few weeks' wages due and, along with his savings, Nelson would survive. He would be back amongst the guts, gore and gouge of London life. The life that most people experienced in a heartless city crammed with money—stolen or otherwise—in the hands of a few.

He was sad that he would miss his colleagues. Over the

years, he had got to know them well, especially Cedric. He would miss some of the residents who had been kind and friendly. They were aware that being a porter wasn't glamorous by any stretch of the imagination. He would miss Ford and Flowers in particular. They had done well in a tough world where failure wasn't recognised by those who reaped the jewels of success. How he wished he was in their shoes instead of renting some shit place in an obscure piece of London Town. And, dear old Miss Holroyd, he won't be there to place a flower on her goodbye carriage on its way to the heavens. Nothing is forever, he surmised.

Not more than an hour after Nelson had departed Mortingbridge, Cedric stood rather impatiently, yet excited, waiting on the edge of town. His friend, Joe Swift, was late for their trip to Kempton Races. Two of his horses were racing. Cedric had bought a new coat and trousers—his first in years. His usual second-hand attire was bought in one of the local charity shops. It rather irritated him to pay so much money for two items of clothes, but as he was going to the races for the first time, he didn't mind. Besides, he wanted to give a confident impression to Joe. Also, he didn't want to look out of place in front of Joe Swift's wealthy friends. He'll be judged alright, as we all are, rightly or wrongly most of the time. Cedric had been judged, rather harshly he thought, most of his life, mostly by people who didn't know him. The only problem with judgement, Cedric constantly thought, is that it stigmatises people. And that can lead, occasionally dangerously, to a false impression of someone or something.

An impressive blue Daimler pulled up alongside where

Cedric was standing, hand in pockets, looking out into infinity. He had high hopes for a successful day among the elites.

'Morning, Cedric. Jump in,' said Joe Swift, rather flustered.

'Hello, Joe. How is it going?' asked Cedric, who was once again anxious but looking forward to experiencing a racing world he knew nothing about.

'Sorry I'm a bit late, had problems with a horse,' said Joe.

'No problem, mate.'

They sped off at speed down country roads that Cedric had not seen before. Big houses with lawns and orchards lay back from the busy roads, which were used by drivers as a convenient shortcut. New shiny expensive cars stood in nearly every house. What a secure way of life, Cedric thought. He would like to have been a residential gardener in one of those grand houses. Left to his own devices, his own tools and shed, life would have been magnificent. No Richards to keep heckling you. No constant resident phone calls to mend this or that. And no night work. Sleeping alone in his centrally heated, cosy double bed, Cedric fantasized of a world that would never materialise!

'This is the M25. It's a circular road around the outskirts of London,' said Joe.

'Yeah, I realised that. I've seen it many times before.'

'Kempton Park isn't that far from here. We turn off at junction 12, then junction 1 of the M3, which leads us to Hampton Court. From there, it's only 20 minutes on the A308,' he said.

'Have you been here many times before, Joe?' asked Cedric, unaware that his friend, Nelson Trussington, had been fined for assault and sacked.

'Many times,' he said with a grin on his unshaven face. Joe was hoping that Cedric was going to enjoy the day out after many disappointments during his lonely and unwanted life. He hoped it was the first of many. Joe smiled to himself, thinking that if only he had found Cedric years ago, he'd invited him to live with the family. But, in reality, all pie in the sky. All he was able to be was a genuine friend. Meet from time to time for a beer or meal. He thought that Cedric would welcome it. Cedric, or anyone else, couldn't go back to repair the damage inflicted upon him. Besides, that wasn't Joe's responsibility.

Optimistic of a successful day, Joe pulled into the racetrack car park. With his binoculars slung over his shoulder, and race card in hand, he paid their entry fee to the course. As time was short, they walked straight to the paddock where some of the jockeys were mounting their steaming powerful beasts. Inside the paddock were assembled owners and trainers. They were moneyed people, no doubt. Cedric eyed them all, wondering how rich they were, how they made their money and what they spent it on. The women stood alongside smiling, wearing expensive clothes and carrying the latest handbags. Punters packed the scene with anticipation.

'You got a horse here, Joe?' asked Cedric who felt a little uneasy in a strange environment.

'No. I've got two horses running today. The next race, I've got Blue Pearl running. The race is over three miles. We call them chases as they jump high fences and it's difficult in these muddy conditions. My other runner, Devils Back, jumps over a two-mile hurdle race. They are a lot smaller, but as it's the end of the season, I'm hopeful,' Joe said as he pointed to the track, trying to explain to Cedric the difference between the two.

'That grey horse, Rose Galore, is owned by my friend, Tommy Ferguson. It should run well. It's won several races in the last three years,' Joe tried to explain. But Cedric found it all above his head for the time being. It would take time and patience to understand racing culture. If he was honest, he wasn't that interested.

'That horse there, Cedric,' he pointed. 'With the yellow colours. He is owned by another friend,' he concluded as the horses galloped past on their way to the start of the race. 'I'm going to back the favourite horse with a book maker, Henry Deeds. I've got an account with him.'

Cedric stood, sipping his beer as Joe made his way to a line of bookmakers. They were all shouting something at somebody but he didn't have a clue what it all meant. He knew they were called tick-tack men. Cedric saw hundreds of people, mainly men, in the grandstand, most of them were looking through binoculars. He could just about see the little figures of the runners way across the other side of the track. Beyond that, he thought, he could see a railway station. But everything was blurred and confused.

Loudspeakers announced that the race had started. He vaguely understood the commentary. Joe, who was at the side of Cedric, started shouting at the horse he had backed. As the race progressed, animated punters uttered loud cries of encouragement. Shouting, screaming and whistling from all around appeared to engulf Cedric. He hadn't seen or heard anything like it before. It felt like the world had come to an end. It reminded him of the Derby he saw, all those years ago.

Unlike this racetrack, Cedric thought, at least on the open downs, one could walk for miles free of any hindrance.

'The bastard got beat,' said Joe, who appeared not too disappointed. 'He is a bit of a rogue, that fucking horse, but never mind. There's always next time.'

They leant on the paddock rail, sizing up Blue Pearl's chances of winning the next race, a three-mile steeplechase. Joe invited Cedric to join him and others inside the paddock. Cedric didn't feel confident enough. The thought of many people looking at the assembled made him feel insecure.

Joe thought the five-year-old looked in good shape. He had grown in the last year into a fine chestnut gelding. The yard thought he had good prospects next season. Sid Price, Joe's trainer, was optimistic about his future. Mind you, when you're paying hefty stabling fees, the trainer has to play it cagey. With only six opponents, the horse stood a good chance of winning. Mind you, the favourite had beaten him on a previous occasion. Cedric watched the horses being led around the paddock by their stable handlers. All the interested parties—trainers, owners, and so on—bunched up as though conspiring to carry out some misdemeanour—they certainly didn't want their voices overheard.

With jockeys mounted, they walked their animals out onto the course and galloped to the starting post.

'I'm off to put a bet on, Cedric.'

Cedric assumed he was starting to enjoy the scene unfolding before him. He felt confident about himself, his worth and his future. If challenged about it though, he wouldn't know what to say. It was probably all fantasy. However, he found the various accents, sights and sounds interesting in the spring sun. The focus on the beasts, he realised, was paramount. Itching fingers anticipated the next winning gamble.

The same cacophony of noise bellowed out from the loudspeakers. For a few minutes, Joe couldn't hear himself think. There was nowhere to hide from the dim. This way of life was certainly not for him.

'He finished second. Never mind, he'll win sometime,' said Joe, who had covered his costs coming runner-up.

Inside, Joe felt angry by the way his horse had been ridden. He thought he should have won. The jockey was caught dithering as they jumped the final fence. He was going to have a strong word with the trainer. When it came to money, there were few boundaries!

Thousands of discarded tickets, race cards and newspapers littered the ground. Unimaginable amounts of money had exchanged hands that day. Cedric was shocked that people willingly handed over enormous sums of money to gamble on a horse they knew very little about. It all amounted to blind faith. No doubt, some punters had lost everything. It wasn't impossible to imagine that many had committed suicide over the years, due to their short-sighted actions. They gambled the family silver and lost. It wouldn't have ended with their own demise either. Family, friends and colleagues, also could have experienced their own lives being affected by someone else's misdeeds.

The boy originating from a rundown Catholic children's home had witnessed decadence on a grand scale. That's what he thought, anyway. He came to the conclusion that it wasn't for him but still hoped to meet Joe again. He told him he had enjoyed himself, but he didn't want to offend the one person who tried to make his life more bearable. Cedric really felt confident in Joe's company. But he had low expectations for himself. His emptiness went deep. Joe helped bolster that desolation. For that, Cedric was eternally grateful.

It was not surprising that there were occasions, however, when Cedric fantasized about owning those large amounts of money he had seen squandered. The thoughts of owning racehorses, an expensive car, having a sexy girl on his arm all added fuel to the isolation that always lurked not far from his barren soul. Why wasn't he successful? Why had he drawn the short straw in life? Cedric was an outsider! That wouldn't change, how could it in his position? Besides, he knew that life was based on superficiality. It wasn't the individual that people were interested in, but the wealth they possessed, he continually felt. He had enough awareness to recognise that if he presented with money, people would fall all over him. Regardless of who he was.

The church bells shook the old foundations of St Saviours as it rang out to welcome the assembled. Judges, barristers and other notable people lined the front benches of the Georgian church to celebrate the life of one of their own. Miss Winifred Holroyd was held in high esteem by colleagues during her long career at the legal bar. Mighty with words and a stickler for detail, she had fought them all on the London court circuit. Many had given her a hard time fighting their legal cases. In court, adversary was the name of the game. She had defended some of the most hardened criminals. Guilty or not, she always found time to speak with them after their cases were finished. She often had a drink with a few old rogues after persuading the jury of their dubious innocence.

Honest, kind and genuine amongst her friends and colleagues. Her frail old body had finished its life's journey in unknown circumstances. What drove her to end a rich endowed life was a mystery. With progressive infirmity, Miss Holroyd probably thought she'd had enough of struggling.

Her supportive counsellor, Mr Matthews, played the organ that echoed deep mournful music in memory of Miss Holroyd, who lay in the wooden coffin nearby. After many years of losing them, one was hopeful she lay there with false teeth in her mouth. It would have given her face that extra smile. Mr Matthews alone, though she did inform Cedric on one occasion, knew the extent of her emotional abuse at the hands of her stepfather. Since childhood, she had battled with flashbacks but fought hard, throughout her life, to overcome those humiliating experiences. It was, no doubt, why she remained a spinster. She didn't get emotionally involved with anyone, although there had been one or two short relationships when she was young. She invested her time and energy into legal work.

Most of Oaks Lodge's residents and staff were there to say goodbye to a woman who most found to be friendly and kind. Though most residents spoke sparingly, from year to year, to her. Due to the average age, residents much preferred their own quiet space. That was Miss Holroyd, solitude had become her life. Although her eyesight worsened, she attempted to keep reading novels and legal journals. Memory recall cruelly hindered enjoyment.

The Reverend Pimple spoke of her diligent adherence in supporting the downtrodden in court. How he knew of this is a mystery. In life, they met no more than half a dozen times.

In his position, it was assumed joyous speculation to be an appropriate consideration. However, she did donate monies to small local charities where Pimple was on the management.

David Richards spoke well of his former resident. He was a little peeved that he now had to find a new resident to pay the exorbitant Cleanaway maintenance fees. This was followed by several colleagues who gave short, yet sincere, cogent speeches. The occasion dictated conformity!

After the congregation, Cedric made his way back to Oaks Lodge for another evening shift of pandering to the whims and whimpers of his seniors. He was astute enough to realise that most residents sitting in that unpleasantly cold church were pretenders. It wasn't due to the loss of Miss Holroyd that they attended, but because of their class conditioning. Not to have attended the church service would have been judged as letting the side down. Most of them were cynics, similar to the people that one met most days. Cedric knew that the Lodge was a whispering gallery of lies and deceit. He probably made his contribution as well. Being a poor, self-confessed communicator gave him the opportunity to overhear malicious conversation.

Cedric stood thinking about his friend who had been fired for hitting Richards. It pleased him to no end to think of his boss flat out on the floor after being floored. But he had a heavy heart knowing Nelson had not only lost his job, been fined by the courts, but he was also now homeless. Somehow, he must find his whereabouts so he could meet him.

At around 9 pm, Richards turned up at the Lodge. As bold as brass, he pushed his heavy bulk through the door, resembling a spoilt teenager. This was his territory and he wanted to make sure others realised he was back in charge. With his ego still bruised from the assault, he pointed at Cedric to explain his next move.

'Hello, Cedric. I observed you attended the funeral. Good, that was expected of you. A new porter, Derek Tranter, will be starting work tomorrow at 8 am. I've already explained duties to him, but make sure before you finish your shift that you show him around. OK?' said David Richards.

'Understood, what about the vacant flat, will he be living there?' asked Cedric cautiously.

'As he is local and drives, he won't require accommodation,' said Richards, whose lip was still swollen from the pounding Nelson gave it. 'By the way, if Nelson Trussington phones, tell him to contact me. I don't want that prick in this place. OK?' said Richards with a no-nonsense tone in his voice. 'Before I forget, I've given Tranter a written contract. No excuses from him, either.'

'Sure, Mr Richards.'

His master's voice had spoken. Cedric had his orders to carry out. He was looking forward to meeting his new colleague in the morning. He had not heard the name Tranter before. Was he a drinker in his local pub, he wondered? Anyone that works in this piss poor joint must be hard-up for a job.

The man Cedric wanted to see most of all appeared at reception. David Ford, as usual, was dressed immaculately in a dark blue suit. The socialising cavalier was at it again, ready to hit the drinking clubs of London with a pocket full of money. He might be nearly 71 years of age, but his attitude of enjoying life was much younger. Cedric had often wondered what

David Ford got up to when he left the Oaks several nights a week. Of course, he was a drinker and gambler in some of the big joints in town, but instinct told Cedric something else was happening. Not for a minute did he think he was serving soup to the embankment homeless, or praying to the wretches of St Martin's-in-the-Fields.

'Hello, Cedric,' he said.

'Good evening, Mr Ford. Have you heard, Nelson got the sack for assaulting Dave Richards? He was also fined in the local Magistrates' Court,' said Cedric with a wry smile.

'Really, well done, Nelson. I never did like that area manager. Have you found a replacement?'

'Yeah, he starts tomorrow morning.'

'I hope he enjoys arm wrestling like Nelson did. I'll miss him, he was a good bloke. If you see him, send my best wishes.'

'I will do, Mr Ford.'

'Good news, Cedric, I've hired a new car for our visit to my cottage in Devon. Two friends will be coming with us. Here is the address and phone number of the hire car company. Pick the car up from Hardy's a week before we depart, their premises are in Ashby, not six miles west of this place. You can drive it around to get used to it. Park it here at the Oaks and keep an eye on it, Cedric. You've got my mobile number, just in case any problems arise,' said David Ford rather excited by the forthcoming holiday to one of his favourite sea resorts.

'Right, OK, Mr Ford, I'm looking forward to the trip. I'll pick it up and take it through its paces,' said Cedric who vaguely remembered visiting East Devon on a day trip with the nuns, but wasn't sure.

'Right, Cedric, I'm off for a good evening with friends.

They all drink like fish. Don't forget to pick up the car, and send my regards to Nelson.'

The usual local taxi driver was waiting impatiently for the intrepid David Ford. Over the years, he had spent a small fortune being driven to London, and elsewhere. Mind you, he could afford to splash out, enjoying the fruits of his successes. Companies still sought his expertise on various structural projects years after retirement. His professionalism was held in such high esteem, he could have commanded his own price. But his working days were over. Not even lucrative consultancies would lure him from a self-imposed retreat, back into a cut-throat world.

The usual late evening, early morning, cacophony of overpowering middle-class voices had not happened. Time served lackeys, such as Cedric, were always available to pick up the trash. Just nod, madam, and we shall bow to your every whim. Although recent developments had boosted his confidence somewhat, Cedric still hated arrogant rich bastards. Particularly those residents who lived above him in apartments that were far superior to his own dog kennel. It didn't get easier to accept but there was very little he could do about it. He could commit suicide, a constant reminder, or leave his job, or just walk out and hit the road once again which was a miserable option. The first choice was always available when life became worthless. New employment had been on his mind for some time, if only something was available for someone with few skills and an ageing body. He'd keep looking.

But fantasy and observation gave his shallow life meaning. He could be anyone at any time, when he so wished. His fragile mind helped him survive when he was incarcerated in various institutions. In those places, Cedric could withdraw into an inner life full of delusional dreams. That was escape from his surroundings. No one could get to him, find him or harm him. Inner defences had their merits from time to time. But he had come to realise that being in those hellholes weren't healthy or productive places. If anything, they reinforced his self-image.

Now that the manager had agreed to his two-week holiday, Cedric could plan the various, potential options in Devon. He felt anxious about meeting two strangers, even though they were friends of David Ford. They, no doubt, had money. Ford didn't associate with people who hadn't been successful in life. Although he was friendly to staff at the Lodge, when it came to socializing, his cohort had pockets full of money. Cedric wasn't fooled by kind gestures. Considerate, though, they were. Handshakes and a bottle of alcohol is one thing, but personal company in clubs full of cash, alcohol and privilege was another.

'Hello, good evening, night porter,' said Cedric.

'Bambridge, could you give me a hand? I'm in a spot of bother,' shouted Miss Fulton.

'Yes, of course, Miss Fulton,' said Cedric, who often fantasized smashing the old bag of bones over the head with a hammer. He had a seven-pounder in his bag of tools just six feet from his desk. The worst that could happen, he thought, was spending the rest of his life in prison. Good food and no responsibility. Some sympathetic judge might even send him to Broadmoor. No more hellholes!

'Don't be long, will you?'

'No, I'll be right there, Miss Fulton.'

Cedric walked to the fourth floor holding a bag of tools. He anticipated the same superficial, arrogant words from her. He knocked softly on her front door. Minutes later, a pair of steel-rimmed glasses looked him up and down like a piece of Harrods furniture.

'You are here, Bambridge. Do come in,' she said.

'What's the problem?' he asked the wealthy spinster. Uppermost in his mind, who she was going to leave all her money to when she kicked the bucket?

'That damn radiator over there isn't very warm. Could you look at it? Sort out the temperature for me,' she asked

Cedric looked into his bag and saw that club hammer lurking in the corner of it. He had this intense feeling of crushing her head to pieces with that solid steel. It was so intense that he quickly moved away from the bag and started touching the radiator. The problem was a minor one, all it needed was the temperature knob to be loosened somewhat.

'All done, Miss Fulton,' said Cedric, who felt, minutes previously, overwhelmed by unceasing frustrations. He felt frightened of the feelings he'd just had of Miss Fulton. He was so close to the edge from bludgeoning her to death. Something pulled him back in time before that point of no return. He didn't want to return to that state of intense anger again. He usually kept things inside his head under control, but on rare occasions, intense feelings just appeared. He put it down to the idea that most people just used him for their own needs and paid no attention to the person in front of them. They were deep-rooted problems going back through his life, not necessarily connected to Miss Fulton. She found delight in undermining those unable or unwilling to stand up to her upper-class demeanour. She, of course, wasn't the only person who Cedric had had those fearful feelings for. The emptiness frightened him. But Cedric, although of limited empathy, was unlikely to kill or maim anyone.

9

CHAPTER NINE

Nelson sat on his own in a small, cheap café just off of Peckham High Street. The place was almost full of people down on their luck. They all had their desolate stories. There were the unemployed, homeless, drifters, former convicts and a few people from a local residential home with nowhere else to go. The place didn't exactly attract the most affable. It had seen better days, just like its owner, Solly Greenbaum. Friends nicknamed him 'Solly with the lolly'. He was a fourth generation Jew. His forebears made their way to East London from Russia in the late 19th-century. One way or another, the family had all worked for themselves. Surviving in a city where bodies were cheap and plentiful to employ. The latest owner of the Smiling Cat last painted the former pie and eel shop some ten years ago. It was now peeling and stained from ceiling to floor. Just by chance, it was swept once a week. But it was a café for locals to meet, chat and drink gallons of cheap tea. It was also a haven for novelists or playwrights seeking to expand their work, ably assisted by the friendly menagerie within.

'Alright, Solly?' asked big Dave Gill, a former merchant seaman and inmate of HMP Lamphill.

'Good, Dave,' said Solly, a short, fat man with a thick mop of white hair.

'How's Pete doing in hospital?'

'I saw him the other night. He's a lot better from when I first saw him. His faced looked terrible, smashed to fuck it was,' he said. Pete Smart, locally born, was beaten up two weeks ago by three unknown men. He had been hospitalised since.

'Tea and toast, Solly, please,' asked Nelson.

'Coming up, mate.'

The train from Mortingbridge Station had taken him about an hour to London. From there, Nelson had made his way to Peckham, his old stomping ground for years. Similar to many months ago, when he visited his daughter, he didn't recognise many faces. Most had moved away or;were ten feet under the ground. Working and living many miles from London must have been different over 12 years; a place quickly changes. City life means a transient existence. He had phoned his daughter and told her that he'd been sacked for chinning his former boss, but he hadn't yet been to visit her and the children. Mindful that he didn't want to be a burden on people, she had her own worries bringing up children without a husband around. No God, around these parts, dishing out money!

The day he arrived back in London, Nelson had found himself a decent bedsit. Sharing the facilities, it was just ten minutes from the rail station. It was a quiet cul-de-sac, ideal for someone of his age. The other three residents were all mature men. No loud music, no drugs or loud aggressive sex parties. He was past all those games.

Nelson knew he had to get his act together, and fast. Although he had savings, after the third week, he decided, reluctantly, to sign unemployed. He was entitled to a benefit or two. Besides, his rent was over £400 a month. He hated the whole job centre culture. He was instructed by a female worker with tattoos on her tits, how to apply for benefits using a computer. There was some kind of contract he had to sign that demonstrated he was looking for work. He would do any kind of work just to be rid of conforming to the institutional mentality of the job centre staff.

Nelson was getting itchy feet. He couldn't adapt to his new life for much longer. Looking on computers, in newspapers, journals and local adverts for a job was getting him down. Even a toilet attendant job looked rosy. It wouldn't be long before he started indulging in crime again, he thought. This job-seeking wasn't for him. Of course, ideally, he would have loved to have found a job. A regular wage sounded great but was a million miles from his grasp, he surmised. He realised by now that he had fucked up big time by punching his former boss. That, and being fined, would deter employers from giving him work. He could always preach to youngsters in prison to stay away from crime, he contemplated. Or apply for a position as a mercenary in Afghanistan.

Cedric was outside the local station, waiting for his old colleague to arrive. They had made arrangements to meet, by phone, over a week ago. Nelson was surprised but delighted to hear Cedric's voice so soon after his departure. After being accosted by tramps, prostitutes and street sellers, Cedric was pleased to see his friend walking towards him.

'Hi, dear brudder, how are you?'

'Hi, Nelson, I'm well. How are you getting on after so many years living in the sticks?' asked Cedric as they firmly shook hands.

'Not so bad. It's not easy living in London, you know.'

'Fancy a tea somewhere?' asked Cedric.

'I know just the place down the road,' said Nelson.

The two men walked along the uneven, dirty, packed pavements through a small street market until they reached the Smiling Cat. It was the sort of café Cedric was used to. Rougher the better, he thought. As usual, it was full of those rootless souls so familiar to those parts of London. They found a small table where they could sit. Nelson went to order refreshments at the counter.

'I often come in this old dive. Something about it appeals to me,' said Nelson.

'Yeah, I know what you mean, mate. Most of these old cafés have been sold as Indian and Chinese takeaways. Fucking shame,' said Cedric with a gloomy face.

'What's it like at the Lodge?'

'Same old place. Residents keep phoning mostly in the early mornings. Treat you like shit, mate. Well, you know that, of course. New porter is a decent bloke. Lives locally and drives an old car. Same agency workers, and David Ford sends his regards by the way. He thought you should have given Richards a severe beating. He misses the arm wrestling with you,' said Cedric, who missed working and occasionally socializing with his friend. They had known each other for many years, and it was probably the closest Cedric had ever been to another person. He felt safe in Nelson's company. He knew people wouldn't take liberties when the big fellow was around. For one reason or another, he didn't have the confidence to say that to Nelson. Cedric was too placid.

Both men had repressed so much during their difficult lives. It had occurred to Nelson, at certain times during the last few years, that he needed therapy to sort himself out. With the best of intentions, the demands of life take over. Due to the position he was now in, there was not a great deal he could do, about it right now, and probably never would.

Cedric was another matter. He was probably unaware that some sort of counselling would help his chronic anxiety. With all the support available, Cedric wouldn't be capable of sustaining long-term, intense counselling. You could safely say that both men were incorrigible. They, and many others, are not to be condemned by a system that found little time to encourage them to be someone. They missed the boat, as they say in money parlance.

Although neither had a great start to life, many from a similar background have done well. Joe Swift is a case in point. From a working-class family, he worked hard throughout his life to make millions. Money doesn't simply appear in your hand, but give them a chance, people will thrive. Supportive family and a good education are not the only necessary requirements for a successful life. Cedric, Nelson and many others failed, because they lacked drive, ambition and motivation also needed to excel. In their case, both lacked the emotional and intellectual skills to challenge deep-rooted personal problems.as they lived

'Some good news, Nelson. I'm driving Dave Ford and his two friends down to Devon on holiday. He's hired a new car. Fucking fast it is. I'm really looking forward to it. Not been there before,' said Cedric enthusiastically.

'Great stuff, brudder, how long you going for?'

'About a week. I'd forgotten those old hags, the nuns, from the home, took us there once for a day's outing.'

'You landed on your feet. Boss man has given you time off?'

'He said, I can take it as a part of my holiday. Mean bastard, isn't he?' said Cedric.

'Fancy a beer down the road, brudder?' asked Nelson, who was getting itchy feet sitting amongst the dossers. He didn't mind those cafés, but within reason. When people begin to associate you with places fit for the dregs of society, they give you a wide berth. He hadn't fallen that far yet. Besides, his pockets were crying out for some extra money. Villainy was on his mind. He knew one or two old faces were still around from the days when crime was a way of life. The word had got through the grapevine that Nelson was back in the manor.

They walked for about 15 minutes, down various side streets until reaching a small Victorian pub called The Watchman. Nelson knew the streets like the back of his hands. As youngsters, he and others had been chased by the police on many occasions. They had hidden up trees, under vehicles, on top of sheds, in neighbour's gardens... you name it, they had been there.

'Morning, Jack, how's it going, brudder?' asked Nelson who was anticipating an old face to turn up for a beer and chat. Uppermost in his mind, though, was money. Failure to be, somewhat, successful at making illegal money would mean obscurity in his eyes. The bloke he expected sat in the corner of the old bar.

'Hi, Nelson, good to see you once again, mate. The last time I saw you was months ago when visiting your daughter,' said the pub owner, Jack Grimes. Now about 65 years old, he remembered when Nelson and his friends used to rule the area. They had a fearsome reputation for being ruthless with anyone who got in their way. The gang used Jack's pub to plan various crimes. It was raided several times by police hoping to find guns, drugs and stolen goods. But they never did! That was all some time ago.

'Yeah, I'm back living up the road after years of graft elsewhere,' he said, the usual smile not far away.

'What you having, Nelson?' asked the pub owner.

'By the way, Jack, this is my friend and former colleague, Cedric.'

'Alright, Cedric?'

'Two pints of lager, Jack, thanks.'

The two men made a beeline for the man dressed in a white suit. This fellow looked the part if first impressions were important. Bald head, gold watch and rings on his thin long bony fingers. Many years ago, Sammy Burns was a regular in the pub and often in Nelson Trussington's company. They had done plenty of crime together. One or two successful robberies, amongst many others, they had carried out. The former partners in crime hadn't met for years until last week when, just by chance, they saw each other outside the local cinema.

'Alright, brudder, how's it going?' asked Nelson who was hoping this fellow was going to put cash his way.

'Alright, Nelson?'

'Meet my friend, Cedric.'

'Alright, mate?' asked Sammy, who looked like a prize fighter with a flat nose spread all over his face and several scars down his right cheek, he was a frightening sight for the squeamish.

'What's occurring, Sammy?' asked Nelson, probing for money to be made.

'Not a lot, mate.' Nelson had realised that Cedric's appearance was something that concerned his friend. He wasn't going to talk shop with him around. He was too old in the tooth to accept strangers at face value. Sammy had survived by using his wits. For all he knew, Cedric could be a plant, grass or whatever.

'Cedric, could yer buy two more pints? Here's the money. Cheers, mate.'

'My round, Nelson,' he said. Cedric made his way to the packed bar. He felt uneasy being in strange company, but for different reasons to Sammy Burns. He felt insecure among a lot of tough-looking blokes. He was savvy enough to realise what sort of pub it was. Time was marching on, he must be on his way back to the Lodge after finishing his beer.

'Who is that bloke, Nelson?' asked Sammy after Cedric had departed.

'He's a friend. Harmless enough.'

'I'm not talking about work in front of him, mate. No offence, he could be anyone for all I know.'

Half an hour later, both men stood outside Peckham Station chatting about another meeting. But Nelson was anxious to return to The Watchman pub and resume the conversation with his friend and, hopefully, renewed partner in crime.

'Good to see you, brudder. Give my love to Dave Richards.' Both men laughed at the thought.

'It was good to see you again, Nelson,' said Cedric.

'I'll phone you some time. Enjoy your trip to Devon. Send Dave Ford my regards, the old pussy.'

'Cheers, Nelson,' said Cedric as he disappeared into the bustling crowded station.

Regardless of those who owned plenty, Nelson was going to give his utmost to try and take his share of it. Why should he go without when there was plenty around for everyone? He'd had enough of being told what he was, what he could do and when to do it. This was the last throw of the dice. He was single-minded, full of courage and strong-willed, he wasn't going down without a fight.

'What you got in mind, Sammy?' asked a desperate man pumped up for action. He craved the thrill of stealing other people's money, jewellery or anything of value. Whatever they had, he would grab with delight. As much as he liked Cedric, he would be a liability when it came to crime. He didn't have the bottle for it.

'This job requires two people—you and me. Every Friday, around 7 pm, a young bloke carries several thousand pounds cash in a briefcase to his parked car. He works for Maynard, a large cash and carry along the high street. The car is parked at the back of the premises. The long walk from the shop to the car is about 500 yards. The public don't have access to the car park. It's for business only. When he arrives, we jump him. Give him a good hiding if he deserves it and scarper, right? I've sussed the job several times. He leaves at the same time every Friday. And the suitcase isn't chained to his wrist, right, Nelson?' explained the accomplice. 'By the way, a reliable source informed me about this cash.'

'I wanna have a look at the job for myself,' said Nelson.

'Sure, brother. Today's Thursday. I'll meet you here tomorrow at 6:30 pm and we will take a look together. Start rubbing those big hands of yours, ready cash is on the way, my son,' said Sammy Burns.

Burns lived about eight miles from the pub in a small privately-owned house. No doubt, it was bought from the proceeds of crime. Now 64 years old, the old lag had served several lengthy sentences ranging from armed robbery to fraud. He was mean, nasty and ruthless. He'd worked with the best and fought the toughest. Burns, even now, was a no-nonsense character. Nelson was in capable hands if he wanted to make money. Mind you, Burns wasn't untouchable. Plenty like him had come a cropper.

When Nelson arrived at the same pub, full of apprehension, his friend was sitting in the same corner seat.

'Alright, Nelson, still interested?' asked Burns.

'You bet I am, must have a beer before we go. What yer having?'

'Large scotch, mate.'

Returning from the bar, Nelson acknowledged a few old faces. Rough diamonds he had known from the days when villainy was rife in this part of London.

'Cheers, Nelson.'

'Good luck, brudder.'

'Right, as we agreed, we'll walk down the high street in about ten minutes, and watch that bloke carry the cash to his car,' said Burns. 'We can follow him to his car and then grab his suitcase. Any resistance, we will have to give him a few on the gob. We'll have to quickly put on balaclavas and—'

'Tell you what we should do. I'm not known around here, remember? I've been working away for many years. You watch the bloke come out of the shop with the cash. You put your hand up once he has passed you, and signal me. I'll walk around to the back of the car park, it's dark now, and jump him. You can follow the bloke and see me in the car park. I think that's the best bet,' explained Nelson.

'Look, let's give it a trial run tonight. If all goes well, we will do him next Friday, right?' said Sammy Burns.

As planned, the two walked to the high street and watched the worker walk to the car holding the suitcase, just as Sammy Burns predicted. Afterwards, they agreed the following Friday would be payday. 'Start rubbing your hands, my son!'

The following Friday, the two men met in another pub. Somewhere off the beaten track where they weren't known. They wore lightweight, dark clothing for an easy getaway, with balaclavas and gloves inside their pockets. Once they had the money, Sam Burns would drive off with it. It would be shared out later on. Nelson would return to his bedsit. No CCTV cameras around that part of the high street.

It was a routine job for Sammy, he'd been in this position many times before. Once he had psyched himself, there was no going back on his plans. He would park some distance from the car park. The suitcase he would place in a rucksack on his back, hoping no one would see him transfer one to the other.

As for Nelson, he had been shitting himself with nerves all week. His working life in Mortingbridge had been another world. His own small flat, meagre wage and a quiet existence, he thought. What was wrong with that? He had kept repeating to himself all week, like a mantra. He was giving himself a hard time for stupidly smashing his former boss in the face. If he was honest with himself, the job was a doddle. Now, he was on the verge of returning to serious crime after years of going straight. He'd promised himself to spend more time with his family. He adored his grandchildren and, in time, would become a regular, reliable and loved grandfather in their lives. His actions, in the next few hours, might blow those dreams of becoming someone dependable to smithereens. Yes, a decent, foreseeable future could all become shattered fragments of these realisable dreams. Was he really going to take a chance tonight and steal the cash? They'll get about £3000 each. That's if Burns' source is reliable. He could pull out of the job, but if he did, his name would then be worthless in most quarters of the manor. If they were both caught, they faced many years in prison.

They stood in the car park, hidden behind a large parked lorry, prepared for action. It was cold, dark and the wind blew hints of fear. Both men were pumped up to rob the ready cash from the unsuspecting male.

'Where the fuck, is he?' Nelson anxiously asked.

'Don't worry, mate, he'll be here soon,' whispered Sammy, who had a large hammer in his jacket pocket, just in case the younger man put up a struggle. They meant business.

They heard him approaching the unlit car park. Nelson had agreed to be the first to surprise him with as many punches as it took to knock him unconscious. He'd do the business, good and proper. With 15 stone of physical might, it wouldn't take him long.

Carrying the suitcase, the young man was about to open the door of the car when several sickening blows knocked him to the ground. He lay there prostrate and unconscious. Sammy immediately grabbed the case, put it in his rucksack, and made off with it before the victim realised what had happened to him. Nelson slapped him a few more times. Pulled the body into the back of the car, tied a scarf around his mouth and hands, and did a runner down the road. It was all over in a couple of minutes. No one was around to witness the robbery, that's what they hoped for.

Both men would not contact one another for some time. Police enquiries would be extensive and thorough. Within minutes, Police swarmed the area like locusts. Any locally known criminal could expect to be questioned sooner or later. Many ran to ground. Trussington and Burns anticipated having their collars felt. Both men, if it were known, were shitting themselves right now. Violent robberies always attracted overwhelming media coverage.

The next day, late morning, Nelson attended the job centre. He hated the place with intensity. But turning up on time was important. Showing he was eager and willing to cooperate, it would demonstrate to staff that he needed a job and state benefits. It would take attention away from unwanted prying eyes. Also, if interviewed by police, they would realise, Nelson surmised, he had little money. Originally, he hoped that the money they had stolen would give him a few months break from registering unemployed. But he knew that was asking for trouble. Just sit tight and wait until police activity quietens down.

Burns, on the other hand, didn't need ready cash. He owned his own home and had money in the bank. For all intents and purposes, he lived a respectable middle-class existence. He kept himself away from the public gaze. Those who knew him thought he was a decent everyday chap. How looks can deceive!

'What you been doing to find a job, Mr Trussington?' asked the worker assigned to him.

'Doing my best, darling,' he said.

'OK. But how many jobs have you applied for?' asked the elderly white woman.

'Quite a few, madam,' he said. He pulled out copies of jobs he had either emailed, written to or phoned. Half of them, of course, were false. Some of the names he found from looking in the local newspaper. The rest from a mind prepared for most eventualities. These civil servants, he realised, praised the conformists.

'That's impressive, Mr Trussington,' she replied. 'Keep up the good work. By the way, are you receiving your correct benefits?' she asked.

'Sure am, madam.'

Laughing under his breath, he walked out of the packed job centre, passed a group of noisy smokers, several with barking dogs outside, and down the road.

IO

CHAPTER TEN

The new porter settled in well at Oaks Lodge. Those residents, who had contacted him for whatever reason, had commended his pleasant and helpful nature. One wonders how long that will last with the likes of David Richards' presence. But, Derek Tranter, aged 55, slim, short with a ginger beard, had worked for many difficult, if not dangerous, individuals—15 years of army life had hardened his resolve to humanity's indifference. He had, himself, been bombed, shot, stabbed and generally knocked about by ruthless people whose only concern was maximum damage. With that in mind, Oaks Lodge was a doddle compared to his inglorious days in the army. Derek lived locally with his wife and son. Driving a newish Ford—his one luxury—after 12 hours on duty, he could return home to some peace and quiet. After viewing Cedric's flat on one occasion, he was so relieved that home was only ten minutes away. Having lived in military barracks, tents, sheds and other accommodation far worse, he nonetheless sympathised with Cedric. Derek's one abiding memory was sleeping next to human excrement for five days. He was in his 20s when he and his platoon came under enemy bombardment. They were pinned down inside a huge latrine! After that experience, everything smelt of roses.

'Good morning, porter speaking,' said Derek, whose squeaky voice sounded like a young boy.

'Good morning, Derek. How are you?' asked David Ford.

'Fine, Mr Ford. And how are you? You must be getting excited thinking about your holiday... today, isn't it?'

'Yes. Has the hired car arrived, yet?'

'Yes, sir. It arrived about half an hour ago. Cedric has given it a quick wash and brush up. It looks superb. The silver Citroen really stands out as a luxurious car,' explained the porter in a deferential manner. 'Cedric is waiting here at reception if you would like a word,' he said.

'No, that's alright. Tell him I'll be down in a few minutes,' said David Ford in his usual mild manner. It was only after a night of bingeing that he became mildly hostile. Otherwise, his front was one of calm. But most of the time, he loved humming various pop songs and hand wrestling, well, that's the impression he gave to others. Wait, and not too long, for the contradiction in people.

Cedric was hanging about outside waiting near the car, feeling rather anxious as usual. The thought of driving three men on holiday, two he had never met, was a daunting task for him. Cedric hoped they were friendly, similar to David Ford. He had bought a few pieces of second-hand clothing from a small charity shop. Three shirts, two pairs of trousers and a hand-sewn tweed jacket made up the bulk of his clothes. In addition, he had bought a second-hand case. Unfortunately, it reminded one of being a leftover from war, surplus to requirements. For once though, he stood out with his film star, look alike appearance. Stanley Laurel came to mind unfortunately.

But inside, he was desperately lonely. Being invited on holiday by David Ford had been, literally, a lifeline for him. After intermittent periods of relative stability, recently, he had serious thoughts of suicide. Not seeing any way out of the constant misery that tormented him, Cedric had made certain plans to jump in front of a local train. He had visited the station, on several occasions, to find the most conducive position for maximum impact. That's how near he came to ending his miserable life. By showing confidence in Cedric, giving him responsibility of driving four people to Devon, Ford had completely changed his outlook. At least for the foreseeable future, Cedric felt uplifted by someone willing enough to give him a chance. Life was worth living once again for the porter at Oaks Lodge.

Cedric had collected the new hired car from a small company in Wellton, some ten miles from Oaks Lodge. David Ford was a personal friend of the owner of the business. They had known each other for many years, from the days they both worked in engineering together. Similar to Ford, Kevin Butcher used to be a hardworking, successful person who loved to drink and gamble. Over the years, he had remarried and moved to the small village where he bought the business. Occasionally, they met to reminisce over a few beers, when money flowed in abundance and was safely deposited in false bank accounts.

'Enjoy the holiday, Cedric,' said Butcher.

'Thank you, Mr Butcher,' Cedric replied.

'Be careful of that old dog, David Ford, he'll lead you astray if you're not careful,' he laughed.

'Oh, I will. He's a good bloke.'

'He sure is. Give him my best wishes.'

Cedric drove the car for many miles, pretending he owned the powerful machine. People looked at him and the car as he drove through many villages at speed. If only real life was like this, he thought. His own home, a new car, money in the bank and a wife to love and support him. Several times he loudly revved the car when stationary at traffic lights. The silver car drove like a sleek bird. It appeared to hover above the ground, such was Cedric's imagination. Full with fuel, and the red leather interior polished soft and comfortable, there was no stopping him until he finally parked at the Lodge. It dwarfed the old bent Ford belonging to Derek Tranter, who came out to meet his colleague. Cedric felt like a million dollars.

'Nice one, Cedric,' said Derek.

'Yeah, I'm looking forward to driving down to Devon,' he replied. Deep down, he was full of anxiety, but the car had, at least, given him something to focus his concerns. He was determined to make the best of his time on holiday.

'The car looks superb, Cedric,' said David Ford who had just appeared, pulling a large black case and holding a small brown briefcase!

'It certainly does, sir,' said Cedric, who was sucking his lips and scratching his head in anticipation of something.

'Look, Cedric, when we are on holiday, or any other time, please call me David. Otherwise, my friends will think I'm your master or Lord of Lodge Manor or something ridiculous. They both have a wicked sense of humour and are inveterate piss takers,' said Ford as he laughed loudly at himself.

'Sure thing, David,' said Cedric rather shyly. He wasn't quite sure what he was hearing from one of the Lodge's grandees. He constantly reminded himself, throughout the years, how tough and uncompromising he was. But he had always been decent to staff. Never took a high-handed approach, unlike some, as being different due to having relative wealth. Be careful, though, Cedric.

'You'll get to know them, Cedric. We're away for at least seven days, so let things unfold, my friend. I've known John and Phillip for many years. All three of us, not to mention Kevin Butcher, have worked on several large constructions around the world. We've had some fucking ding-dong holidays, I can tell you, Cedric. Tales that would make your cock stand up. Just be yourself with both of them. They have an open mind, they are not stuck on class or education or achievement. Mind you, that's not to say they are against making money by doing your best because they are not! Both have big houses somewhere, I forget where, Cedric. It isn't that important, is it? It will come to me in a minute where they live,' he said in his most judicious manner.

'Thanks, David,' said Cedric with a hint of innocence in his uneasiness.

'Right, Cedric, my dear boy, we had better hit the road. It's past 11 am and we have to pick the other two urchins up along the way,' said a reassuring David Ford. Cedric placed both cases in the boot, which opened automatically with a push of the key. His confidence further boosted by what had just been explained to him, Cedric drove out of Oaks Lodge anticipating a new and exciting experience.

Having looked and studied a road map of the journey for the past week, Cedric was aware of the first destination—Flakstead. They pulled up outside an old 16th-century renovated building. John Tribe had bought the dilapidated grand house some 20 years ago. Many thought he had gone nuts to take on the hard work needed to modernise his pet project. His wife nearly walked out on him, his kids left him until they relented, and neighbours complained about noise and dust. Undaunted, John kept at it. Rage and red wine compelled its completion some four years ago. He was now on good terms with most people, including the Sikh lady from the local fresh air monitoring service.

'Morning, chaps, I hope all is well. Hello, you must be Cedric? Dave told me about you. Thanks for driving us reprobates on holiday,' said John, aged 74, tall, slim with a sturdy athletic body.

'Hello, John,' said David Ford. 'Cedric is a great guy. We'll get to know each other, I hope, over the next few days. A few pints of wallop soon releases inhibition,' Ford laughed.

'Once again, good to meet you, Cedric,' said John, shaking his hand.

'Right, shall we hit the road?' said David.

With case in hand, John followed the other two out to the car. Cedric drove off feeling a little nervous. He'd never been a very good conversationalist, alright in pubs he knew, but he felt out of his depth with intelligent men. Nonetheless, he was going to try his best, dig deep and just expose himself to new experiences. He had nothing to lose anyway. He would still have a job, wage and flat when he returned. Utopia!

Three miles further on, the car pulled up outside the home of Phillip Knox. A modern detached build, similar to the rest of the road, with new cars, trimmed hedges and utter silence. No children could be seen, though the occasional howling dog, some way off, could be heard guarding the manor. Knox and family had moved into the newly built house not long ago. He loved moving around. He found it difficult, even at aged 75, to settle down in any one place. His wife supported his roving around the country mentality, even though she loved the present establishment in Millstead. It appeared that Knox was still restless for action, while most men his age had settled for the armchair and occasional gardening. Apparently, his attractive wife wasn't slow in coming forward to entertain younger men when her husband was elsewhere.

'Hello, Phillip. Please meet Cedric, I've told you about him, haven't I?' insists David Ford.

'Hi, Cedric, nice to meet you,' said Phillip, another slim, spritely looking man, who appeared, not surprisingly, full of energy.

'Time is getting on. Shall we hit the road, Cedric?' asked Ford.

'Goodbye, honey,' Phillip said to his wife.

With the car full of cases and men, Cedric didn't waste time putting the miles behind him. It was a warm, sunny, late spring day. It was ideal conditions for a holiday in Devon. Cedric had never been down this far in the West Country. At least, he didn't think his parents took him there, but in all honesty, he couldn't remember. The subject confused him. He had dreamt of the Cornish Riviera, seen photographs of the sunny, sandy coastline and advertisements on railway hoardings. Now, the real place was less than 200 miles from where he sat behind the hired car.

As the other men quietly talked shop, Cedric concentrated on the road ahead. He was acutely conscious that he didn't want to mess things up after hours of preparation. Much was expected of the porter from Oaks Lodge. Besides, Cedric was aware of some of his own unmet needs. This holiday, with three successful men around to help, might just give him the opportunity to unravel the frustrations that had haunted his life. He had to be brave about opening up to men who could, given the opportunity, help him understand the knots and binds entangled inside him. If anyone could, it would be these mature and worldly men.

As he drove along the A34, via Oxford, to meet up with the M4, his thoughts turned briefly to his friend, Nelson Trussington. After visiting him in London, Cedric had convinced himself that way of life wasn't for him anymore. Nelson had acted impulsively, and he had paid a high price by losing his job and accommodation. One consolation was that Nelson had his family around to support him. But the thought of dirty, smelly bedsits, crowds of faceless people, noise and crime stung Cedric's conscience. As much as he disliked those who had power over him, and always had, he felt he had an obligation to refrain from doing wrong. On many occasions, he had been tempted, given the opportunity, to steal from vulnerable residents. In other places, he also felt the powerful urge to steal anything of value. Yet he had refrained from doing so at the last moment. He cherished his freedom. The experience of being incarcerated, many years ago, in prison had left an indelible mark on him.

Nevertheless, the overriding thoughts in Cedric's mind were the futility of life. Ford had always been decent to him and all the staff at Oaks Lodge. However, he was mindful of their respective positions in life. He didn't want the holiday to make him all starry-eyed and stupid, allowing others to easily manipulate him into thinking he was one of them. Cedric knew where he belonged, no problem. He didn't want to blind himself into thinking otherwise. Keep your feet on the ground and all will be fine.

'You're quiet, Cedric,' said David, who for the past hour and a half had been either texting or engaged in small talk about sport.

'I'm just concentrating on the roads, David. I want to make sure we all arrive in one piece,' he replied.

'I appreciate that. Now, we are on the M4, shall we stop at the service station coming up in about five miles? Decent place, I've been there before. Good grub... well, it was three years ago,' quipped Ford.

They pulled into Ashley Services, which was full of vehicles of all sizes. Rubbish blew around the large car park. Flattened flowerbeds had been walked upon by countless feet. People congregated outside the building endlessly smoking and chatting. Soaked fag ends piled up on the ground next to the litter bins. Not exactly an inspiring place to enter, thought John Tribe. He prayed the food and drink would be more visibly enterprising.

'Four coffees and traditional breakfast for all, I hope?' appealed Phillip. All were in agreement as they found a corner table that had been cleaned. Quite a rarity in motorway establishments as piles of used crockery and cutlery are usually left to the flies.

'Well we've made good progress Cedric. You don't hang around my friend,' said Phillip, who had a disproportionately small head compared to the rest of his sturdy body.

'Yeah, it's going well. We've been on the road for about two hours, we travelled some distance along the M4. Lots of traffic though,' he said, mindful of the company and how he presented himself.

'You been in any of these places before, Cedric?' inquired John.

'Nope, first time for me, John,' he said.

'You haven't missed very much, I can assure you,' said David who, when employed, constantly used these human zoos.

'Don't tell porkies, Dave, you and I have been using these washed out facilities for years, haven't we?' John reminded his friend and fellow bruiser.

'True, mate.' He winked acknowledgement at his friend.

'Here comes the grub,' Phillip reassured.

An hour later, they were heading for the M5 motorway. The traffic had thinned out, the sun disappeared, and three men sat sleeping and snoring. Cedric turned on the radio, very silent, to listen to classical music. From a young age, he had been enthralled by the music of Mozart, Beethoven, Brahms and many more. He couldn't tell who was playing what at any one time. He couldn't read music, but he was moved, sometimes to tears, by various classical pieces of work. One instrument or an orchestra, they were all sublime to him. He never told anyone from his background, otherwise, he would have been ridiculed and further undermined. So, in public, punk rock took precedence and it still does. Occasionally, playing the few punk records he still possessed, the memories gave him reassurance and comfort from a time he still cherishes.

With eyes fixed on the road, the internal map ever present, Cedric briefly recounted some of those faces from the heady punk rock days. He wondered how many were still living. What had they done with their lives, gone on to develop a good job and happy marriage, perhaps? How he'd love to turn back the clock to experience those late nights and early mornings, jumping up and down mindlessly, listening to crazy music. The smell of cannabis, beer and sweat stormed his imagination. Men and women having sex in the toilets never left his fantasies. They were so brazen, yet so spontaneous. He wondered where they all ended up.

'Where are we, Cedric, old chap?' questioned David Ford, who had just woken up after napping for some time.

'We are on the M5, Dave, heading for Taunton where we need to branch off and take the A39 via Bridgewater, along the coast road to your cottage. Do you fancy food and drink? According to this map, there is a Little Chef six miles further on,' said Cedric eagerly.

'Great news, I'm hungry already,' John remarked.

'We went in there, Dave, you may recall, about 15 years ago when we were working on a large construction site near Barnstable,' said Phillip. He added, 'I remember that you fancied the young Indian woman who served us that afternoon.'

'Fuck me, Phillip, you have a razor-sharp memory,' said David.

'I know, I fancied her too,' laughed Phillip.

Unlike the last establishment, this one was nearly deserted. Masses of faded daffodils, flowering valerian and pruned roses made the place cheerful. Very little rubbish and few discarded cigarettes could be seen around the small, privately owned café. Once out of the car, all four of them rushed for the toilet. Soft music greeted their grunts and strains. What a sight—four old men, all holding their bag of jewels, looking straight ahead with eyes fixed on the tiled wall.

David Ford did the honours by paying for all the food and drink, but the Indian woman, it appeared, had moved on from washing dishes and mopping floors.

'Where we driving to next, Cedric?' asked John.

'Well, we're on the A39. We drive via Bridgewater, along the coast road to Sandridge Bay where the cottage is, four miles west of Lynton.

'Great stuff,' said David with an air of expectation.

'How many miles to go, Cedric?' asked Phillip.

'It's about 20 miles from Minehead. Add another six or seven from here, so about 30,' said a flagging Cedric, who had never driven so far in one day. But he didn't want to show the others he was tired. Keep positive and upright, he kept reminding himself. He felt important being asked various questions. Well, he had a serious task of driving four men to Devon. Just think, he reminded himself, he had the power, if he so chose, to kill the lot of them in a crash with another vehicle. Something like a 40-ton truck should be powerful enough to inflict maximum damage, he fantasized.

'Tasty cottage pie, better than the old girl's back home but don't, for fuck sake, Dave, say that to her, will you?' said John as he shrugged his bony shoulders.

'Yes, I will let the cat out of the bag alright. Just wait until we get back home,' laughed David Ford who had known John's wife for many years. She often laughed about how her husband's renovations had considerably aged her. Furthermore, she claimed, it had made him impotent!

'Like it, Cedric?' smiled David.

'Yeah, handsome, mate,' replied Cedric with a rare smile on his worn face. A face rarely noticed by others, but within lay untold stories that, given the opportunity, would interest people. He didn't have the confidence to express those experiences. When he fleetingly thought about them, he ridiculed himself for thinking such nonsense. Who would listen to him? Nevertheless, he realised that behind the steering wheel, he was in charge. All their wealth and prestige cared for nothing, if he decided to end their lives, it would be all gone.

For about 15 minutes, all was quiet as they scoffed, most earnestly, the food in front of them. A rampaging bull wouldn't have moved their old, sagging backsides such was their hunger. From plastic, processed food earlier to home-cooked fair, and this meal was also cheaper. Cedric lapped it up. He loved his food even though he wasn't the most discerning shopper back in Mortingbridge. On this occasion, he was going to make the very best of anything offered. After all the driving, he was becoming more tired and irritable. He just wasn't used to being cooped up in a car with three relative strangers. Loners, like him, are used to their own company. He hated explaining information to people, even though David had discussed the pros and cons with him prior to departure. But there will be times on holiday when they will go out on their own, gallivanting, which will give Cedric space. Right now, he needed five minutes to himself. Things were too intense, so he wandered off to the toilet again. He sat in the cubicle taking deep breaths. It helped him relax and think straight after fantasizing of intense death.

'Cedric doesn't say much, Dave?' inquired John Tribe.

'As I think I told you both, he's had a hard life. I'm not aware of the details but I'm basically surmising from what his boss told me. He's a porter where I reside, chaps. That much I told you both. He and another porter have a small flat each at the back of Oaks Lodge. I've not seen them, but apparently, they are rather sparse. Cedric is a decent chap, friendly and keeps himself to himself. No problem,' David remarked.

'He seems a decent enough bloke. Good of him to drive us on holiday. Besides, he's not compelled to follow us around for a whole week, is he?' added Phillip.

Ten minutes later, Cedric returned to the table. He was mighty thankful for some time to himself while sitting on the toilet seat. That 30 feet of space between him and his fellows had given him the impetus to sort out his mind needed to drive the final 30 miles.

Back in the car, seat-belted and comfortable, Cedric drove off along A39. Either side of the main road, thousands of saplings had been planted. It had brought some wildlife back to the area. Hitherto, it had been barren for many years. Beyond, thousands of acres of ploughed farming land beckoned. The only living beings were hundreds of rooks scavenging the furrows for food. They were a reassuring sight, drilling their beaks into the baked soil. Cedric always noticed these things. Nature had always interested him. He fantasized about walking over hills that lay beyond, wearing his rucksack and holding treasured maps bought by his parents. He'd just remembered that he forgot to bring that old sack with him. He'd bought it some 25 years ago when travelling around Britain. It had seen action alright, just like its owner. No problem, he thought, buy one down there.

After their fill of food, all was quiet once more until David made a request for soothing music. Cedric was only too pleased to turn the radio on to classical music. He preferred the silence. They were approaching Bridgewater, which was unusually busy, and to Cedric's dismay, full of road works. Sweating navvies toiled six feet under the ground. Supermarket trolleys littered the empty holes already dug to replace the Victorian pipes. Every 50 yards, some buffoon stopped them holding a red flag.

'I bet you know what I would like to do with that bloody flag, don't you, Dave?' laughed Phillip.

'Not up his arse, surely, Phil?'

Eventually, the gang of four escaped the clutches of local officialdom. The works of Debussy and Elgar had saved the day, or at least helped soothe Cedric's frayed nerves. Now on the coast road, it would be another hour until they arrived. They soon came across Moor Wood, which was on their right. Perched high, it sat there precariously above Bridgewater Bay. Three cyclists stretched their legs along the narrow road. Just before Porlock, Cedric looked across at bleak Exmoor. Out of nowhere, the thought of the senior nun, at the children's home where he once lived, crashed into his consciousness.

Within seconds, he labelled her the 'Exmoor Beast,' a very apt name for one who did so much damage to vulnerable youngsters.

'There it is, Dave, Sandyridge Bay, 500 yards,' said a jubilant John. This was all familiar to the friends who had been down here many times. It was understood, by the women, as being a week out for the boys. It was time to get away, be carefree and let your hair down. Amongst other activities!

The four men walked down from the pebbled car park to Sea View Cottage, a 19th-century former fisherman's shack. David had extended it five years ago by adding two single bedrooms. The timbered dwelling now comprised of four small bedrooms, a kitchen, bathroom and a dining/lounge room. Mrs Hook, a local elderly woman, was the unofficial caretaker. She cleaned the interior and maintained the small rocky garden. She also oversaw that the few people who rented the cottage were well-informed. Especially when descending the steep wooden steps to Sandyridge Bay, which had claimed its fair share of accidents. Prior to visiting, Mrs Hook usually washed the linen, cleaned and stocked up the fridge-freezer for David. Of course, he generously recompensed her. As for the money, he didn't let on.

Ensconced in the small lounge, they sat there drinking red wine and eating local pasties. All were pleased to have arrived after six hours of travel, Cedric in particular. He felt absolutely shattered after the long drive, but it boosted his confidence for the week ahead. All unknown territory, untested ground and unfamiliar faces to be sorted out, he had been thinking to himself for some time.

'Thank you, Cedric,' all the blokes agreed in unison.

'We'll have a beer later,' said John. 'Those two have to go out soon so we can wander down to the only pub.'

'Don't get him pissed,' said David.

David Ford and Phillip Knox were down in Devon, primarily, they hoped, to make lots of illegal money. More the merrier, they all hoped. John Tribe was a part of the collaboration. He had stayed behind with Cedric around, just in case evidence was needed later on. Besides, there was Ford's briefcase to look after! Dressed formerly, with serious intent on their faces, they drove off, heading for a secluded farmhouse near Marton, on the western side of Exmoor.

A middle-aged man, fat with greying, greasy hair greeted them at the front door. Heavily bearded, the tall figure of Ian Hedges showed his two clients into the large lounge. They had been here before, several times, on business. Hedges had lived alone, in his expensive pile, for at least 20 years. The proceeds of crime, no doubt, pay handsomely for the man who lived a semi-reclusive life. Hedges' nearest neighbour was 500 yards.

'Large scotches. Cheers, chaps,' said Hedges softly. 'Well, what can I do for you on this occasion?' He shrugged his shoulders as if he wasn't that interested, one way or another. But, of course, that was all a front. When it came to making money, pound signs registered in his grey matter. The only people that ever visited him, by his request, was to make money.

'Cocaine,' remarked Ford.

'Yes, of course, we have business to sort out, don't we, chaps?' said Hedges in a carefully reassured voice. 'Now, how much do you require, how and when are you going to pay and will you take it back by car, or have you made other arrangements?' He then further added, 'Would it not be wiser to buy this white gold nearer to your home?'

'Well, Ian, the nearest place we know is London, and that place is too big and competitive for us. They blow your legs off if you get in the big boy's way. We'll pay in cash. Leave the rest to us,' answered Ford in no uncertain terms.

Hedges walked out of the room. The two remaining men scanned the wealth in front of them. Famous pictures by various artists adorned the flock-covered walls. They assumed they were the real deal. Expensive carpets, furniture and jewels were there for all to see. Ford knew they were worth big money. They also realised that one of his bookcases held priceless scrolls. Hedges was a shrewd operator, he had to be in a hate-ridden drug world. Otherwise, if he made a mistake, just one, there were plenty who would bury him ten feet underground for a price.

With that in mind, Hedge's whole house, inside and out, was on CCTV. Even though they had done deals before, the two buyers were rather dubious of Hedges. He was a crook of the highest order. It was either drive 200 miles, have a holiday at the same time, where very few people knew them, or play around with the big boys from the smoke, which was a proposition they didn't relish one bit. They were all in their 70s, and all agreed this was the last cocaine deal. It was time to call it a day. They all had enough money. They didn't want or need for anything material. John was rather reluctant travelling on this occasion. He only did so out of genuine friendship. They were, of course, using Cedric as a front. Get him to drive, be a skivvy and generally act as someone who could be told what to say, and to who, if needed. That was the idea, anyway.

Hedges returned to the room holding a small plastic bag containing white powder. He placed it on the small coffee table.

'Right, there you go. Try that stuff with your machine before we start the real business of negotiation,' said Hedges arrogantly.

'Let's see what we got,' said Phillip as he reached for a small pen-size-shaped machine in his inside pocket. He scooped a small amount of the powder and placed it in the machine, shook it several times, and waited two minutes. 'Hey, presto, chaps, that's the real stuff, cocaine,' said Phillip, pumped up with excitement.

'Right,' said Hedges sharply. 'What are you prepared to pay for it, and how much do you want to buy? The more you buy, the cheaper it becomes.'

They gave him a price. He didn't agree.

'Try again, lads, nowhere near it,' said Hedges curtly. 'I tell you what. Go out to your car and discuss the price among yourselves but I've told you the minimum price for the minimum weight.'

They sat in the car for an hour tossing and turning, not sure, undecided and somewhat confused about what the dealer had put before them.

'Shall we call it a day, Dave, before we commit ourselves to something we might regret? Every time we deal with Hedges, he ups the price, the bastard. We've all done well over the years. Being middlemen has made us less vulnerable to the gangsters. If they found out, they would cut our bollocks off,' Phillip gravely commented to his friend.

'Now we are here, Phil, let's go for it,' said David, who was by now very anxious. He added, 'We've got £50,000 in that account which we can withdraw at any time. We've given the bank prior notice. It's all legitimate. Let's conclude the deal. The final deal we're all getting on as it's becoming too stressful.'

'Right, Dave. If Hedges agrees to the deal, we'll meet him back here in three days with the money, in exchange for the cocaine. Similar to other times, we'll keep the stuff in your suitcase and carry on enjoying the rest of the holiday,' suggested Phillip.

They returned to the farmhouse with their proposal. After half an hour of hankering, the two sides came to an amicable arrangement. The cash and cocaine would be exchanged in three days, at a time to be arranged but no more than one hour's notice. This would allow the buyers some sort of security up until that time, and if needs be, they could cancel the deal. They doubted whether Hedges kept any illegal drugs in his home, he was too smart and devious to be caught with his pants down. His supplier, no doubt, lived near but where, would be like finding a needle in a hay stack. This cocaine skunk left no smell behind him.

That's the impression the men had got over the past years dealing with him. Other than business, he said very little that could incriminate himself. Hedges always covered his tracks squeaky clean. There were no flies on the snake from Exmoor. No doubt, they both agreed, Hedges had given much thought about how they would lay their hands on a large sum of money, in cash. They wouldn't put it past him, about informing other crooks, of a large amount of cash to be had, if only he knew where it was hidden. The buyers had never told him their whereabouts, or where they actually lived near London. Mind you, Hedges probably had them followed or checked out their background. His freedom depended on it. Nevertheless, the stage was set, the scene was scripted and words prepared for the final foray into the world of buying illegal drugs. For the old men, from a respectable middle-class background, one more trip to the farmhouse and it's all over.

Early next the morning, John prepared the breakfast in the white-washed timbered kitchen. Not one of his most skilful activities but what the hell when you are on holiday, away from the women, and enjoying yourself. That's what he tried convincing himself, anyway, by frying eight eggs and several large pieces of bacon. Two pans sizzling on the stove, bread in three toasters and a large pot of coffee ready for the masses to devour. He was looking forward to an easy slow day—swimming, laying in the sun and drinking cold white wine. He and Cedric had a few beers together yesterday. As he was preoccupied, anxious for his two friend's safety, there was very little conversation. Now they were back in one piece, they could all relax.

'Morning, John,' said Cedric, who had enjoyed his company in The Lobster Pot. He wasn't cocky or arrogant, just a decent bloke exchanging superficial information about his experiences.

'Hello, Cedric, you alright? Help yourself to some grub.'

'Delicious, mate,' muttered Cedric.

'Eat as much as you like.'

'Does that apply to me also, John?' said an eager Dave, who had just walked out of his bedroom still wearing his pyjamas. Weary-eyed after a restless night worrying, concerned, about what lay ahead tomorrow. One thing was for sure, it would be the last drug deal. Phillip followed, fully-dressed, not long after. He, too, had finished the drug game.

The four men sat there eating, all engrossed in their own thoughts, but no one spoke. The one thing they had all agreed upon was a relaxed day on the beach. Well fed, dressed in beach clothes, carrying large towels and four bottles of white wine, the men gingerly negotiated the precarious woodworm ridden steps. Phillip had never been that keen walking down to the beach, aware that a few innocent souls had fallen to their deaths.

Sandyridge Bay was between two high columns of rock. Outside of summer holidays, it never attracted many bathers or sun seekers. It was ideal, a small inlet for David Ford and his friends to lap up the warm weather, swim in the chilly sea and doze on sun loungers. It was custom made for the oldies. Very few children or barking dogs were ever around to upset the silence.

'Place the wine in that rock pool over there, Phil, it will keep cool there,' said John, who was mightily relieved after last night's brief discussion with his two friends. He had agreed overwhelmingly to their suggestion that the deal tomorrow will be the final one. He too had had enough of the intense anxiety that increased every time they indulged in drug dealing. He was too old. He couldn't take anymore. It would be the final car journey tomorrow to Barnstaple, driven by Cedric, to withdraw the money from the bank. David had pre-arranged for the cash to be ready for collection around midday. So worried was John, that he usually took a mild tranquilliser before collecting the cash in £50 notes. If he could, he would leave the area right now, without any hesitation. But he couldn't desert his friends... that was a step too far. His conscience made sure of that.

'Sure thing, John,' he replied.

Other than Cedric, who couldn't swim, the others had dressed in their colourful swimming outfits and ran, with mounting enthusiasm, into the sea. The outsider was on hand to look after the clothes. But Cedric was enjoying himself sitting on a lounger, wearing shorts and a shirt, lapping up the peaceful atmosphere. No phone calls from demanding residents. The first day had gone well for him. He had enjoyed going to the pub, had slept peacefully in his own bedroom and it was a rare occasion to have a large breakfast cooked by someone else. He was soaking up the attention.

With no one around, he took the company mobile phone out of his pocket. He hoped he could get a signal in this small cove.

'Hi, is that Derek? Just a very brief call, mate,' he said.

'Yeah, how's it going, Cedric? Are you enjoying yourself in Devon?'

'I am. It's sunny down here right now. The other blokes are swimming in the sea. What a life this is, Derek, I would love to live here on my own in one of the few small cottages,' he answered.

'I won't bore you with things here. Just to say, the boss arrived yesterday to inspect the place. He strutted around like General Shitfart, as if he owned the fucking place. I'm not surprised Nelson chinned him,' Derek muttered sarcastically.

'OK, mate. Must go, otherwise, he will have a go at me for

using too much phone time. I was gobsmacked when he allowed me to take it with me.'

'OK, mate. Take care,' said Derek.

Cedric sat there listening to the hypnotic waves crashing on to the shoreline. Long pieces of seaweed littered the beach. Large herring gulls watched him anticipating mouthfuls of food. They were so brazen, only several feet from Cedric, they pecked at anything resembling edible. He forgot about their ferocious beaks and went back to a peaceful state of mind. If only everyday life was like this, he thought. He realised that the other three men had the wherewithal to indulge in this lifestyle at their leisure. The thought of doing so irritated him beyond belief. To shed that internal burden, his thoughts turned to his friend, Nelson Trussington. If only he were down here with him. Cedric realised how he missed spending occasions with the bloke who called him brudder. Listening to his brash statements and carefree attitude, Cedric hoped some of it would rub off on him. He wasn't addicted to people, he had always preferred his own company, but Nelson was somehow different.

'Hi, Nelson, how you keeping, mate?'

'Well, fuck me, brudder, if that isn't my dear friend, Cedric. I'm well, how are you? What's that sea noise I can hear? You robbed someone and done a runner, mate?' he asked in bewilderment.

'I should be so lucky. No, I'm on holiday in Devon with Dave Ford and his two friends. You remember him, the bloke you had arm wrestling matches with?' said Cedric with an air of confidence.

'No, fuck me, brudder, he must like you. That's right, you

told me some time back. What you doing right now, you eye-ing some pussy?'

'I'm on a quiet beach. Only a handful of people here. While they are swimming, I'm using the time to see how you are.'

'I'm still living in South London, the place you visited me, you know. Still trying to find a job, no bastard wants to em-ploy an unskilled gangster like me, mate.' But Nelson wasn't going to say anything about villainy over the phone. Besides, although he liked Cedric, Burns would be mad if he found out he was advertising their illegal activities.

'Take care, mate. I can see Ford and company walking up the beach as if they own the gaff.'

'And you, brudder. Cheers.'

The three drowned rats eventually returned to their seats in the sun. This was much to the disappointment of Cedric, who had dreamt of wonders far above his potential during their absence. A different environment—sea, rugged coast-line, few vehicles, even less inhabitants and thick wooded ar-eas had the porter thinking deeply about his last few years left on this earth. How he would give all he had, which, of course, was very little, to live along this coast. Why not me for once? He thought to himself. He even wondered if he could live in David Ford's cottage. He could be the full-time caretaker, maintenance and gardener. No wage was necessary, Cedric could live off his savings and state benefits. In a few years, he would be eligible for a pension. It was the perfect set-up for him. If people rented the cottage, he would be willing to share for a week here or there. No problem. He had given serious thought about asking the owner if it was a realistic proposi-tion.

'Alright, Cedric, been tanning yourself?' asked David.

'For a while but I burn very quickly in the sun,' he replied.

'Cedric, could you fetch two bottles of wine, please? I've also brought four beakers down along with fruit and biscuits under my seat,' said a smiling David, who felt, at this moment, on top of the world. Tomorrow wasn't on his mind right now.

'Cheers to you all,' said John, who drank half of his full beaker in one gulp.

'Good health, everyone,' bellowed Phillip. 'I hope we have a superb holiday together,' he said as they drank and ate their fill. All three had been stimulated by swimming a considerable way out. The sea was now warm and clear. The sky above was light blue with white flecks. The outline of shearwater, gannet and cormorant were identified flying high above. Others landed on the cliffs nearby. Small human features could be spotted walking the coast path beyond them to the east.

'Nelson sends his regards, Dave,' said Cedric.

'Oh, that sounds good from the big chap. How is he, by the way?' came the request from David.

'He's fine. He now lives in London.'

'Well, good on him. Please return my regards, Cedric.'

It was late afternoon, and the May temperature was cooling down for the night. All agreed it was time to walk back to the cottage, change their clothes, and head down to the pub for an evening meal. Once again, they gingerly negotiated the steps, resting several times. Some of the ageing timbers had seen more productive days. The climb was hindered by their consumption of alcohol.

The three friends had been using the pub intermittently for over 20 years. The landlord of the Sailors Rest, Patrick

O'Keefe, had joined their company on many occasions for an evening of songs, jokes and booze.

'Hello, you old seadogs, how good to see you all once again. Other than John, who I saw yesterday with your dear friend, I haven't seen you since last year when we hit the rum bottle, I vaguely remember,' laughed the landlord, whose purplish face was a strong hint that he was regularly on the wrong side of the bar.

'Hi, Patrick, are you well, my friend?' asked David Ford, who looked smart in his brown mohair suit and matching suede shoes.

'What's your poison, lads?' inquired the landlord, aged 66, tall, slim and wore thick rimmed glasses.

Four pints of that local bitter, please, Pat,' said John. They sat down at the nearest available table, within ear shot of the landlord.

'Cheers, lads,' said David. 'I hope it puts hairs on your chests.'

'Good health, Dave. I feel thoroughly invigorated by the swim in the sea. Nothing like the sea beats all those chlorine filled baths and lidos,' said Phillip enthusiastically.

'Enjoy the beach, Cedric?' asked David.

'Yeah, it was peaceful. While you lot were swimming, I followed various birds catching fish and taking it back to a nest up high in the cliffs. What powerful animals.'

'Yes, I wouldn't relish a bite on the arse from a herring gull.'

The small pub was typically decorated for that part of the world. There were shells, rope, sailor's hats and low beams—predictable paraphernalia. Pat depended on tourism to earn a decent living, although he had, by now, made enough money to retire. O'Keefe and his wife bought it 30 years ago, when it was in desperate need of renovation. They ploughed in money and hard work to make a thriving business. Over the years, he had made some extra money buying stolen spirits, cigarettes and fish. It appeared everyone was at it in these small villages, where work was seasonal, incomes unpredictable and bent gear always available at the right price.

Four more beers, please, Pat,' said Phillip.

'It's still warm, fancy sitting in the small garden at the back?' asked David.

They all trouped out, with beer in hand, to a sheltered spot full of lemon balm, rosemary and forget-me knots. A small elder shrouded the small table where they sat. All was peaceful and quiet, save for someone mowing a lawn nearby. The beer was soon swallowed down the hatch. Dave went to replenish the stocks. While inside, he had a crafty, single whiskey with the landlord just for old time's sake, he convinced himself.

'Must phone the missus tonight,' said John. 'Otherwise, she will think I done a runner.'

'She should be so lucky,' laughed Phillip.

'Yes, John, women around that age start thinking about toy boys. Be careful, my friend!' Hoots of derision broke out from the guys, including Cedric, who was feeling the beer loosening him up.

'Stop taking the piss, you bunch of nomads,' replied John.

'All have a beer.' Cedric didn't wait for any replies as he shot to the bar and returned in five minutes with four more beers. The alcohol was flowing. People began to relax their inhibition.

'When you going to move away from that geriatric ward, Dave?' asked John, laughing from ear to ear.

'It's a smashing place, the Oaks, isn't it, Cedric?' Dave insisted he agree.

'Yeah, it's not a bad place. I've worked and lived in worse,' said Cedric hesitantly, but he held back his true feelings about the place. Guy Fawkes and dynamite came to his mind.

'How long you worked there, Cedric?' asked Phillip.

'About 13 years.'

'Fuck me, Cedric, I admire you. I couldn't work and live in the same place,' he said.

'Where you from, Cedric?' asked John.

'Well, I don't really know... I was brought up in a children's home somewhere in Dorset. I was adopted by decent parents. They treated me well, really,' muttered Cedric.

'That must have been difficult living in a home?' John questioned.

'It was run by nuns. They could be fucking terrible sometimes,' he said, reproachfully. 'It was heaven moving to Wiltshire and having my own bedroom.'

'Sounds like you have had a tough life?' inquired David.

'It's been tough at times. Especially unemployment, sleeping rough and hunger,' he quietly responded. 'The last years have probably been the best so far.'

With the temperature dropping further, they all moved back into the bar. After another beer and an enjoyable evening meal, they decided to retire to the cottage. All were now feeling tired after hours of vigorous frivolity. They said their goodbyes to the O'Keefe's, hoping to return before the end of the holiday. Uppermost in their minds, not surprisingly, was the drug deal tomorrow. None of the three slept well that particular night.

In the morning, everyone felt somewhat subdued. Alcohol was one reason for the extended silence at the breakfast table, but the other was becoming more polarised. Unspoken words sent volumes of distrust across the table. They all glared towards the floor, resembling monks praying. No one offered to break the ice! The three friends knew each other so well that they could read and understand their body language. It wasn't too late to cancel the deal with Hedges. They could have their cases in the car in no time at all, and be back on the road within minutes heading elsewhere. Cedric, though, was used to prolonged bouts of silence. Besides, he found it pleasurable at times. But the other silence, the one he was unaware of, had the capacity to cripple the decision that they all had to agree on. As it was late morning, David Ford pushed, cajoled himself into making that decision, otherwise, years of friendship could be destroyed.

'Excuse me, Cedric, but I need to discuss something important with my friends in the bedroom. Please don't take it personally, will you?' apologised David, who assumed that Cedric had no idea of the intensity being played out in front of him.

They finished their coffee and made their way to the place that would, unequivocally, decide the day's modus operandi. Stress has its limits until all is shattered. They didn't want to reach that fatal point.

'Right, my dear pals, here is what I propose. Cedric drives

you, John, to the Barnstaple Bank at about 1 pm. Make sure he stays in the car as I don't want him to view the transaction with the bank worker. Place the money in the suitcase and drive back here. Now, the crucial point is this: when do I phone Hedges and what time shall we meet him?' Ford gravely remarked.

'I agree with you, Dave, and 1 pm is fine by me. By the time I return, can I suggest you phone him about 3 pm? We don't need too much time between the phone call and the meeting, just in case of security or other unforeseen problems,' replied a flagging John. 'What about you, Phil?' he asked.

'Yeah, I'm in agreement with you both, but one more point. Is it more secure for one of us to stay in the car, either outside his home or elsewhere, and, of course, all keep our mobile phones open just in case we need to instantly communicate? We've done similar before,' he said.

'Yeah, I agree with all that. Perhaps its best that you, John, stay in the car outside Hedge's house,' suggested David.

'OK, no problems, Dave.'

'The final, and most important, point is when we return with the cocaine, unlike before, I suggest on this occasion we put the briefcase holding the stuff in the loft of that outside shed. You never know if people have seen things in the past. Walls do have eyes, as well as ears, lads,' emphasized David Ford in a carefully reassured voice.

At around 1 pm, Cedric and John made their way, on the A39, to Barnstaple. Cedric wasn't told why they were driving there, and he certainly didn't ask. He knew his rank. As far as he was concerned, it was an enjoyable drive across Exmoor and through several small quaint villages, forgotten by modernity. The very fortunate souls, he thought. Wild flowers grew in abundance along the quiet main road. Either side of it was farming country. The lush green grass sparkled in the afternoon sun. What a contrast it all was to the crowded dirty streets that Nelson experienced every day of his abysmal life, thought Cedric.

Cedric parked in the high street, while John, wearing his neat green suit, walked into the bank, holding the suitcase. He resembled, Cedric suddenly thought, one of those office types, who used to walk over London Bridge and throw a few coins into his cap when he was homeless. But seeing the well-dressed, healthy overweight people of this area, he assumed there were very few, if any, homeless. As usual, his mind would instantly fantasize over its immediate surroundings. Sometimes, he saw things in graphic details. His eyes were drawn towards an ageing cob horse. The stout white male was harnessed to a delightful four-wheeled cart, full of timber and two well-oiled axes. That was the sort of life he craved, once again. To work in a forest, selling produce to local people. Just a horse as a companion, he declared. Cedric didn't ask for much, but even that was no more than a dream. But it kept him going. The alternative was damaging self-harm and deep-rooted vindictive abuse against the world.

However, he held onto the fantasy of living in Ford's cottage. If it materialised, Cedric's life could substantially improve. The bleak emptiness could be changed. There was a different way of life to be had if only he knew how he could change his present conditions. He had already dreamt about painting the inside of the cottage. The garden would be designed to an attractive display of shells, rocks and old sailing memorabilia. He would encourage people to add their own pieces to it. He would also buy fish caught by local people. God, please help.

'Right, Cedric, apologies for the delay. The old codger couldn't find his glasses,' said John, who was actually questioned in detail by the manager about the large amount of cash. But all, he hoped, was soothed over.

'No problem, John,' said Cedric who loved the idea of watching people from a secure distance. Just observing, he could be anyone at any time. Such was the case in the children's home, where they were locked up for the night in cold dormitories. Mind you, given the opportunity, he might well have risked severe punishment if he had been one of the fortunate boys who regularly stole food.

Within less than an hour, they had arrived back at Sandyridge Bay. Inside the cottage, they were greeted with a large glass of wine. Phillip was preparing salad, which would accompany the two large dressed crabs he had bought from the local fisherman. It all seemed light years away compared to the austerity of Oaks Lodge, thought Cedric. The three collaborators appeared to be more grounded after their soul-searching discussions. It wouldn't be long before David picked up his mobile phone and arranged that final meeting. Over the years, some of the previous deals had all been difficult, not only due to financial negotiations, but the accumulated stress involved in dealing with snakes like Hedges. Given the opportunity, he would sing like a canary, as they say in criminal circles. But all was nearly at the end!

'Right, tuck in, everyone. Help yourselves, I'm not your fucking nursemaid,' bellowed Phillip.

'Yeah, great stuff, Phil,' said John, who looked well pleased.

'Thanks, Phil,' said Cedric.

'Thank you, mummy,' laughed Dave, whose stress levels rose every time he thought about that phone call. 'Oh, by the way, Cedric, the three of us have to go out sometime late this afternoon. Please feel free to do whatever you fancy. Why not explore the coast path?' David suggested.

'Yeah, good idea, Dave. I've brought my boots with me.'

'But, Cedric, be careful of those nudists who gallivant up there. I'm told they pin you down, get out old bill and give it a good pull.' They all laughed at another of Dave's absurd jokes.

'All have another large glass of wine, lads?' asked John, mindful that was his third glass as he needed to have his wits about him later.

There was a general discussion about the evening's activities. Should they go out in the car for a drive along the coast for a meal, or stay locally, or even buy wine and food and spend the night in? There was no consensus, but all would be sorted out after Dave had made that phone call. The time was right!

He walked to his bedroom. He was breathing heavily. After five minutes of deep breathing, he prepared himself. With the phone held in his left hand, the right hand went to push the buttons but it started trembling uncontrollably. Fuck it, he said to himself. Get yourself together, you've done this many times before. More deep breathing followed. He tried, once again, and succeeded in contacting Hedges.

'Hello, my friend.'

'Hello, you OK?' he asked.

'What time shall we meet?' asked David, who was feeling rather anxious.

'About 6 pm. No later, alright?'

'OK, 6 pm.'

David Ford gave out a mighty sigh of relief. His hands were still slightly trembling. He checked inside the briefcase, once more, to see that the 50 £1000 bundles were correct. Also, the small meter to check he wasn't buying rubbish, and small scales to weigh the correct amount he was buying. All was set for the finale!

He returned from his bedroom with an artificial smile that informed his two accomplices the deal was on. It was tangible that Ford, who would be the mouthpiece for the deal, was feeling immense guilt. It was something that he would have to deal with when he returned to Mortingbridge. His conscience kept snapping at him to be brave, recognise and accept what he had done to others! He was the one that led his two friends into selling cocaine in the first place. He promised them big money with little hassle. They could have refused his offer but continued.

'Well, it's about time we set sail, lads. I've got everything in the suitcase,' said Ford, rather subdued.

'OK. I'll drive, Dave,' John held the car keys in his hand. He wasn't looking forward to the next hour or so. His thoughts were concentrated on his family, the home they had all built together and how he wished he was there, right now, having dinner with his family.

'As I said, Cedric, enjoy yourself. Have you got enough money? We'll see you later on,' said David Ford.

'OK, Dave. Oh, by the way, you don't have a rucksack I could borrow for this afternoon, do you?'

'Have a look in the shed.'

'Thanks. See you later.'

The three friends drove off, along the A399, to their last drug deal. The day was overcast. Several rooks pecked and ripped at the wayside carcass of a dead fox. That about summed up life, thought Phillip. Show any weakness and you're devoured. Something his father had constantly drummed into him when young, vulnerable and naive. Had he, somehow, misunderstood the message?

John pulled into a small lay-by 200 yards from the farm-house.

'Right, Dave. I'll stay in the car with my mobile open. If there's any danger, I'll text one word: danger. That means police cars or any other vehicle, which I suspect is involved with Hedges, OK?' said an emphatic John Tribe.

'Right, John. Let's go,' said David Ford.

The car pulled up outside the farmhouse. David Ford, briefcase in hand, and Phillip Knox walked slowly up to the large oak door. Phillip pressed the bell. There stood the large bulk of Hedges, a smirk on his face. Large money signs racing through his devious mind. He showed them into his home, the place they had got to know well over the years.

'Right, Dave, we have agreed on the amount you want to buy, right? And we have also agreed on the price you'll pay for the cocaine, right?' said the seller with an unequivocal and forthright attitude at the forefront of his mind. 'There is the cocaine. I'm sure you want to taste it and weigh it.'

David Ford reached for both the instruments. The weight

was correct, and after testing it twice, he knew the cocaine was the genuine stuff.

'Right, they are both OK,' said David Ford, who was anxious about whether the deal was being filmed on a hidden camera, and if there were tough heavies ready to pounce once he produced the cash.

'You've got the readies?' asked Hedges.

'Of course,' David pulled out the bundles of cash and placed them onto a small coffee table. Likewise, Hedges pulled out from under his seat a small machine that calculated the cash, £1000, each bundle separately. He was satisfied that it was correct. David put the cocaine and paraphernalia into his briefcase. The men shook hands and departed.

After a few miles, on the way back to Sandyridge Bay, John was the first to ask a question. He had to, after sitting inside the car for nearly an hour of suspense, unaware of the outcome of the deal, he had to hear it with his own unfettered mind.

'Everything went well, Dave? No problems?' he asked, near frantic with, anticipation.

'Yes, all is well, John. Everything weighed. The cocaine was the real stuff. He weighed the green music, all correct. Well done all of us. Phew, I'm fucked. No more, as we all agreed. Enough is enough, we're too old and fragile for this high intensity game. It's for younger people who have the energy, drive and motivation. Absolutely no more for me, I've had a belly full!' said an exhausted David.

'There's something evil about that farmhouse, its intangible but my instincts warn me to stay away from the fucking place. From the first time I took my first strides in the place, the walls appeared to try and crush my feelings. Sounds ridiculous, I know, but that bloke, I shouldn't think, has rarely spoken to another person or seen much of the outside world. It wouldn't surprise me if he has dead bodies hidden away in his cellar, amongst the rats and vermin that are prevalent around these ways.

'John, stop at this village and we can buy a few bottles of plonk and food for tonight. I don't fancy going out, do you?' asked David.

'No, neither do I, Dave,' said Phillip.

David Ford bought anything in sight such was his preoccupation with cocaine in the car. Anything that would get them pissed enough to change their consciousness for a while. Loaded with four bottles of red wine, four steaks, various fruit and vegetables, Dave Ford threw the lot onto the back seat of the car. If there hadn't been people around at that moment, he would have taken a drink straight from the bottle.

Back at Seaview Cottage, all was quiet once again. The first wine bottle was consumed within 30 minutes, such was the relief. At the forefront of Dave's mind, in particular, was where to safely hide the cocaine until their departure back home. He didn't want it left inside the cottage, just in case they were visited unexpectedly by someone. Other times, they had used various places to hide their acquisition, sometimes changing it every other day. Dave had thought of burying it in his garden, deep in the sand. But after considerable thought, he agreed with others to hide it in the loft of the outside shed. The shed was about 20 feet long, ten feet wide and formerly used by Dave, and once leased to a local carpenter as a workshop. He had built a gantry some time ago, to accommodate kayaks, timber and other miscellany. The cocaine would be safe and dry up there, and out of the way!

'Cheers lads,' said Phillip, opening the second bottle of wine. 'I'll stick those steaks in the oven on a medium heat so they are well cooked. It's not the best of meat. I'll also cut all the vegetables, sprinkle with herbs and spices, and leave them all for about an hour or so,' he explained, now relaxed after two large glasses of wine.

'Where did Cedric go, Dave?' asked John.

'Fuck knows, mate. I hope he's enjoying himself, though.'

Cedric arrived back three hours later. He looked energised and refreshed from taking a ten mile walk on the coast path. The sea-salt had, somewhat, browned his lean features. Up there, among the clouds, as he saw it, he was in his element. Alone, free, the wind blowing in his face and various birds screeching at him, all added up to the most enjoyable day in ages. Why couldn't he move down here, he thought? He didn't necessarily have to live in Dave Ford's cottage. It would be terrific if he could, but there were plenty of other ways of living around the West Country coast. The big detached houses he had passed hours earlier, he kept mulling over in his mind were a case in question. He could write to some of them to enquire whether they required a residential gardener come maintenance person. There were different ways of looking at the prospect of living near the sea. He would, when on his own, give the subject more consideration. He needed space, time, silence—all enforced conditions originating from St Michaels.

'Hi, Cedric, did you enjoy the day out?' asked Dave joyfully, now into his fourth large glass of wine. 'Where have you been? I hope one of those decadent nature lovers didn't rob you of your trousers?' he ribbed Cedric.

'I've had a long walk along the coast path. I really enjoyed it, the longest walk in ages. My old legs are now feeling tired,' he said.

'We've kept hot food in the oven for you, Cedric. Eat as much as you wish,' said Phillip, who was looking forward to sea fishing tomorrow. 'Fancy sea fishing tomorrow, Cedric?' he asked. His cheeks were blushed red by the consumption of alcohol.

'Not for me. I can't swim, and besides, I'm frightened of the sea,' he explained.

The night wore on. The three friends continued laughing and joking about previous holidays. Great times, but soon faded into the past. They shared the last half a bottle of wine. All of them excited by the prospect of sea fishing with Graham Hind, a local fisherman renowned for catching an abundance of crab and consuming large quantities of rum. They ventured out to sea every year they went on holiday together. Looking half-wrecked on wine, they thought it wise to hit the sack.

Cedric, however, remained on his own, thinking of tomorrow. What could he do, where should he go? The opportunities were endless. He must make the best of the few days he had down there. Perhaps read newspapers and shop adverts for gardening vacancies, or, he thought, he could write out his own advert requesting work. Leave his, or rather his employer's, mobile phone number, and see what happens, he thought. Before jumping into bed, he decided to have one last look at the sea. That ageless, fathomless wonder had always bewildered him since childhood. Stories from the nuns of various sea monsters had bewitched countless generations of children from St Michaels. Even today, he could recount those haunting stories as he surveyed the dark sea. A part of him still believed those fairy tales, recounted so eloquently by the young Irish nuns.

At 6 am the next morning, Cedric was awoken by the terrific noise of someone shouting and knocking on the front door. 'Police, police, open up immediately before we knock the door down,' could be heard a hundred yards away. The whole household was abruptly shaken to its bones of the calamity coming from outside. David Ford, in his pyjamas, quickly made his way to the door.

'What is this?' he shouted from inside, confused and frightened.

'It's the police, open the fucking door, otherwise, we shall break it down.' Behind the officers stood the artillery, comprising of two police cars and a large van.

'I'll give you five seconds,' shouted a uniformed officer.

David pushed back the internal bolts, unlocked the latch and was confronted by several police officers.

'I have a legal warrant to search this cottage. Step aside.' Six officers, one had a headstrong dog on a lead, rushed into his home. The full force of the law was now upon them.

'Search a bedroom each. Take the dog in every room. Give every inch of this place a thorough search. Leave nothing unturned,' demanded the senior officer. 'Is your name David Ford, and do you own these premises?' he asked.

'That's right. These men are all my friends. We're down on

holiday,' said David, trembling in anticipation of the consequences to come.

'I'm Superintendent Hay from Barnstaple Police Station.
Give your names and addresses to my officer. All of you stay
in this dining room until we have completed our search,' he
said with a voice of absolute authority.

'What are you looking for, officer?' asked Ford who, of
course, knew why he was there and was praying that they
wouldn't find the cocaine. Right now, he and his two friends
could only think of one thing. Had they been caught?

'I can't tell you that, sir,' remarked Hay.

'Would you mind if we made coffee, officer?' asked Phillip,
who had a hangover from the binge the night before.

'No, stay where you are,' said Hay rather sternly, who realised that drugs were somewhere there, hidden away safely,
but the dog would eventually find them.

Another officer, older than Hay but inferior in rank, approached him 20 minutes later. His face looked grim.

'Nothing so far, governor,' he said.

'Search the car and outside building,' he demanded. 'Is
both the car and shed open, Mr Ford?' asked Hay, who looked
impeccable in his neatly pressed uniform, glittering with various badges on top of his shoulders. The symbol of a life dedi-
cated to public service, no doubt.

'Yes, they are open,' he said with a resigned look on his
face.

'Take the other officers and the dog, and give it a thorough
search,' he directed. His tall, stout demeanour ever present
wherever he trod.

Four officers and the Alsatian looked inside the car and

boot. Various papers, tools and tapes were found. All legitimate. The dog smelt and sniffed everything in sight. It hesitated but found no drugs. The last resort, to find the intended cocaine, was the large shed at the back of the cottage.

It appeared that the old dilapidated shed hadn't been used for some time. However, one keen-eyed experienced officer, Andrew Dell, realised that, among the cat shit, cobwebs, spiders, dust and other crap, someone had recently been in there. The old door had been opened. Foot marks had scuffed the rotting floor. They led him to the sealed loft above, at the end of the shed. He and the other three officers removed old, ageing bicycles and various tools to one side. Up the ladder, Dell pushed open the hatch to reveal a dark, musty space. His torch revealed dead rats, birds, their nests, and rotting timber. In one dark corner, hardly visible, was a brown briefcase leant against the wall. He climbed in for a more detailed search.

'Dave, place the dog on the ladder in front of you and push it up through the hatch,' asked Dell rather excitedly.

Dell encouraged the dog to sniff around, pointing him towards the briefcase. Immediately, he became excited, started barking and scratching at the worn leather. The officer opened it up, which revealed two bags of white powder. They had hit the jackpot. Their information was correct. They had got them. There would be no wriggling out of this illegal cocaine possession worth a fortune on the open market.

'Well done, boy. We've got the bastards,' said Dell, patting and rubbing the dog's head. Sandy, the police dog, had been handled by Dell for six years ever since he was a puppy. They had worked on many successful searches and raids together. The dog's prize was a rubber toy to chew.

The superintendent was quickly summoned by his sergeant to view what they had just found. He looked at it, felt it and knew immediately it was cocaine. Superintendent Hay had justified the cost of surveillance, personnel and transport. He was delighted by the outcome. Another pip for that bulging shoulder was justified.

Supported by his five officers, Hay walked to the living room where the four men had been apprehended. The following he had performed many times:

'I am arresting the four of you for illegally possessing a Class A drug under the misuse of drugs act 1971. Anything you may say will be...'

The four men were handcuffed and put into the van and taken to Barnstaple Police Station. There, the humiliation began. All four were photographed, fingerprinted, personal possessions taken and individually locked in a cell until the next morning. Before that, each one was interviewed and signed a statement. Cedric was gutted that he had also been charged when he was totally ignorant of what the others were doing. He tried to explain his position, and reason for being with the others. He didn't have a legal leg to stand on. As far as the police were concerned, he was in possession, along with the others, when the cocaine was found. His only chance of being discharged would come from the evidence of the others who could verify his innocence. From the station, they would appear the next day in the Magistrates' Court and, afterwards, if bail was refused, sent on remand to Exeter prison for seven days.

At midday, a tray of food for each prisoner was passed through a tiny hatch in the cell door. Cedric, of course, had been in police cells before. He knew what to expect if they were sent to prison. Before, he had pleaded guilty to various charges. All minor compared to charges he now faced. Fair enough, he thought to himself, but on this occasion, he was fucking innocent. Those bastards next door knew it. Cedric was fucked if they didn't confirm his innocence. Just think, he kept questioning himself, all the time they were down in Devon, they were drug dealing. It was all a sham the holiday spiel. What devious fuck pigs they were, all of them. They probably all had previous convictions. When he thought of all the pretence that Ford gave him and Nelson at Oaks Lodge, it made him so angry, that if he saw him again, he would do him an injury. For sure, he would see him, and the others, in the dock tomorrow. Given the opportunity, he would confront them. Failing that, he would deal with Ford in prison, he convinced himself of that.

It was not surprising that Cedric had always been a loner. He usually recognised bullshitters, charlatans and conmen from a mile off, but on this occasion, he was taken in by Ford's silky-smooth words. There he sat, in a cold cell, with no solicitor or anyone to help fight his corner. Acceptance seemed to be setting in already. What was the point in fighting anymore when all you received was lies, pretence, shit and futility? That word contradiction had, once again, surfaced into Cedric's awareness.

Cedric lay on his hard cell bed looking up at the dirty grey concrete ceiling. His thoughts focused on one action. He had come close to pulverising his body. Head-butt the wall until he lost consciousness. Severe damage this time was all that was needed to end it all. But, on this occasion, something held him back from jumping off the precipice to oblivion. Could have been his new-found friendship with Joe that gave him the courage to resist those pernicious thoughts. Or the confidence he had gained out of driving three strangers to Devon and socialising with them. Perhaps he had restrained himself, knowing that he was an innocent man. No one could take that away from him.

The other three sat numb and motionless in their cells. The suffering of others, who had taken cocaine, and no doubt, there had been victims, rampaged through their conscience. All of them were profoundly guilty of what they had done to others. Life would never be the same again, for themselves or their families. The poisons they pedalled for years had, no doubt, changed the lives of countless individuals. Thousands washed down the pathologist's drains. David Ford's wife knew what he was involved in and wisely decided to say nothing but left him for good, aware of his devious behaviour. All she was able to call him on departure was a double-faced money-grabbing bastard. She assumed the other two spouses never knew of their husbands' illegal drug dealings. Now, a potential life imprisonment awaited their presence.

Phillip Knox and John Tribe were just as complicit. Although Ford had initially set the cocaine deals up with the blokes who made the big money thereafter, they were led by greed to feed their insatiable appetite for more. But all three had made sufficient money, legally from their professions, why continue after years off of the police radar? Their grandchildren cherished their every step. Similar younger people

would have ingested the poisons that the three friends pedalled for profit.

Cedric realised, that all those return taxi journeys from
Oaks Lodge to London were to negotiate drug deals in clubs
with the people who made the really big money. Ford supplied the drugs. The public dealers had slaves who wrapped
the drugs in small packets to flood the market. Young, rootless, vulnerable and exploited, they're the sort of people those
millionaire gangsters used. And what's more, they were paid
nothing except to receive the poison they craved to stay alive.
The three friends—Ford, Knox and Tribe—did not participate
in that level of abhorrent activity. Nevertheless, without sup-
pliers, there would be no illegal drug deals. When he set up
deals, Ford used to always meet a different male at a different
location. He, or the other two, never met the ringleaders.

What part, if any, did Hedges play in the arrest of the
men holidaying at Sandyridge Bay? That is a difficult question
to unpack. That they had been valuable customers over the
years is correct. Just from those deals alone, Hedges would
have made a lot of money. The men were no financial or legal
threat to him. As they lived at least 150 miles from Exmoor,
they certainly weren't there to take over his patch of clients.
Besides, all three men were in their 70s and unlikely to start
touting for vulnerable youngsters to muscle in on Hedges'
manor, which could have pulled the money strings for those
in London, thereby carry out his business in relative geo-
graphical safety. Did he actually grass on them, if by doing so
the police would leave him alone, then it's possible he had.

The following morning, the four men stood shoulder to
shoulder in the small wooden dock. Wearing the same

clothes, washed and fed, the initial shock of being arrested had somewhat subsided. The defendants didn't speak to each other prior to the hearing. They looked around the courtroom with innocence and vulnerability. Two police officers sat feet from them, contentedly reading a newspaper. A young female solicitor sat alone on the front benches, playing with her mobile phone. This was familiar territory for Cedric. He wasn't that concerned with Magistrates' Court, it was the higher courts with judge, jury and barristers that made his anxiety levels rise. Right now, he was thinking that Ford's cottage was a lost cause. Instead of the possibility of living there, his only real concern was spending most of his retirement in clink. His coast fantasy now ruined.

'All rise in court,' said the police officer as three magistrates took their seats.

The clerk of the court asked the defendants to confirm their names. The crown solicitor stood up to outline the case. But before he did, he informed the magistrates that Cedric Bambridge had no case to answer and was free to leave the court. As he was about to step down from the dock, David Ford whispered to him.

'All three of us told the police you were innocent, Cedric.'

'Thanks, Dave,' he said.

The officer escorted him to a small musty room, just outside the court. The usual offensive institutional smells lingering of urine, bleach and smoke.

'Well done, Cedric. Here's your valuables, please sign for them,' he said without looking at him.

'What about the hired car?' Cedric asked, wondering how he was going to travel back home.

'That's been impounded,' he said. 'You will have to make your own arrangements to get home, mate.'

Cedric wasn't concerned. He was free. No more court appearances, he kept reminding himself. Well, at least they did the honourable thing by him and allowed the not guilty to walk free. He wondered whether they would plead guilty to drug dealing. In all honesty, he thought, what else could they do? He was a lackey and enjoyed the self-labelled status.

CHAPTER ELEVEN

Meanwhile, an exhausted yet jubilant Cedric Bambridge arrived back at Oaks Lodge. After two packed noisy trains and a slow bus, he was so pleased to be home. Even a dog kennel was five-star luxury when he considered that hours previously he was looking at the prospect of visiting Exeter prison. Wow, he pinched himself. I'm back here to continue my job. He left his case in the car park and walked to the garden to look at the plants that he and Nelson had planted. Bees and butterflies hovered around the flowers, drinking their fill of nectar. Daises, buttercups and speedwell covered the thick, green turf. Spontaneously, he fell on his back to the ground. It felt so sound, supportive and secure. He looked straight above him into infinity. All the accumulated anxiety of the past 24 hours fell into the soil. He hadn't felt so good in ages, such was the intense relief of being free. We crave for things our minds are fixed upon. Being an outsider had its merits, Cedric knew. Marriage or relationships he didn't need, though he occasionally thought about friendships. They too had their problems.

Expectations of others was something he couldn't measure. On his own, life was much less complicated.

'You alright, Cedric?' asked Derek Tranter, who found Cedric sleeping on the lawn.

'Yeah, Derek. I was lying on the lawn and thinking about the absurdity of life, I must have fallen asleep.'

'I saw your case in the car park but couldn't find yer. I thought you did a runner out of the Lodge for good. Anyway, Cedric, you're back early. I thought you were having seven days in Devon with Ford?' he enquired.

'You wouldn't believe it, Del. Let's have a cuppa inside before big bollocks arrives, and I'll explain what happened. It's like something out of a crime novel, honestly,' said Cedric incredulously.

As the two men walked slowly towards the reception area, David Richards pulled up in his flash car. If you wanted to feel bad about yourself, he was the person to guarantee you success. His big bulk hauled itself out of the car. Its presence had spoken. Occasionally, Cedric wished he had the guts, like Nelson, to punch his ugly face. But unlike his friend, he didn't want to eat crumbs living in a poor area of London.

'Hello, Cedric. Thank you for phoning me to explain your early return. Shall we go into the tea room and discuss what happened?' said Richards, who was anticipating an exciting account of David Ford's demise. Always happy to expunge the shit out of other people's decline, that was the shareholding boss. He had worked hard, though, from his parents' unreasonable expectations, to a minor Soho acolyte and now a shareholder of Cleanaway Ltd. Not surprising, therefore, that his anticipation of most outcomes was high. Who knows, perhaps behind that hard exterior there was a decent person.

'Could you explain in some detail what happened in Devon? From the arrest, the charge of cocaine possession, court appearance and your discharge. I need to know for legal and other reasons, Cedric,' asked Dave Richards, who didn't want to miss a word that involved a resident, or probably, former resident in Ford's case.

'Well, boss, it was something like this...'

'Look, take your time, OK? Think about the details. We have plenty of time, so think about the police, the three men who have been charged and your part, if any, in the cocaine,' said Richards, trying to grasp the situation.

'Well, as you know,' Cedric's breathing was laboured and he found it difficult to think straight. 'I drove Dave Ford and his two friends down to Devon for a weeks' holiday,' he said. Anxiety, once again, had invaded his inner life. Must be careful what he said to his boss, otherwise, he could lose his job. Those grimy London streets haunted him. He didn't want to upset Richards, who had the power to hire and fire, because Cedric knew at his age that he wouldn't survive being surrounded by the masses.

'Right, Cedric, what next? Take your time,' insisted Richards.

'Erm, well, we went to the beach and then the pub. Later, on the second or third day, the three of them had to go out somewhere. Oh, I remember, before they went out, I drove John, Dave's friend, to a bank in Barnstable. He went to the bank, holding a briefcase, while I stayed in the car.' Cedric was becoming confused. He racked his consciousness for more information, so his boss would take him seriously. Don't upset that bloke in front of you, he kept thinking to himself.

'Then what happened, Cedric?'

'Well, after we returned from the bank, they all went out in the car. I went out walking on my own, and when I returned to the cottage, they were all there. I think, yes, that's right. We had wine and food, it was an enjoyable evening, I recall, Mr Richards,' said a mumbling Cedric. What had he done to deserve this life, he constantly thought, when his subconscious reminded him of what one of the nuns had told him, and several other boys. They were impure. That God had sent them to the children's home to atone their sins. Those words had held him back during his life. He was no good, due to those pernicious words uttered by a young woman, just a few years older than him, he recalled.

'What happened next?'

'Well. We all went to bed, then around 6 am, there was loud banging on the door. It was the police. Four, five coppers and a dog, they searched the cottage and the shed. The bloke in charge told us we were being arrested for possession of a controlled drug. I was so confused, I forget what he actually said, but it was something to do with Misuse of Drugs Act 1971, I think that's what he said.'

'Then what happened, Cedric?'

'We were taken to Barnstaple Police Station and charged. This is the piece of paper they gave me. The next day in the local court, they dropped all charges against me. That's when I phoned you about it all,' said Cedric as he sobbed into his hands.

'Well, it's been a terrible—'

There was a loud knock on the door.

'Come in,' said an irritated Richards.

'Apologies, Mr Richards, Ms Fulton just phoned requesting your assistance,' said Derek Tranter. It was rather early
for her to phone. Perhaps the whispering grapevine had found
her ever listening ears.

'Right, Derek, I understand.'

'Thank you, Cedric. I'm sure it's been a difficult time for
you. It is important that my boss understands the nature of
what happened to one of our residents. Keep our discussion
confidential. I'll inform other staff not to speak to the press
or anyone else who doesn't live here. OK? And, don't forget,
you still have four more days of your holiday left.'

'Thank you,' said Cedric, pleased to hear he could spend
some time away on his own from problems that always appear, to lurk somewhere, unseen. His old case in hand, full
of broken dreams yet again, he walked to his flat. There,
he thought, he'd feel safe after the upheaval of the last few
days. But to his horror, he found that someone, during his
holiday, had broken into his flat and trashed the place. Although most of it worthless, even the old furniture had been
broken, his pots and pans smashed on the walls and clothes
ripped to pieces. The mindless shitheads had urinated on his
treasured soccer annuals, valued novels and hallowed punk
records. Most tragic of all, his only photograph—a black and
white one—of his parents had been torn in countless pieces.
Cedric was mortified at the carnage before him. He fell to
his knees and sobbed uncontrollably. How much more must a
man take before he is finally kicked into submission?

'Hello, David Richards speaking.'

'Hello, Mr Richards, how are you, my dear?' Ms Fulton asked in a quiet, friendly manner. No doubt, there was some serious information gathering to be had behind her self-righteous, frail exterior.

'I'm well, thank you. I hope you are too?'

'Yes, rather, Mr Richards. I saw you drive into the car park earlier and I thought, that's if you have the time, could you come up for a few minutes?' she asked, full of excitement and cunning.

'Yes, of course, Ms Fulton. There are one or two things I have to sort out, then I'll be there,' he said.

'Derek, you finish at 8 pm, don't you? Who's on the night shift, is it the same agency chap? What's his name?'

'Stan Cliff, he's from the same agency as the others. Good worker and gets on well with residents. He's done quite a few shifts recently,' said Derek who knew Cliff socially, and they had worked together years ago in construction.

'That's helpful. Tell him to keep coming in until further notice. OK, mate?' said Richards in an unusually friendly manner.

After inspecting the ground floor and plants for any sign of dirt, Richards made his way up to Ms Fulton's retreat. He opened the front door, as he was usually permitted to, and walked into the lounge. A sea of books lined the walls. Magazines were stacked on the coffee table. Books on international politics were spread across the floor. She kept her brain active, that was self-evident, but due to her deepening depression, she had recently been prone to phoning any time of the day. Of course, she was entitled to, but it was out of character.

'Good evening, Ms Fulton.'

'Hello, please sit down in the mist of all this clatter,' she said, her piercing brown eyes alive as ever. Looks can deceive, though, as many have found out.

'How can I help?' asked Richards.

'I was flabbergasted, listening to the evening news on Sky, to hear the awful news of Mr Ford and his two friends, charged with cocaine possession and intent to supply,' she said, pinching her scrawny neck in anticipation.

'I'm not aware of that news. I shall have to phone around to find out what has happened. Thank you for telling me. How are you keeping? I remember you informed me a few months ago of your depression. Has medication helped?' asked Richards, who was afraid the breaking news of Ford would soon be on everyone's lips. There was nothing he could do to stop it. It really wasn't his responsibility he was only concerned with the good name of Oaks Lodge.

'Well,' she hesitated, 'I'm not so bad. Sometimes things get on top of me. This problem has been around, on and off, for some time. Occasionally, I feel so low.'

'Would you like me to send for the doctor?' he asked, concerned that she might harm herself.

'No, no, thank you, my dear,' she said but her anorexic frame shouted otherwise.

Approaching midnight, Tom Flowers appeared in the reception. As usual, he was well-dressed, trimmed moustache, for a night out in one of London's shadowy night clubs. That much he had in common with David Ford. Now single and retired from engineering, he often took a taxi into the metropolis. Not to play chess, however, but to hobnob with those with deep pockets, and flaunt with shallow, gaudy young women.

At 77 years old, and an inveterate night owl, one must appreciate his stamina and fortitude amongst those money-grabbers. Was he another resident, searching by night, seeking out criminality in the concrete jungle called London?

'Good evening, Mr Flowers. You're bright and dandy, as always, sir,' said young Stan Cliff, aged 33, in desperate need of a full-time job. Full of soft soap, he would do and say anything if it got him a regular income.

'Hello, Mr Cliff, you're becoming a regular fixture nowadays,' he inquired.

'Yes, I'm hopeful they give me a regular job someday.'

'I say, did you hear about Mr Ford, one of our residents? According to the news, he and others have been charged with drug offences,' he remarked.

'No, I haven't heard that,' said Stan Cliff.

'Yeah, I hope it isn't true for his sake. That's a serious charge, that is. Anyhow, all the best, here comes my taxi,' said the Errol Flynn of Oaks Lodge.

'Hello, night porter speaking,' said Stan Cliff.

'Say, could I speak to David Ford, please?' the unknown male voice spoke.

'Sorry, he doesn't live here. Goodnight.' That was the instructions given to him by his boss.

Minutes later, another external phone call, it could only be the press or someone trying to get information, or hoax or prank calls. These situations are a paradise for the nighthawks. Those who have countless problems pick up their phones, or turn on the numerous gadgets out there to create havoc. Instant news becomes instant reaction. If you have a crap in a Fulham Broadway alley, within minutes, you're likely to receive a text or email from a Chinese takeaway in Florida.

'Good evening, night porter.'

'Good evening. I'm trying to contact my uncle, his name is David Ford,' said the softly spoken female voice.

'No one of that name lives here. Goodnight.'

Within minutes, Stan was overwhelmed by internal and external phone calls. As he spoke to a resident about Ford's drug charges, three journalists were taking photographs of Oaks Lodge. He immediately ran out to explain they were on private property. That's what the boss informed him to tell anyone who ventures onto the Lodge soil. He felt superior doing it. Power at last, he gloated. Stan also phoned the police to ask for their support. One car did arrive not long after, and the hacks were told, in no uncertain terms, not to enter the premises. They could stand in the road, but go any nearer and they would be nicked.

'Yes, sorry, Mr Black, our conversation was rudely interrupted by journalists taking photos of Oaks Lodge. What did you want? I've forgotten,' said a flustered night porter. Not only was he seeking attention, his usual 2 am comfort, but he was also trying to prise information out of the night porter.

'Is it true about our Mr Gould?' he said in a drunken voice.

'Sorry, who is Mr Gould?'

'You know, the chappie in the news. He lives in apartment two.'

'Mr Ford, that is.'

'Sorry, how silly of me. Would you like a nightcap, my dear boy?' asked Black.

'I'm afraid I can't, Mr Black, I'm very busy right now but hopefully another time, goodnight, sir.'

So, it continued, unabated, for several hours, until Derek Tranter calmly walked into reception unaware what lay ahead.

That same morning, around the time Black phoned, three men were hiding in woods belonging to a large private estate. Wearing black overalls, balaclavas and gloves, they had been waiting two hours for security guards to leave the unoccupied premises. On the ground was their bag of tools to open various secured doors and windows of the early Georgian Manor, in West Berkshire. Reliable information had informed the thieves that inside was full of jewels, pictures, books and furniture. The upper crust owners were away on holiday, ensconced in their inherited Scottish castle. They were shooting deer with friends on a Highland Moor, land long ago stolen.

As there was far too much to take away, their only target was one item—jewels. They had been given computerised detailed plans of the ten-bedroom country pile. The information had cost them thousands. But the family jewels, dating from the 15th century, would repay that outlay many times over if successful in negotiating the modern alarm system. Once that was unravelled by an expert, Sean Derbyshire, the rest was a doddle, according to their information. Sean didn't graft for peanuts. He didn't have to after a succession of successful heists.

He had known Sammy Burns for many years. They served time together before they both learnt to keep away from police. Nelson was introduced to him only during the last few weeks. Nelson's reliable reference was Burns. That satisfied the man who had the brains to make them all financially healthier. The fourth man, known only as Victor, was the car driver and wouldn't be needed until they made their escape. He was parked several miles away but near enough to be ready in minutes if needed. They were all in mobile phone contact.

It was about 2 am when the guards eventually left Heydon Manor. Well hidden amongst the ageing conifers, the three men made their way to an outlying building where the main electricity supply had to be switched off. Their rustling movements made some birds take flight. Owls could be heard nearby. Being completely camouflaged, it wasn't dangerous for the men being caught on the CCTV cameras. They wouldn't be checked until the next day. Nelson's steel crowbar opened the large, re-enforced steel doors. They all stood still for a moment to listen for any unsuspecting noise. The manor stood in 100 acres a mile from the nearest village. Any artificial lights could be seen a distance off by the public.

Sammy and Sean went inside the small building, as Nelson stood guard outside, armed with his three-foot jemmy. Using a dim light to read the electric circuit system, Sean worked diligently to disarm the source of power that closed down all cameras and alarms inside and outside the building. Many hours of meticulous studying of the plans had been successful. He went back over them to make sure he had disarmed anything that could be triggered once inside the house. Sean was satisfied that he had covered all eventualities.

They stood outside the building where all the electricity supplies were housed. They secured the doors with wire. Nelson held the large bag of power and hand tools. The silence was overwhelming. The intensity of the moment made them aware of each and every minute sound. The only independent security light, that couldn't be switched off, shone from the front of the house. That was no problem for them. They knew the easiest way in was through a side door, adjacent to the kitchen. Once again, the mighty jaws of the jemmy easily prised open the door. They were inside another world. Nearly all the interior was suggestive of a world far removed from the modern one, where the three thieves now stood. The ceiling plaster, woodcarving, balustrade, wall and floor decorations, chandelier, even the old ceramic sink most of it nearly 300 years old. Some of it originally installed in the early 18th century. Who knows, possibly graced by King George 1st. No doubt, its extravagance was paid for by the excessive profits of industrialisation.

They immediately made their way to the master bedroom, where a small wall safe was located. The tall resplendent pelmets and thick drapes gave them added cover from the outside. It also helped reduce the noise of the powerful hand drill. Using a dim light, Nelson gave the electric drill to Sean. Sammy held the plans, as Sean drilled around the thick lock. Fortunately, the metal was soft 19th-century iron, and not as strong as modern materials. In 40 minutes, the hard drill had penetrated around the safe lock, and Sean, using a small club hammer, smashed it out. He pulled open the door. Four small, square trays glittered into his eyes. There the beauties sat—diamonds, sapphires, rubies and other precious stones. Their information was spot on. They had hit the jackpot.

Sean handed them down to his two accomplices. Also inside the safe were the deeds of the house, various bonds and private family trusts. They decided to leave them, although they thought the private bonds, unseen by H M Inspector of Taxes, should be sent anonymously to various national newspapers.

The four trays spread out on his master's bed looked as if their days of worrying over money was finished.

'I can't fucking believe it,' said an ecstatic Nelson, handling glittering top-notch diamonds, with his large firm hands, for the first time.

'Well, lads, it's a good morning's work. After my contact has completed his work on them, and taken his cut, we'll have six figures each. It's only with great fucking reluctance that we have to leave all the other priceless stuff. But we're out of our league trying to fence pictures or furniture. Besides, we haven't got the space in a small saloon car to take most of it,' said Sean Derbyshire.

'That's right, Sean. We don't wanna go over the top,' remarked Sammy Burns, who was already thinking that this would be his last job, but that's what all villains say... until the next time comes around.

'It's enough to make you cry, though, lads, when you see all this wealth to leave it behind. If I had my way, I would even take those turkeys hanging in the kitchen,' Nelson laughed. 'Good times ahead, brudders,' he said.

'One word of caution, lads, don't rush to spend. Just continue your everyday things. Same food, pub, car, whatever. You both know the score. You know the eyes of people miss very little,' said Sean, who wasn't going to make a fatal mistake. In his case, it certainly was the final heist. He had invested his ill-gotten gains very shrewdly over the years. He and his wife were retiring to the French countryside. They had bought a smallholding some years ago. For most of that time, he had planned robberies, entertained gangsters and milked a few goats that he had inherited from the estate agent. It was a perfect rural idyll for both of them. Sean and his wife were socialised in a rundown area of Manchester, where dogs ate as much as the kids. The terraced housing was full of dry rot, overcrowding and petty thieving. Sean carried a bigger helping of life around with him. From nicking supermarket food, trashing motors for the insurance money, and housing benefit fraud on a large scale, he eventually met the blokes who really mattered. He'd done his time, like Sammy and Nelson. But now, it was his turn to enjoy a life off the beaten track in France.

The next day, social media spin had got the vibes of a massive jewel heist in affluent Berkshire, where family tofts, originating from Conquest, lived. One of them, Lord Shank, had been turned over for £10 million. That's the spiel his solicitor sung to the waiting media outside the high, steel gates of the enormous estate. An estate owned by a succession of Lords and Ladies who benefited from the suffering of others. The three rascals had taken their share of the ill-gotten gains accrued by those who are now establishment figures. At least one aristocrat had been kicked up the arse.

So incensed was Nelson at the time, though he said nothing to the others, he wanted to set fire to the place that symbolised grotesque exploitation. In fact, he wanted to shit all over the bedsheets and imagined Lord Shank returning to witness the rancid brown pile all over his inherited silks. All three men could only imagine the countless people who had toiled, over the centuries, from dawn to dusk for pittance.

But, of course, they all knew that they had to keep a tight lid on their hostile feelings. They couldn't rewrite history!

12

CHAPTER TWELVE

Mr Justice Khan walked out dressed in a long scarlet robe, black sash and fading white wig. He took his seat up high, overlooking mere mortals below. He kept his head still and fixed on papers in front of him. It felt like an hour, but in reality, maybe several minutes he kept them waiting. There was no sound at all. Intense times for all concerned, as his authority immediately permeated the packed courtroom. Barristers of all schools knew him as a stickler for manners, time wasters, he scolded and, worst of all, would openly warn anyone who was stepping out of line. Enough said about the ageing judge.

He eventually looked down at the assembled, a slight nod to old adversaries and half a smile to newcomers. After another two minutes had passed, he was ready for the prosecution counsel to open proceedings against those in the dock.

Ford, Tribe and Knox had spent three months, on remand, in Exeter Prison. No champagne, large scotches or lobsters on the menu there! Considering the gravity of their offences, it was a relatively short period of time to wait. The probable reason for this outcome was that they all decided to plead guilty. With the overwhelming evidence against them, they had very little opportunity to manoeuvre. They decided that it would be more practicable, amongst other considerations, to retain the same solicitor and counsel. All sing from the same hymn book, thought John Tribe.

During their enforced tenure at prison, they had all been busy instructing their solicitor about the case. This had been conducted over several sessions. The solicitor listened, they explained and legal costs rose every minute. Mitigation being their only saviour, they were most concerned, as were their spouses, about the prison sentences they would inevitably receive.

Ford was rather aggrieved that only his young nephew came to visit him once... he was hoping to be included in his will. No others bothered, although he did receive several letters from friends and colleagues. When in trouble, friends and family run for cover. He didn't expect any London gangsters would write to him, wishing him an enjoyable time! This was one occasion when money wouldn't buy them freedom.

Conversely, Tribe and Knox received weekly visits from various family members. It kept up their morale. As they were on remand, fresh clothes, food and other materials were a most welcome source of supply. But most of all, it was the emotional contact that kept them going. The smiling faces, warm kisses and gentle reassurance. They realised the short-sighted stupidity of what they had been doing. That, of course, is the usual reaction when you face adversity. Piss on your shoes, Cedric should have told them. Do your time.

They had certainly shit on him and rubbed it in. He was so pleased the bastards were staring at long prison sentences. He wouldn't shed any tears. The defendants braced themselves for substantial sentences. They were fortunate that no further charges relating to previous drug deals would be brought before the court. Otherwise, they were looking at spending their remaining days in prison.

The prosecution QC, Percy Mills, was known as a wily old fox with an enduring smile upon his ageing, battle-hardened face. He outlined the case against the defendants in a clear, precise and meticulous manner. Emphasizing the devious plans to travel to Devon, withdraw £50,000, meet up with their supplier and then return to London with the goodies. He went into detail involving the logistics the defendants used to open different bank accounts. Similar to other experienced advocates, Mills was a consummate seasoned actor. It was a game of eloquent words, played out for him on high.

Only once throughout the whole proceedings did he look up at the judge. His eyes fixed straight ahead, though mesmerised by an outstanding debt or wishing he was in the bar quaffing claret. His ears like early radar systems, his short, fat body didn't miss a word. His heaving frame had been treading the West Country courtrooms for at least 30 years. He was equally known in the pubs for his outrageous wit and drunken schoolboy jokes. Aged 64, he was popular with the young barristers, those craved to learn his skills over bottles of claret.

'With regards to the defendants,' he said, 'their actions speak loud and abundantly. All of them over 70 years old, educated, professional men who had the negotiating skills to

256 - BARRY MERCHANT

maximise their booty,' said Mills, who brought a wry smile from some of the assembled.

After cross-examining the two senior officers who were involved in finding the cocaine in Ford's cottage, a formality, he concluded his case for the crown.

Defence lawyer, Sidney Silver QC, tried to make the best of a lost cause. His mitigation was based more on trying to address the heart, not the head, of the judge. He emphasized their lowly position in the drug chain, but Mr Silver realised his pretentious appeasement fell on deaf ears. The battling counsel tried, in vain, to portray the defendants as willing victims, who didn't really understand the murky world of illegal drugs and its evils.

'In their middle-class position, they hadn't experienced the world of the weak, wrecked and forgotten users who ingested what they sold,' said Mr Silver, who tried passionately, forcibly, yet abysmally to explain their criminal actions. He was treading water, as far as the judge was concerned. He had heard it all before. A million times!

'To conclude, my Lord, they were three naive old fools, who thought they could make some pin money on top of the considerable wealth. Money wasn't the motive for the serious charges they now face in court today. It was a once in a lifetime experience that went too far. They apologise profusely to all who have been affected by their irresponsible and illegal actions,' he said. Another handsome pay-day for the ageing well-versed public school-educated barrister.

Before sentencing the three men, the judge was informed that one defendant, David Ford, had a previous conviction for possession and supplying of drugs. That was 40 years ago, of which he was sentenced to four years imprisonment. The other two defendants had no previous convictions.

Due to their age and financial positions, the judge did not require social or probationary reports. The final duty for the judge was sentencing. After retiring to think about the case, the judge told the prisoners to rise.

'You have all pleaded guilty to possessing, with intent to supply to another person or persons, a controlled drug. This comes under the Misuse of Drugs Act 1971. I have taken into consideration what your counsel had to say. I have also considered your ages, and your previous professional careers. In light of what I have been informed today:

David Cecil Ford, you are sentenced to ten years imprisonment. And you will be fined the sum of £50,000.

Phillip Knox, you are sentenced to seven years imprisonment. And you will be fined the sum of £50,000.

John Tribe, you are sentenced to seven years imprisonment. And you will be fined the sum of £50,000.

Take them down,' ordered the judge. He had not been fooled by the well-paid pleadings on their behalf.

The whole legal proceedings were concluded in less than six hours.

There were half-muffled screams and shouts to be heard from the public gallery. The defendants' families had made their feelings known by reaching out to the men they loved.

'See you later, sweetheart,' shouted Tribe's wife.

'Oh, no, I can't believe it,' cried another.

'Love you, Dad,' came another supportive voice from Knox's two sons.

The middle-aged female court attendant sitting nearby

asked the families to keep quiet. Her grey face wasn't impressed by the emotional rants of over-excited people. Years of sitting down and just listening to countless cases had made her insensitive and indifferent of those endless souls suffering for their loved ones. Understandable, one wouldn't argue against.

'Please stop shouting in court. Otherwise, I shall have to ask you all to leave,' the attendant informed the families, in no uncertain manner, that they weren't in a public house or watching a football match. It was all in a day's work for her. Deference to those below in the court arena was her only narrow concern.

That evening, Cedric Bambridge had just minutes earlier started the night shift. As he made tea in the staffroom, it was being announced on the television of the sentences handed down to the three men he went on a short-lived holiday with.

'Yes,' shouted Cedric as he punched the air in jubilation. 'They got what they fucking deserved.'

With Richards' instructions in mind, he had to proceed with caution. But now it was public knowledge, there was very little he could do or say to residents about the matter. Social media was very different. His boss told him what to say to phone callers of dubious origin. Also, journalists were to be kicked off of private premises, or phone the police, Richards emphasized several times.

Cedric sat in the reception area thinking about the holiday that never materialised. Just before police burst into the cottage and ransacked the place, he enjoyed being with three men he didn't know. They all appeared to be decent and friendly blokes. They all sunned themselves, drank wine under a parasol and felt relaxed under the blue sky. Cedric had enjoyed the personal discussion he had with John in the local pub. John had suggested that Cedric might enjoy visiting his home sometime to meet his family. His confidence grew during an evening of excess alcohol and food. He felt like one of the lads for the first time in his life. They confided in him, which shocked Cedric. No one during his life had ever disclosed that type of personal information before. Mind you, he hadn't been in that particular kind of company before. But it indicated, so Cedric surmised at the time, that they thought him an OK guy. But they were setting him up as a fool. Never mind, he thought, they weren't the first, but they will certainly be the last. It exhibited his lack of worldly experience. It was correct, he reflected, he was unable to read body language, along with all its nuances and hidden messages. Cedric knew he was naive, easily duped and prone to ridiculous bouts of fantasy. They were in prison for the foreseeable future, however, he was free to come and go. He had a job, home and a small wage. Days off was time for walking, travelling on buses and trains, and basking in the summer sun. There were fish and chips, a few beers and visits to the flowers that he and Nelson had planted years ago in Marsh Wood. In the scheme of things, not momentous endeavour, but he was free as a bird, unlike those buffoons locked up behind bars.

'Good evening, night porter,' said Cedric.

'Hello, good evening, Bambridge. I was phoning about that horrible news concerning Mr Ford. Ridiculous sentence, wasn't it?' commented Ms Rees, who although somewhat of a recluse, missed the occasional discussions she had with the late Miss Holroyd.

'Yes, Ms Rees, it was rather harsh, wasn't it?' said Cedric, laughing all over his face. He only wished it had been life imprisonment. She didn't know, and he wasn't about to inform anyone, that he was there. Cedric knew the aged criminals would serve most of their sentence in an open prison. Being similar to holiday camps, Cedric had once served time in one, so they wouldn't be deprived of most things. Fresh air, relatively good food, exercise and social activities abound in those places. And it made Cedric's blood boil to think they were prime candidates for parole. He knew that they would serve less than half of their original sentences. When he was in prison in his early 20s, he met old men who had served many years for stealing a pittance compared to the cocaine dealers he had the misfortune to meet.

'Well, take care, Bambridge,' she muttered.

'Goodnight.' Well, at least the residents were calling him by his surname once again. He felt reassured. He felt accepted by some people, even if they thought him to be inferior. That's the lot in a life of a flunkey. Were residents happy in their self-made prisons, reading their books, research papers and bibles? Maybe, maybe not, it all depended upon conditions. Yes, of course, Cedric had realised that people incessantly played games. What for? He couldn't care. He was no different; he had tried to get his own back on the residents. He let them think they were superior to him, and so it continued. How absurd life really is!

Outside phone calls continued barking. Cedric handled them as his boss had ordered. Two blokes were seen taking photographs of Oaks Lodge from the road. Cedric was disappointed that they didn't take a mug shot of him. If only the journalists had realised what treasures were to be had. He could have revealed all to those undeserving scumbags who loiter, hide and flash their cameras, what really happened in Devon, but it wasn't worth a second thought. He'd had enough of it all.

'Good morning, Mr Black, how are you?' asked Cedric, who was anticipating the pissed old chap would phone at some stage murmuring incoherently, as usual.

'Hello, my dear boy, how are you, Mr Bambridge?' asked the pathological attention seeker. It was passed 2 am, and the inveterate alcoholic was mumbling, gurgling and talking an alien language. Cedric was used to it by now. He had heard that voice and frequently experienced its evil smelling mouth for many years. All part of the service he provided.

'I'm well, sir. How are you?' asked the night porter.

'Well, to be honest, I'm a bit drunk. You know me by now, my dear boy. Would you fancy a tipple later?' he asked, praying that Cedric would agree. Owning plenty of money, like most residents, but saw very few people to enjoy it with. He was a tragicomedy with the lead role. As Cedric had questioned for years, were they happy?

'I'm busy right now, Mr Black. Maybe later, sir.' He had been saying the same thing for years, around about this time of the morning. Occasionally, Cedric did go there for a quick drink hoping, in the meantime, to be included in his will. He often wondered who would inherit the old buffer's wealth. He was single, owned an apartment worth at least one million pounds, yet it appeared there was no obvious person, or persons, to inherit. Over the years, there had been a succession of men visiting him. They could have been lovers, friends or colleagues, but no one had appeared in the last three years or so.

'Is that you, Bambridge?' asked a quiet, fading voice.

'Yes, that's right, Ms Fulton.'

'Please, could you come immediately? I don't feel well.'

'Of course, I'll be there in two minutes,' he said. What was it this time that needed urgent attention at 3 am?

He jumped up from the reception chair and rushed up to the third floor. The door was wide open. He walked in, not knowing what to expect. The whole sitting room was in disarray. She was the kind of person who usually, until of late, kept everything in order. She was fastidious in the extreme. Civil servants, Cedric was informed, have that ability to locate anything, anytime when required. That's the nature of their profession.

'Hello, I'm not well,' she said, her voice distinctly losing its strength by the second. Cedric was in a panic, he hadn't encountered this type of behaviour from her before.

'How can I help, Ms Fulton?' He had a quick scan of the room, hoping there might be a trinket, ring or small cash he could flash into his pocket.

'I'm not well. I've been taking too many of those pills,' she pointed to a small, labelled bottle on the coffee table. Several small brown pills were scattered around it.

'I'll phone for the doctor,' he said, his hands shaking as he fumbled inside his pocket for the mobile phone. At that moment, Ms Fulton fell to the ground unconscious. Anxiety reared its ugly head. He hadn't been trained to deal with this type of problem. He picked her up from the floor and sat her on the sofa. He put his arms around her and reassured her all was well. He hadn't phoned for a doctor yet. What should he do? Ms Fulton was unconscious, and he didn't want to leave her. Should he phone for the ambulance, or doctor, or the police? He continued to hold her in his arms. Her breathing was shallow. He felt like running out of the room to safety. His conscience scolded him. He placed her head on a pillow and phoned the ambulance. Her warm, thin body was losing its fight for life. Has she taken an overdose? His instinct told him all was certainly not well.

Ten minutes later, the blue light of the ambulance lit up the building. Cedric was there to escort the two hurried workers to Ms Fulton's apartment. It appeared that she was still unconscious. One gave her artificial respiration, while the other prepared to use a small canister of oxygen. The former got no response from the lifeless body. He quickly ran downstairs for the trolley. The older worker turned her on her side and phoned the local A&E department to warn them of a casualty that would soon arrive. As they were unable to communicate with her, she was kept on her side for a while. She was lifted onto the trolley, made comfortable and swiftly taken down to the ambulance. Within minutes, the vehicle sped out of Oaks Lodge and made its way to the hospital.

Cedric didn't touch anything in her apartment, but was surely tempted. He was mindful that the police, Richards, and any number of people could start asking questions. After locking the front door, he made his way down the stairs, passing three residents before he arrived back at reception. Cedric shook uncontrollably after the trauma of trying to help Ms

Fulton. The frail old dear didn't look at all well, he kept thinking. It was not the first time this sort of intense anxiety concerning the welfare of a resident had happened, and it wouldn't be the last.

None of the staff had received first aid training. If Cedric had, he would have known how to proceed. But instead, he panicked. Should he ask Richards about introducing first aid, or keep quiet until he mentioned the subject? Either way, Cedric wasn't enthusiastic about how to help a person who could be dying. Giving CPR, a word he saw written on the worker's clipboard, didn't appeal either. He preferred that the professionals should be involved with medical problems, not porters and cleaners. With regards to Ms Fulton, he'd realised that residents had informed him she hadn't been well for some time. In fact, she informed Cedric, on several occasions, that she wasn't well. He had collected prescriptions from the pharmacy for her. After going to the library and looking up the name of the prescription drug, he realised she had depression.

As anticipated, several residents, woken by the ambulance, phoned to seek an explanation for its presence at Oaks Lodge. Panic had set in. What could he say other than what he had experienced? Personally, he was most concerned by what had happened to Ms Fulton. Would she pull through and continue to live at the Lodge? In 12 years, Cedric had seen many residents die of various illnesses. Had he done his best for Ms Fulton? The inevitable looked close!

With those usual worries uppermost in his mind, Cedric was on his way to meet with Joe Swift. He had liked Joe, even though they had only met on two occasions. He was a decent, friendly and sincere man, he thought. Mind you, Cedric had said that about other people's qualities and had been mauled, turned over for lack of insight. But his instinct told him that this guy was above board, he meant what he said. Bedsides, Cedric had nothing to lose by visiting him. It still bothered him, somewhat, that he couldn't place Joe at school. It didn't surprise Cedric for he had been an introvert, quiet, shy, lacked confidence. Had no girlfriends, he couldn't even remember feeling a girl's breast. Whereas, Joe was a leader—gregarious, tough and uncompromising. People look up to those types of men, he determined. Not surprising, therefore, that he had done well in life. But was he happy? Cedric didn't know and wasn't that concerned. Personal wealth... well, that was for other people. He would keep walking in the same direction. With many painful experiences behind him, he was now contented with his lot in life. Money, family, sex and education was for others to enjoy. It just didn't interest him.

'Morning, Cedric, how are you?' asked Joe Swift, who had just pulled up in another expensive car, which had belonged to his late wife. He didn't have the heart to sell it. Sentimental, that's all it was. Something to hang on to amongst the tears, anger and love he felt every day in abundance. Joe had thought many times about trying to pull some old floozy from the internet. When all considered, what would he achieve at 62 years old? Sagging arse, fat belly, short-sighted, balding with a limp cock in the bargain. Now, that advert would attract some lovely beauties, dare say he laughed to himself many times. Nothing could or would replace his darling wife. Besides, he had three adult children and five grandchildren. They kept him moving on his size ten, flat feet. With them, and his racehorses, and other male friends, he was contented. He didn't relish the idea of waking up in the mornings next to some beached whale, minus false teeth and layers of rouge.

'Jump in, Cedric, we'll go back to my place in Doveton. I thought you'd prefer something informal. It's nice and quiet down there, so quiet you can hear the old lady next door farting every five minutes,' said Joe with a smile beaming from his face. 'Mind you, the au-pair might be sun tanning herself in the garden,' Joe laughed. 'Only kidding, Cedric.'

'Yeah, that sounds good, Joe. Go to your place, I'd love to.'

'You alright? What you been doing with yourself?' asked Joe.

'Other than working, I've been out walking. I walked in the Cotswolds, did 50 miles in three days. Bloody enjoyable, that was. I've been to the Picture House a few times. How's the horses, Joe?'

'It's the flat season now, so my horses are having a good time munching and getting fat on that old green stuff. All they do is shit. The lazy sods aren't earning me a bean,' Joe said, who also indulged in flat race gambling. Although a staunch national hunt supporter, he and his friends loved the big race scene like Goodwood, Ascot and Epsom. With a fat wallet and keen eye, they adored mixing with the super wealthy in the bars and restaurants. Some of the racehorse owners pay millions for a yearling horse. Hoping that, at some stage, they will be handsomely rewarded as a successful stud acquisition. That kind of money was out of Joe's league. He didn't want to get his fingers burnt playing around with the really big boys.

'I like your new car, Joe. Lots of seats in it,' said Cedric, who was fascinated by the different names of cars around, but most of them, he thought, all looked the same. The pricey ones like Joe's two cars, though, looked the bee's knees.

'Yeah, thank you. It's called a Volkswagen Touram. It used to belong to my late wife. She was a nightmare behind the wheel, but elsewhere, very placid. We bought it so we could drive our family and friends around. Mind you, she drove, and I drank. She loved screaming around the old country lanes. Right nutcase behind the wheel, she was, Cedric. You would have liked her company, I think. She came from a one-parent family. Never complained about it, she got on with the life in front of her. I liked her late mum, right fucking scream, she was, Cedric. Embarrassing at times, especially when we drove out for a drink. She'd go to the bar as bold as brass, and bring back a bottle of wine and three pints of beer. My wife only drank a half-pint when she was driving, so that left her and I to down the rest. She used to fall off the chair, stumble into bushes and mouth abuse at anyone. But I loved her company,' said Joe as he drove up the track leading to his large house.

'Blimey, what a lovely place, Joe,' said Cedric, who had never been invited to such a grand family palace before. He had noticed thousands of similar houses during his wanderings. Fantasy usually took over for a while. He wondered what they did behind those high walls. Swimming pools, parties on the lawn and lots of people enjoying themselves. If only, he thought on countless occasions, he could be there amongst those wealthy elites, drinking a beer with the landed gentry. But, of course, only fantasy. He was just contented to be invited to Joe's home.

'Have a cold beer, Cedric,' said Joe as they sat on the large patio.

'Cheers, Joe. I haven't seen you for some months, have I?'

'It must be about three months, I suppose.'

'You may recall from one of our phone conversations that I was going to Devon for a week?'

'That's right, I remember that. How did it go?'

'Bloody nightmare, Joe,' exclaimed Cedric, unsure what to tell him. As it was public knowledge, and he was put upon by Ford, he thought, why not explain what happened? Speak out for once and be heard. 'It didn't go well. To cut a long story short, Ford, the bloke from Oaks Lodge, and his two friends were charged with possession of cocaine. Early one morning, about 6 am, police raided his cottage. There were about five coppers and a vicious looking dog. They got us out of bed and pushed us all into the living room, while they ransacked the fucking place looking for drugs. They eventually found the cocaine in the outside shed, somewhere.'

'Sounds like a crime novel,' spouted Joe.

'Yeah, it does. They pleaded guilty at Exeter Crown Court, and all three received hefty prison sentences. Incredible,' said Cedric.

'So, that means, they were using you to drive them down to Devon and back, with illegal cocaine. You were totally ignorant about all this?' asked Joe, whose narrowing eyelids summed up his feelings.

'That's right. The police charged me with possession, along with those pricks. It was only in court the next day that the prosecution dropped the charges.' He further added, 'So much for their respectable middle-class values where morality is a mockery,' said Cedric, who was visibly shaking out of anger for those impostures whose only way of life was illegality and deception.

'Why did they drop the charges?'

'Well, as I was leaving the dock, Ford told me all three of them informed the police I was the innocent party.'

'Have another beer, Cedric.'

'Cheers, mate.'

'How many years before you can retire?'

'About five more, I suppose,' said Cedric, full of delight at hearing the word retire. 'I'm now 61 years old, I think, so a few years off yet.'

'Look, Cedric, how would you like to live here for the rest of your life? It must be a bolt out of the blue to be told something like that, I can imagine, but I'm sincere about it.'

'Well, I'm gobsmacked, Joe. I don't know what to say. I mean, I would have to think about it, mate,' said Cedric, full of joy and bewilderment.

'Sorry, my friend, this must be a shock. You wouldn't have to pay any rent or any other payment while you live here. Just pay for your own needs, like mobile phone and personal items. How does that grab you?' asked a smiling Joe, who genuinely wanted to support Cedric and give him a secure home where he could live in peace and quiet. He would have his own large bedroom. There was a large garden where he could, if he wanted to, grow his own vegetables and flowers. He could please himself what he did with his days.

'I'm just overwhelmed, Joe.' Cedric began to cry, unaccustomed to such kindness. All that he had ever fantasized about could now become a reality. He sobbed uncontrollably into his handkerchief. His life came flooding back before him, a life of hardship, injustice and pain.

'Sorry to shock you like this, Cedric. I realise there would be much to discuss. And, don't forget, you don't have to move in right away, whenever you want to.'

'That's the most marvellous thing that has ever happened to me, Joe,' said Cedric, who was moved by all that was unfolding in front of him.

'Just take your time over the decision. It's a lot to think about. I must be honest with you, I've lived on my own since my wife died, and I get lonely sitting here some evenings craving for just small talk. Or knowing there is someone in the house. My children have to be, of course, with their own families. They have a life of their own to fathom out. But, of course, we certainly wouldn't want to live out of each other's pockets. As you know, I have my horses and friends. No doubt you have your own interests. But small, yet enjoyable, things like breakfast, beer down the pub or gardening we could indulge together,' emphasized Joe. 'But no all-night parties with over-aged groupies,' he joked, trying to help Cedric relax and assure him that he wasn't alone and abandoned by a heartless world, craving mass consumerism.

'I can't believe all this is happening to me.'

'Just take your time, Cedric. Fancy another beer?'

'Please, Joe.'

They drank in total silence for a few minutes, both trying to assimilate what they had just discussed. Joe would appreciate the affable company of Cedric. Neither knew each other, but both had enjoyed the handful of times they had met. Before those meetings, it had been nearly 50 years since they last cast eyes upon each other. But his instincts informed him that Cedric would live like a door mouse. His needs were few, and being independent, would ask for very little. He assumed that he hadn't much money saved, but it would be sufficient until his pension arrived. Of course, he wouldn't see him go short of anything, but would have to tread softly, as not to upset him. The man had been a long-life loner, so he would naturally have recourse to himself. It would be like a huge gravitational pull.

Joe wasn't feeling any sort of superficial sentiment towards Cedric. He'd been honest with him. That he had his own personal, selfish reasons for asking him to live at Doveton. Of course, there was a part of him that couldn't forget that abandoned little boy who hid in the corner of the classroom. How could he forget? Whatever conditions had brought them together, Joe didn't know, he just wanted to make the best of the years left. If he died before Cedric, then the will would make arrangements for him. If Joe contracted an interminable illness, which necessitated hospitalisation, then Cedric could live on at Doveton, or somewhere else, that would be payable by Joe. Whatever the various living scenarios might be, they would all be healthier and more comfortable than Oaks Lodge.

Joe took Cedric for a conducted tour of the house. Cedric was mesmerised by the size of every room. Each one had its own unique interior. Different coloured walls and ceilings, expensive furniture, beds, cupboards and hung pictures. Cedric had seen similar apartments at Oaks Lodge, but never in his wildest dreams would he ever have thought that one day, one could be his home.

'This bedroom should be yours, Cedric, if you, at some stage, move in,' said Joe, hoping his friend would agree to it.

'Blimey, Joe, it reminds me of a picture I saw in a magazine called Cosmopolitan in the dentists,' he said, a large smile beaming from his face. It was similar to the other rooms. It was enormous in size, creative in context and comfortable in variety. Cedric was lost for words. All his chattels could fit in one corner. He couldn't imagine living the rest of his life in this bedroom. That room alone was larger than his grimy flat.

'I'm pleased you liked it, Cedric.'

Before lunch, they walked slowly around the long, wide garden. Large borders, beds and tubs full of flowering summer plants perfumed the environment. The dense variety looked similar to one of his favourite television gardening programmes. The mowed lawn reminded him of the hallowed turf of Wembley Stadium. The surroundings evoked in him one special book he had enjoyed reading at school called 'Through the Looking-Glass'. He had entered a fantasy world full of kindness, security and hope. At the bottom of the garden was a large shed, full of tools, compost heap and an attractive gazebo, where Joe and his wife used to sit, kiss and hold hands in the evening shade. Joe held on tight to those vivid, heavenly dreams.

An exciting area, Cedric thought, where he could have tea, read the newspaper, feed the birds and talk to the spirits. He loved personal space out of the way of the gibbering masses. Like small nooks and crannies, where he could smell tree bark, moss and lichen. These things had been important for him ever since he was a boy. Initially, to hide from the nuns, but as he grew, he realised the tiny wonders to be had, all by oneself. That self-awareness had been an integral part of being an outsider. You are outside of other's values, needs, expectations and so on. He could be himself, not what others wanted of him.

'If you wanted to, you could grow what you required, Cedric. Make this part of the garden your own,' said Joe, aware that Cedric, as a loner, would enjoy being on his own in a peaceful place.

'I would love to grow vegetables. We could eat them for our dinner,' he said.

'It's early days, Cedric. When you go home later, give it some thought about moving in. Just take your time.'

'Yeah, thanks a lot, Joe. It's really kind of you. I was thinking about when your family visit you, I would find that difficult. You know, I've lived all my life on my own and might find it too challenging to adapt to another life. It's not that I'm not grateful, I really am, but family and friends are sort of group people, I'm not. My friend, and former colleague at the Lodge, Nelson, would give anything to be offered the opportunity to live in, well, near paradise on earth.'

'That's OK, Cedric. You don't have to meet lots of people if you don't want to. Different arrangements can be made. I'll explain and they'll understand,' said Joe, who wanted to put down the right conditions for Cedric to think about. Joe was convinced that they could both, as they aged, live enjoyable, and most of the time, independent lives together. To those ends, he was committed.

'Anyway, Cedric, let's go and have some food. I've cooked. Crab salad, ice cream sundae, chilled wine. What do you think?'

'Sounds delicious, I've not had crab for 40 years. When I was dossing about in Norfolk with a bloke I met in prison, this old sea-dog felt sorry for us and gave us one already dressed. Fucking handsome it was.'

'Well, come on then, let's go inside and tuck into some food. I'm starving,' said Joe.

What did all this information mean? Perhaps, Cedric was a control freak! He was certainly a contradiction like most people. Many times, he had wondered what it was like to be oneself. He'd overheard people say these things, yet it confused him. What did it mean? Was he being himself, or acting out a part, unconsciously, for other people? He had come to the conclusion that others have the power to give you an identity, which didn't necessarily apply to the person in question. Occasionally, he felt he had lived a million different lives, all given to him by other people. The loner, Cedric had concluded, fulfils other people's frustrated desires. But no sooner those feelings arose, he would repress them. Best locked away from his consciousness, he thought.

Regular fortnightly phone calls, exchanged with Nelson, had materialised in meeting him for the first time since London. During that time, Nelson had moved home twice. Years ago, that wasn't that unusual for either man. Longest employment for both men was Oaks Lodge. Other than that, they had constantly moved around. Sometimes due to employment needs, occasionally because they didn't have the money to pay the rent, and other times told to leave by the landlord. As for many people, life is a constant struggle trying to find decent accommodation. Any place to lay your head, sleep, eat and shit—just the basics of life catered for.

He was excited, anxious and sad to be leaving his job and home for the last 13 years. He wanted Nelson to know about his good fortune. In time, perhaps, he could come around and meet Joe. Cedric, however, didn't want to get things out of all proportion. He had been let down cruelly many times before. He still didn't believe in sincerity. If it didn't work out at Joe's house, well, he'd just have to move on again. With savings, he could rent a decent bedsit or flat. Council accommodation was even possible. Cedric wasn't afraid of work either, he'd wash floors, pans, toilets... anything to earn a few bob. No, don't worry about the orphan from the kid's home, he'd be fine on his own. It was time for a change anyway, so moving to Joe's home was a part of that arduous, fragile journey.

'Hello, brudder, good to see yer,' said Nelson, giving his friend a large hug.

'Hi, Nelson, how's it going, mate?' inquired Cedric, whose smile provoked a million dreams.

'What you been doing with yourself? I hope you haven't been thrashing that old bill too much?' laughed Nelson.

'Long story, mate, you wouldn't believe it.'

'Try me. Anyway, what you having to eat and drink? I thought you would like to meet in this old garden. It's owned by the council, but the café is managed by a private business. They're Italians. Nice people. I would love to shag his wife.'

'Yeah, I'll have the all-day brunch and a pot of tea, please, mate,' said a relaxed-looking Cedric.

It was a delightful Edwardian building. Similar to many of those old houses, it was privately owned until after the last war when the family, due to bankruptcy, sold it to the council, which had renovated it. Ever since it has been a successful enterprise. The current managers, the Fabio family, had been there ten years. Everyone knew and liked them. The mass of different coloured roses and hanging lobelia had been donated by them. Three generations of Fabio's sauntered around the place, where they sang and joked with customers. From a safe distance, Cedric was impressed by his friend's choice.

But what caught Cedric's imagination were the extravagant colours used to decorate the house. Buttercup yellow paint covered the front. A black weather vane sat on top of the chimney. It hardly moved in that late summer sun. Kids ran about on the large lawn, chasing each other and kicking balls at the War Memorial. He vividly remembered when his new parents had taken him to the local park. He found it difficult mixing with other kids. Cedric would sit on the outside alone, watching other children play. He'd just sit there, as he did in the home, not interested in others around him. Yet all the time, he craved to be one of them. Laughing, shouting, running and generally being caught up in the melee of the moment.

'There you go, big boy, one brunch and tea for two,' said Nelson.

'Where you living now, Nelson?' he asked.

'I'm renting a little flat near Brentwood in Essex. It's a comfortable place. The village has a few shops. Friendly people, unlike where I was living in London,' he said. In reality though, Nelson had bought a handsome flat in Suffolk two months previously with proceeds of crime. He and his two accomplishes had made some big money from their jewel heist at Heydon Manor. But he wasn't going to inform Cedric, or anyone else. Experience told him that people can't keep their mouths closed. Inform one today, the whole world is talking tomorrow. Fuck that, he thought. He didn't like Cedric, never had, it was all a charade. He was no different to anyone else. In fact, he thought him scum of the earth. The same as the other riff-raff he had worked with at Oaks Park. At his age, with a good life ahead assured, Nelson wasn't going to jeopardise it. No way, brother!

'That's good news, mate. By the way, a belated birthday greetings, do anything special?'

'That was months ago, bro. Yeah, I gave the whole family a great treat. We all flew to Jamaica for three weeks. There were eight of us aboard that big old bird that flew us into Kingston Airport. Steel band music made it feel like home. The extended family were there to greet us. There must have been about 20 of 'em. Most of us had never seen each other before. My uncles, aunts and so on... there were so many faces, we were overwhelmed with joy. They made us all comfortable. There was plenty of boozing, dancing and pussy. It was a great experience, brudder,' Nelson said vociferously.

But it was all bullshit that he had told Cedric. Not one word was truthful. He hadn't flown his forgotten family anywhere, least of all to the Caribbean. Nelson had never been anywhere near the place! His children received the occasional phone calls, visit and cheque in the post. But he didn't flaunt his money. Gave everyone the impression he just about made out. No more prison for this old lag, he kept his cards close to his chest from now on.

In actuality, he had taken his young girlfriend on a cruise around the Mediterranean Sea. Living an independent life, but discreet about it, his choices were unlimited. Give them a good time and then get rid of the leaches before they suck you dry.

'What about yourself?'

'You know that bloke, Joe Swift, I told you about? Well, he's invited me to live with him in his fucking great mansion. His wife died of cancer a few years ago and his kids have their own families. So, there will only be the two of us. No rent or any other bills to pay. All I have to buy is personal items. There is a fucking great garden as well, mate. Joe said I could use it whenever I want to. It's time for a change, mate, isn't it?' Cedric said excitedly.

'Yeah, you bet it is, brudder. Go for it. Move away from that Oaks Lodge and that prick Richards. You've been there many years, mate, move on. It's a great opportunity. The bloke has money, racehorses, big house... go for it, Cedric. You got nothing to lose, have you? Take what you can while you are able.'

'No, I haven't, Nelson. It's quiet and peaceful there. I've saved some money over the years for a rainy day. If it doesn't turn out well, I can look after myself. I've got to move on from Mortingbridge. If I don't make the move now, some day they'll take me out in a wooden box,' he remarked.

'That's right, mate. Go for it, the opportunity won't come again,' said Nelson.

'How's the family, mate?' inquired Cedric.

'Yeah, they are all well, brudder,' beamed Nelson. Actually, he hadn't seen any of them for months. He phoned occasionally, but that was as far as he wanted to venture back into London. He explained this to his daughter. She was disappointed. He sent her money, made sure she didn't go short!

'Well, hopefully, one day you can visit me, the country squire of Doveton?'

'Sure thing, brudder, no problem,' said Nelson who, after this meeting, had no intention of seeing Cedric again. He had to move on, just like his old buddy from Oaks Lodge. Fresh pastures, succulent grass and a nourished body, thought Nelson about his days ahead.

Cedric was coming to the end of his employment at Oaks Lodge. Other than Richards and Tranter, he had kept a tight lip. He didn't like people knowing his business, even less so the enquiring questions and pretentious farewells. In fact, he had succinctly asked his two colleagues not to inform others of his imminent departure. He'd be pleased not to see any of them again. No parties, cards or presents, that's the way Cedric wanted it. The only farewell he had really enjoyed, with bitterness in his heart, was leaving a few friends at the children's home. Bitterness of the cruel regime that left him scarred for the rest of his life.

On the final day, hours before his departure, he received a letter from a solicitor in London. Reynolds & Co was the name. His anxiety levels automatically rose within him. What could it be? Had Joe Swift changed his mind at the last moment, and no longer wished Cedric to move in? That wouldn't surprise him. The last and only solicitor's letter he had ever received informed him of his mother's death. That upset him greatly. She was the only person who had ever loved him, held him close to her heart and offered him an opportunity to grow. Cedric was becoming frightened of the unknown. Was this more bad news, frustration and disillusionment? He hadn't banged his head on the wall or door for some time, but he was now close to carrying out something he hated himself for. Oh, how intensely he hated himself, after many months of relative, emotional stability. He was now frightfully near to giving in to his demons. But he gritted his teeth and desperately hoped that he would be released from the clutches of despair. He tentatively opened the letter.

On one A4-sized page, there was a cheque for £25,000 clipped to the left-hand side. He ignored the letter as he sat there, eyes fixed, staring at the amount payable to Cedric Bambridge. Most of the foreseeable problems had evaporated in front of him. What had he done to deserve such a large amount of money? He was now set up to live with Joe, but be independent of his goodwill or charity. Just think if this kindness had happened to him years ago, he would have bought a camper van or a highland bothy. He now felt too old for those adventures. But new experiences would follow. All manner of anxieties left his short, slim body. Relaxed, relieved and released from 13 years of bondage. Free from the beck and call of other's needs. Cedric Bambridge, thanks to Ms Fulton's compassion, walked out of Oaks Lodge holding two battered cases full of hope.

13

ACKNOWLEDGEMENTS

There are many people who, at crucial times in my life, have given me their unquestioning support. Without their skilful intervention, my life would have been overburdened and fraught with unsolvable problems. This support applies not just to my literary work, but more importantly, negotiating the pitfalls and problems of everyday life. There are far too many names to mention here. They know who they are, anyway. But I want to thank all of you from the bottom of my heart. Your kindness and friendship shall remain with me forever. I am eternally grateful!

However, the author is also very grateful to his parents, Lis Bird and the Triratna Buddhist Community. Without their love, friendship and support, he doubts he would have travelled the path thus far.

14

ABOUT THE AUTHOR

He was born into a large, poor working-class family of 13 children. Love was in short supply, but food was always in abundance. He was accidentally electrocuted at the age of two. The author suspects that this traumatic accident, along with other painful experiences later on, led to him living a semi-feral existence, wandering from place to place, constantly threatened by inner fears. These tortured, tormented and threatened to engulf him at times. To a certain extent, they are still around today, manifesting themselves as chronic insecurity.

Frustration led him to take chances that only a foolhardy and immature person would take. Consequently, he was sexually abused as a teenager. At the age of 20, the author contracted Dystonia, a neurological condition. The treatment led to 17 years of addiction to prescribed drugs. During this time, he served 18 months in prison.

For years, thereafter, one unskilled job led to another. But through walking the various byways around Britain, the author found peace, contentment, enjoyment and new experiences. Tramping was life enhancing. He met fellow souls along the way who taught him new skills. For a while, he lived a life of self-sufficiency and slept under the stars. Temporary work sustained his few needs. Still an ardent walker, he now, in his 70s, uses B&B accommodation. He has walked many thousands of miles over the past 20 years with a friend. They continue to seek out long distance tracks where flora and fauna flourish in abundance.

He realised he was woefully underdeveloped in certain areas of his life. In order to improve his development, he studied and passed a social science course at the age of 40. It was his first academic qualification. He trained as a social worker at university. Further studies led to an MSc qualification in the efficacy of non-medical therapies for Benzodiazepine addiction. He found various social care jobs, but soon, unfortunately, realised his early socialization was incompatible to the nature of the work! But in spite of everything, higher education was an invaluable experience. It opened up a whole new world of different people and ideas.

To date he has written five books:

Seeking a New Voice (2013)

A Working-Class Saga (2014)

A Quest for Self-Discovery (2016)

A Web of Delusion (2019)

The Outsider (2021)

Lightning Source UK Ltd.
Milton Keynes UK
UKHW021458261021
392872UK00005B/196